PRAISE FOR

Stone in the Crick:

Rebecca Zook's Amish Romance

Book One

"Rebecca Zook, 22, a talented quilt maker in the Amish community of Lancaster County, Pennsylvania, is getting past the point of getting married and starting a family[.] Burgess makes good use of his setting. Rebecca's Amish culture isn't just a backdrop; it's part of her. Her quilts rework images from her family's daily life, such as the saddles and leather goods made by her father, while still honoring tradition. The gentle love story also respects Rebecca's values. **A sensitive story about finding oneself in a community.**"
— *Kirkus Reviews*

"Like a quilt woven with many dexterous hands, Burgess weaves a page-turner tale of intrigue and romance…. A witty novel, full of humor and intelligence, with memorable characters who feel life-like enough to hug."
— Elizabeth Oberbeck, author of *The Dressmaker* (Henry Holt & Co.)

STONE IN THE CRICK

Rebecca Zook's Amish Romance

Book One

Granville Wyche Burgess

ISBN 978-0-9997569-0-4

This book contains the entire text of the edition of this novel originally published by Honeybrook Publishers.

Chickadee Prince Logo by Garrett Gilchrist

Visit us at www.ChickadeePrince.com

First Printing of the Chickadee Prince Edition

GRANVILLE WYCHE BURGESS

Stone in the Crick

Rebecca Zook's Amish Romance

Book One

GRANVILLE WYCHE BURGESS received an Emmy nomination for his writing on the soap opera, *Capitol*. He has also received awards from the CBS/Foundation for the Dramatist Guild, the National Endowment for the Humanities, and the Pennsylvania Council on the Arts.

He has also written for the television series, *Tales From The Darkside*, and for PBS. His musical, *Conrack*, based on the Pat Conroy memoir *The Water Is Wide* had a sold-out run at Ford's Theatre and was attended by President George H.W. Bush and the first lady, Barbara Bush. Mr. Burgess's plays and musicals have been performed throughout the United States. He is CEO of Quill Entertainment, a charitable company whose mission is "Teaching America's Heritage Through Story and Song."

He lives in Connecticut with his Amish-Mennonite wife, Reba.

This is his first published novel.

STONE IN THE CRICK

Rebecca Zook's Amish Romance
Book One

Chickadee Prince Books
New York

*In loving memory of
Mabel Zook Stoltzfus Smoker*

God hath not promised skies always blue
Flower-strewn pathways all our lives through;
God hath not promised sun without rain,
Joy without sorrow, peace without pain.

But God hath promised strength for the day,
Rest for the labor, light for the way,
Grace for the trials, help from above,
Unfailing sympathy, undying love.

God hath not promised we shall not know
Toil and temptation, trouble and woe;
He hath not told us we shall not bear
Many a burden, many a care.

But God hath promised strength for the day,
Rest for the labor, light for the way,
Grace for the trials, help from above,
Unfailing sympathy, undying love.

God hath not promised smooth roads and wide,
Swift, easy travel, needing no guide;
Never a mountain rocky and steep,
Never a river turgid and deep.

But God hath promised strength for the day,
Rest for the labor, light for the way,
Grace for the trials, help from above,
Unfailing sympathy, undying love.

Author Unknown

CHAPTER 1

The afternoon sun beat down mercilessly as Rebecca Zook hurried down the hoof-scarred lane toward the King house. She knew the other women would already be gathered around the quilting frame, patiently stitching away. And talking. After all, that was one of the great pleasures of quilt making, the chance to chatter away about anything and everything. "Did you know Morris Beiler had to buy a new mule because his old one keeled over just last Tuesday, right there in the tobacco field?" "Did you see the color of Mildred Pedersheim's covering in church last week? She ought to wash it before it runs away from her!" "My corn beans just aren't doing so good; must be the caterpillars." For women whose life is full of hard work and the responsibilities of taking care of a large family, a chance to chat is a wonderful thing.

Rebecca had spent the morning working hard at Elizabeth Ansbacher's quilt shop, talking with the customers, which she liked, and doing the books, which she didn't. But she'd always been good at figures, so naturally when Mrs. Ansbacher had hired her almost a year ago, she quickly put her to work making sure the shop stayed profitable. Rebecca didn't particularly like doing the books, but she didn't mind too much. After all, it was good practice if she ever had her own quilt shop someday.

Rebecca walked along at a goodly pace, the beautiful June day putting a spring in her step. She was a fine-looking young woman, with dark-brown hair, a tall, sleek neck, and the fine figure of a twenty-two-year-old. Her eyes were a shade of blue-green that often elicited compliments. Those who knew her more intimately could see a tiny freckle in her left eye. Its presence had bothered Rebecca greatly during her teenage years, but now that she was older, she was beginning to appreciate it as something unique about her. Given the sameness of much of Amish life, anything out of the ordinary was to be cherished, she had decided.

To Rebecca's left as she walked, acres of growing corn marched like well-trained soldiers at a parade, their rows of green stalks swaying gently in the summer breeze. In another three months, it would be harvest time. Her brother Henry and her father, Elam, would hitch the cornhusker to the mules and drive it through the fields. The machine would neatly crop the cobs and feed them into a wagon attached to the rear. Her older brothers, who had already left for farms of their own in other states, would be doing the same thing.

Rebecca often asked if she could help, but the answer was always no; harvesting the corn was men's work. The division of labor was a hallmark of Amish life. "Because that's the way it's done" had usually been the answer to Rebecca's questions about why she could or couldn't do something. It was an answer that had never satisfied her and still didn't.

Not that Rebecca wasn't happy; she was. But she couldn't help feeling that there was something missing in her life. She knew that, as an Amish woman, she was not supposed to be concerned about personal fulfillment. That was for the English, with all their drive to succeed, to make a name for themselves, to make money so they could become rich and famous. Rebecca didn't care about any of that, so she was Amish in that way. Yet this vague sense that there should be more to life than "that's the way it's done" gnawed at her.

Thoughts of this nature eventually brought her to the Kings' front door, where she politely knocked. "Come in!" Lydie's hearty voice rang out from within, and Rebecca did as bidden.

A group of women was seated around the quilting frame. All the Amish women wore the same style, the only difference being the color of their dress and perhaps the design of their black shoes. Rebecca's mother, Mabel, was wearing her usual peach-colored dress, her shoulders draped in a black cape, with a sheer, white covering holding down her light-brown hair. In her late forties, Mabel had the stout appearance of many Amish women, with strong legs and arms, the result of many hours of hard work. She had a stern look about her, which hid a tender heart. Rebecca loved her very much, even though they'd had the usual mother-daughter spats down through the years.

To Mabel's right sat Emily Miller. Emily was the only woman at the quilting bee who wasn't Amish, even though she spoke their German dialect. She was Amish-Mennonite, her parents having left the Amish church when she was a young girl. Her father had wanted the modern convenience of a tractor, and, when caught driving one after repeatedly being warned by the bishops, he had been shunned.

Emily's cape and dress were designed differently from those of the Old Order Amish, but hardly noticeable to the nondiscerning eye. The way she wore her covering was another difference, tied in back and all one loop from ear to ear. "It looks ferhoodled," Rebecca's mother often said to Rebecca under her breath, so as not to offend. "Messy." "Out of line." *Order* had more than one meaning when it came to the Amish, Rebecca often thought.

Lydia Mae King, called Lydia Mae in her youth but Lydie now, the hostess of today's bee, was sweeping the kitchen floor. Rebecca thought how often she'd seen Lydie with a broom, obsessively sweeping the porch and stone walks in the morning and sometimes again at night, as if the broom were an extension of herself. And when the talk turned to men, which it inevitably did at these gatherings, Lydie tended to be particularly harsh on them. "Never trust a man," was a typical Lydie refrain, which struck Rebecca as peculiar since her husband, Omar, was the preacher. They didn't have any children. But when the topic was young ones, Rebecca noticed that Lydie often had a wistful look about her and didn't say much. No matter the subject, Lydie had a calm way of speaking, as if she always had her emotions under control.

Rebecca's aunt, Hanna, completed the foursome around the quilting frame. Unlike her older sister, Hanna was beginning to get a little plump, due to a fondness for ice cream. She had a round face with big brown eyes, and a goofy smile seemed permanently etched on her lips. Growing up, Rebecca had often shared a bed with Hanna, and she felt as if she had two mothers, so close was their relationship.

"Hello, Rebecca," Lydie said in welcome. "We've saved you a chair."

"Becca-Bee!" cried out Hanna in her childish voice. She ran to Rebecca and gave her a huge hug.

"Hello, Aunt Hanna," Rebecca managed to reply when Hanna loosened the hug. "Hello, everyone. Sorry I'm late, but a customer came into the shop at the last minute."

"Buy anything?" asked Mabel.

"As a matter of fact, she did," replied Rebecca. "And it was one of our quilts."

"Glory be!" shouted Emily.

"We'll be rich," cried Hanna. "Rich, rich, rich! Now we can get that new fridge'ator!"

"We'll do no such thing," countered Mabel.

"Will, too! Will, too! Won't we, Becca? Ours isn't worth stink beans!"

The women tittered at Hanna's language, but said nothing. That was one of the privileges, if one could call it that, of having Hanna's condition. She'd been thrown from a horse when she was a little girl — a horse she was not supposed to be riding — and had landed on her head. Certain parts of Hanna's brain had not matured normally. As a result, though she was perfectly capable of making a meal or raking the yard or cleaning and otherwise taking care of herself, she was a bit soft in the head, as the family used to say. Sometimes when Hanna was particularly annoying, Mabel simply called her "dumb."

"I don't know, Hanna. Our refrigerator seems to work well enough," replied Rebecca.

"It don't keep my ice cream hard!" complained Hanna.

"Hanna, will you just let Rebecca sit down so we can finish this quilt!" demanded Mabel.

Rebecca pulled herself up to the table and began to thread a needle while Hanna watched from the side. Emily started the next round of gossip. "Let me tell you what I saw Aaron Peachy do yesterday. You know how they play baseball in the field next to my barn? Well, Aaron changed into his uniform right there in the field!"

"Men got no respect," Lydie chided.

Emily went on. "He used the back of his carriage to shield himself. But still, there were two legs showing, naked to the knees!"

"Children today! No manners, no consideration," intoned Mabel. Emily and Lydie nodded assent.

"I saw a naked boy once," offered Hanna.

"Not now, Hanna," said Mabel firmly. But not firmly enough.

"Seen more than his legs, too."

"Hanna!" Mabel raised her hand in warning, as the others smiled in amusement.

"He had a cute — "

"Hanna!"

"Butt," Hanna giggled. "Cute butt! Cute butt!" she sang. The others laughed.

"You always had an eye for beauty, Hanna," chimed in Lydie, which caused more sniggering among the womenfolk. Even Mabel smiled a little at the absurdity of it.

These were the moments of her life that Rebecca cherished. Small moments, insignificant perhaps, but somehow profound. Well, not profound, exactly, just reassuring. Sharing them gave Rebecca a sense of the timelessness of existence, the feeling that there had always been Amish women sitting around chitchatting, and there always would be.

The afternoon passed, in comforting gossip. How Sadie Smoker, after leaving the Amish to join the English, was living up to her name, smoking cigarettes all over town, even right there in front of the post office. How Jonas Glick was sweet on Gideon Lapp's youngest girl, but couldn't bring himself to ask her for a walk. The weather, the crops, various aches and pains — all spun out warmly from the web of their mutual love and respect.

"Lydie, can I have some lemonade?" Lydie's nephew, Jacob, said as he burst through the kitchen door, smelling of cows and manure, a broad-shouldered man of twenty years, with dark-brown eyes socketed deep into a square-jawed face. He was a plain-looking man, whose shock of black hair was now plastered down on his head, his dirty forehead glistening with sweat. "Oh, sorry." Jacob quickly yanked off his hat. "I didn't know you ladies were quilting."

"That's all right, Jacob," said Emily. "Come on in and sit a spell."

"Oh, no, can't do that, I have a lot more mowing to finish."

"Here you go," said Lydie, handing him a glass of lemonade. "Careful, don't track in any dirt."

"*Denke*, Lydie." Jacob drank the lemonade down halfway. Some of it spilled down his chin.

"Let me get you a clean hanky," Rebecca offered. She took one from the bureau drawer and gave it to Jacob.

"*Denke*, Rebecca," Jacob said. They smiled at each other.

"When are you two going to get married?" Hanna's question shot out at them. "'Bout everybody else is married up 'cept you two. Get to it!" She grabbed Rebecca's hand and attempted to force it on top of Jacob's.

"Leave them two alone, Hanna!" barked Mabel. "How many times do I have to tell you to stay out of other people's business?"

"A thousand!" cried Hanna gleefully. "Tell me a thousand times!" And she grinned one of her lopsided grins.

"Hanna, you act like you're not right," declared Mabel.

Jacob quickly got in his question. "Rebecca, could I see you outside for a minute?"

"Sure." He held the door for her, and they walked outside.

"Ask her! Ask her!" Hanna shouted after their retreating figures.

"Hanna, will you sit down and behave?!" Mabel asked, exasperated.

Hanna ignored Mabel's plea and went to a window to spy on Rebecca and Jacob.

Outside, Jacob got right to the point. "I'd like to take you to the next singing, Rebecca, if that's all right."

"When is it?"

"Saturday, a week from now. Over at the Fisher's farm on Whitehorse Road in Gap." When Rebecca hesitated, Jacob asked, "Are you busy?"

"No," Rebecca said. The truth was, she wanted to be busy. Not because of Jacob, but because she wanted to use the time to work on her secret project. It was hard enough to find the time to do it, and a Saturday night was a good opportunity, because everyone was tired from the week's work and went to bed early.

Jacob interrupted her thoughts. "Then I'll pick you up. Same place as usual?"

"Yes, Jacob, I'd like that," Rebecca responded sweetly. It was true. She enjoyed singing, and Jacob had a beautiful baritone voice. The summer tent meetings always had interesting ministers from other Amish or Mennonite communities. She thought of Psalm 85:6: "Wilt thou not revive us again; that thy people may rejoice in thee?"

"Good! Well, I'd better get back to work. Enjoy your quilting." Jacob dipped his head in good-bye and turned back to the fields.

"Bye, Jacob," Rebecca said. "Thank you for asking me."

"Asking you what?" Hanna said, descending the stairs. She had slipped out while the other women were focused on their quilting.

"To go to the singing with him, Hanna," Rebecca replied. "But you should mind your own business!" She tried to sound stern, but she could hardly ever be mad at Hanna, no matter how outrageously she behaved.

"Hanna Stoltzfus, what are you doing?" Mabel demanded from the doorway.

"Talking with Becca, Mabel. *Lass mich gehen!*" Hanna placed her fists on her hips for emphasis.

"I'll leave you alone when you mind your own business," Mabel responded. "Get your things; we're going home."

"I don't have nothing," Hanna replied.

"Then let's go."

"I'll just say *denke* to Lydie," Rebecca said, reentering the house.

"Me, too," said Hanna, following.

Alone outside, Mabel watched Jacob mount the mower and move off. She had no idea what he and Rebecca had been talking about, but she guessed it hadn't brought them any closer to marriage. Sometimes she wished she had Hanna's way of being direct, asking anything of anybody. She determined to press Jacob's case for him.

As they walked home, Mabel feigned tiredness and asked Hanna to go on ahead and get supper started.

"I can help you, Hanna," Rebecca offered.

"I'd like you to keep me company, Rebecca," said her mother.

"I don't need any help. I'm a good cook," Hanna said, and she moved off quickly toward home. Once Hanna was out of earshot, Mabel began her campaign.

"That Jacob is such a nice boy," Mabel offered. "So polite, don't you think?"

"That's for sure, Mam," Rebecca replied.

"Hard working, too. You'd never starve with Jacob working the land." Rebecca was silent, waiting for her mother to get to the point. "What did he want with you anyhow?"

"He wanted to ask me to the next singing."

"Did you say you'd go?" Mabel looked at her daughter anxiously.

"I did."

Mabel was relieved. "Good!" she said. "And Jacob has such a nice voice," she added for emphasis. "Hanna's right, you know, Rebecca. It's time for you to settle down. Past time, really."

"I know, Mam. Jacob and I are thinking about it." Rebecca looked out over the fields. This was going to be one of those conversations she wished she could avoid but knew she couldn't.

"You oughta do less thinking and more doing," Mabel responded. "At your age I'd already been married four years.

"I'm not you, Mam."

"I'm not asking you to be me. I'm just asking you to get married and start a family like the Amish have always done."

"Do I have to do everything the way it's always been done?" Rebecca asked plaintively.

"Why not?" her mother asked firmly.

"I don't know, Mam. I can't find the right words for how I'm feeling, exactly. It's like quilting, kind of. There are these patterns you're supposed to follow."

"You mean the right way to do things?" her mother challenged.

"Yes, but maybe there's more than one right way to do things. Maybe there's more than one pattern to a person's life."

"You're not making any sense, Rebecca," her mother said in an exasperated tone. "What's wrong with marrying Jacob? He's from a good family. Their barns are always nice, always painted. They keep the weeds out of their fields. They know how to manage."

"But a marriage is not a business to be managed," Rebecca countered.

"Yes it is!" Her mother raised her voice. "How do you think your father and I got along all these years, fed you, your brothers, built a new barn, bought more cows? We managed!"

"But, Mama, what if I want my life to be more than painted barns and managed fields?" Rebecca cried.

Mabel answered sharply. "Look at all this." She gestured to the surrounding countryside. "All this land. *Gut* neighbors, *gut* food, hard work, the love of God. What's wrong with that life?"

"Nothing, Mama," Rebecca replied, her shoulders sagging in defeat. "It's a *gut* life."

"Then get on with living it and forget your big ideas. I'll see you at supper." Mabel marched off toward the house.

Rebecca paused, resting her hands along the top of a fence, looking out. Corn as far as the eye could see. White barns and white houses. Amish neighbors she'd known her whole life and probably would know the rest of her life. Rebecca sighed. *Is this all there is?*

After supper, when everyone had retired, Rebecca sneaked out of the house and headed for the abandoned cottage at the rear of the farm. She didn't exactly sneak, but it was true that she was going somewhere and doing something she had not shared with her family. It felt too special to do that yet. So she found what hours she could to be alone in the cottage when no one would notice.

As she strolled along under a full moon, she pondered Hanna's question. When were she and Jacob going to get married? They had first dated during *rumspringa*, that time of life when all Amish teenagers were supposed to sample the world outside the Amish faith, the world of cars and bars and material goods beckoning from every store window. "Sow their wild oats," was the way some Amish put it. Of course, some teenagers sowed wilder oats than others, depending on how much they wanted to rebel against their parents or their plain life.

This rumspringa was not condoned by the church, but neither was it condemned. Amish aren't baptized when they are babies; they practice adult baptism. And this baptism represents a serious decision to join the church for life, which meant a lifetime of following its tenets. So teenagers are encouraged to spend a year, or longer, learning about the outside world, with some even tasting its temptations, so that when they renounce them, the renunciation is likely to stick.

Rebecca and Jacob hadn't been that rebellious. They'd gone to a lot of movies together, mainly romantic ones. The men and women in those stories had faced troubles, true, but love always won out in the end. There would be a beautiful lake, maybe, and a sunset, and the rush of lush music as the man and woman kissed passionately. Once, at that moment in the film, Jacob had reached over and kissed Rebecca. It hadn't seemed as passionate as the kisses she'd seen in the films, but it was definitely a kiss. It had felt so wonderful. Warm and luscious and sweet.

Rebecca paused on the bridge over their small crick and looked down into the water. That kiss had been two years ago. But somehow the feeling she had for Jacob that summer had not grown as it was supposed to. It hadn't decreased, exactly, but it hadn't grown. It had just sat there, like the stone she now stared at in the crick — a large, round stone that glistened in the moonlight. Was her life with Jacob to be like a stone in a crick, solid but stationary, withstanding life but never flowing with it? And where was that water rushing off to, gurgling with such excitement? *I don't know, but somewhere! Water or stone. The choices of my life.*

With a sigh, Rebecca left the bridge and walked to the cottage. It would be dark inside, but she had a kerosene lantern she would light. The thought of its warm glow made her smile. The thought of what would be beneath that glow made her smile even more. She silently opened the door and looked in on what she hoped might be a new pattern for her life.

CHAPTER 2

The wind blew Gregory's hair straight back like branches in a rainstorm. That's one of the reasons he liked it long, so he could feel it whipping behind him. The wind felt fresh on his well-tanned face, the South Carolina sun warmed the back of his neck, and the steady cadence of the horse's hooves beat a trance-like rhythm into his brain. He closed his eyes for a few seconds and enjoyed the sensation of not knowing precisely where he was, while still knowing exactly where he was. This thrilling sensation was his favorite thing about riding: being both in the world and yet somehow simultaneously removed from it.

Gregory Pinckney was a handsome young man with a chiseled face, warm, brown eyes, an easy smile, and the tanned complexion of a person born and raised in the South. He'd been a good athlete in college at Furman University in Greenville, and he still retained the muscular body of his college days. He had first discovered his love of horses at a friend's house in high school and had persuaded his mother to let him take riding lessons. Of course, she'd had to convince Gregory's father, who thought riding was "foolishness." But, for once, his father had given Gregory what he wanted: a horse for graduation, in exchange for Gregory's agreeing to attend the University of South Carolina Law School. Gregory thought it a fair exchange. Law school seemed like a good option until he figured out what he wanted to do.

A row of oaks, draped with Spanish moss, rose up before him at the edge of the field. He loved the look of the gray moss, like some wacky Santa Claus had tossed it on the trees, the way his family used to decorate their Christmas tree with silver icicles. So beautiful. So peaceful. *So romantic!* Gregory smiled. Not many young men his age spent time thinking about how romantic Spanish moss looked. No, they were too busy getting on in life, making their way in the world, trying to put money in their pocket — the kind of life he was supposed to be constructing for himself. Gregory shook his head, as if throwing away the thought. He was outdoors, doing the thing he loved most. Why spoil it with thoughts of the "real world"?

He entered the woods without slowing down. This was his favorite part, dodging the trees this way and that. They weren't closely packed, and most of them grew fairly straight. He wasn't worried. Bojangles knew this trail by heart; he could run it blindfolded, no doubt. The oak trees gave way to a grove of pines, skinny and tall against the azure sky. Bojangles's powerful legs kicked up the dark, sandy earth with each stride. Closer now. Just past that last stand of pine…

And he was through! The sea stretched out before him like a vast, dark lake. The surf was calm, waves lazily uncurling against the white sand. Seagulls swooped and darted. Three dolphins did their roller-coaster dance in the water. Gregory urged Bo into a full gallop. Horse and rider whipped through the brown sea oats cresting the last dune, down the other side, and onto the beach. The sand was hard, perfect for riding. Ocean on the left, dunes on the right, cloudless sky overhead, setting sun behind. Except for the seagulls' frenzied bickering over a clam morsel, there was nothing but empty shore all around. Freedom.

"How's that feel? Good, huh?" Gregory groomed Bojangles's mane in his stall after the beach ride. He loved the way Bo's ivory hair shone against his palm. "Aren't you a beauty, though?" Bojangles nodded his head as if in response. "OK, don't get conceited!"

Gregory was so glad he had chosen a palomino for his first horse. He loved their versatility. And their muted gold color never ceased to dazzle him. He also loved their history. It was said that Richard the Lionhearted had a palomino warhorse. And Queen Isabella owned one hundred of them and forbade any commoner to own even one. Yes, a very special animal.

Bojangles swished his tail. "Wish we were still out there, don't you, boy? Me, too! 'Cause you know who will be home from work soon. And then…" Gregory stood back and looked at Bo. "Don't you look good, now? Best lookin' horse in all of Charleston County. Gimme a kiss." Gregory puckered his lips near Bojangles's rubbery black mouth.

"Don't you dare kiss that horse, Gregory Pinckney! That's disgusting!" Gregory turned to see his mother, Meredith, standing in the stable doorway. She was wearing a pale-pink, sculptured Chloe dress that hugged her slender body like Saran wrap, and matching shoes. A crisp, new Gucci handbag hung over one arm. Her short, blond hair was cropped fashionably, and bright-red lipstick accentuated her full lips and complemented her red nail polish. "It's bad enough you let him slobber all over you every time you feed him. And hug him! Why don't you hug your mama instead?"

"'Cause I might wrinkle your new dress, and then what would your lady friends think?" Gregory picked up a bucket and began scooping feed into it from the large barrel in the corner. "You off to Charleston for your weekly society foodgrab?"

"We do not grab our food, and you know it."

"Bo does," Gregory countered, dumping the food into Bojangles' trough. Bo began rooting around in his food. "You sure that's not what ya'll look like?" he teased. He liked his relationship with his mother: light enough to joke around, serious when necessary. But they often disagreed what was appropriate when.

"Stop kidding around, Gregory. That's your problem: you're never serious. You take life too lightly." Meredith wobbled a few feet forward in her high heels.

"Look who's talking. What are you serious about?"

"Lots of things. Good manners, fine art, the symphony, managing the household staff, keeping our home neat." As if to confirm her scrupulousness, Meredith picked a piece of lint from her dress.

"No, Lily Ann is serious about keeping the home neat, not you." Gregory ducked under Bo's neck to come closer to his mother.

"I *am* serious; I just hire her to do it. Oh, I am not going to get into a discussion about social relations with you at this minute." She opened her purse, took out her compact, and gave her lipstick a final inspection. "Now, your daddy will be home shortly. Lily Ann will be serving you both supper. Then what will you do?"

"I'll think of something."

"Laura Kingsley's daughter is home from college. Why don't you give her a call and go out, take her to a movie or something." Meredith smiled broadly at her son.

"Mama, I'm too old for her."

"Twenty-seven is not too old to date a college senior. I wasn't even a high-school senior when your daddy was twenty-seven." Satisfied with her looks, Meredith replaced the compact and closed the purse with a loud clack. She glanced at her silver Cartier watch. "Oh my Lord, I've got to go! I won't be back too late. You and your father have a nice evening together. Bye, sweetie!"

She turned, navigated the straw-strewn barn floor in her high heels, and, on firmer footing, moved swiftly down the driveway to her car. Gregory watched her go. She had kept herself in good shape, he had to say that. He knew his father wouldn't stand for anything else. Meredith slipped behind the wheel of her Porsche convertible, backed out of the driveway, and sped off.

A stillness settled over the late afternoon. Gregory wiped the sweat from his brow. Was he really hot, or was he perspiring in anticipation of the evening's inevitable scene? He laid his head against Bo's massive cheek. The two of them stood silently for a moment. Gregory pulled his head back and looked into his horse's huge, brown eyes. "It'll be all right," he said out loud. But inside he wasn't so sure.

"All right, Bo, time for bed." He led the horse to his stall, closed the gate behind him, and walked out of the stable. The large plantation house with white columns loomed ahead. So did the inevitable confrontation with his father.

The official envelope stared up at Gregory from his oak desk in the sunny bedroom at the back of the house. "South Carolina Bar Association," the return address read. Another envelope lay opened, from the South Carolina Department of Social Services. Gregory looked at them both. Two possible futures. One in South Carolina, the other somewhere in Pennsylvania. Two possible careers. Lawyer or…what?

Gregory moved to a window and looked out across the backyard to the tidal swamp across the way. A blue heron stalked its prey on spindly legs. An alligator lay stone-still on a far bank. Turkey buzzards kept a watchful eye from the limbs of a tall pine. Gregory took a deep breath. The sweet and salty air caressed his lungs. *Do I really want to leave all this? Maybe the conversation with Daddy won't go so badly. Maybe he'll understand.*

Gregory returned to his desk and picked up the manila envelope from the South Carolina Judicial Department.

> *Dear Mr. Pinckney:*
>
> *We regret to inform you that you failed to pass the South Carolina Bar Examination. Your score of 108 on the multi-state portion does not satisfy the minimum requirement of 110 points and you have therefore failed the entire Bar Examination without the necessity of grading the essay sections.*
>
> *As this is your third failed attempt to pass the Bar Examination, you are not eligible to sit for a Bar Examination until at least one year following the administration of your last failed examination. (See Rule 402(j)(1), Admission to Practice Law, South Carolina Judicial Department).*
>
> *Enclosed please find an application to retake the Bar Examination. Contact the South Carolina Judicial Department at the above-referenced address and phone number should you have any questions.*
>
> *Thank you very much.*
>
> *Victoria Bruce*
> *Chair, Board of Law Examinations*
> *South Carolina Judicial Department*

Gregory walked briskly to his open window and breathed in deeply a few times. "Why?!" he shouted out to the heron. The elegant bird turned its head in Gregory's direction, then flew off, leaving him with his unanswered question.

The sound of a car coming up the driveway penetrated his mind like a sharp spike. *He's home.*

Gregory's father, Gregory Cotesworth Pinckney — young Gregory was a "junior"–, nicknamed Red because of his hair, poured himself a Scotch in the darkened den where he retired immediately after work each evening. Dewar's, just like his father. *Why doesn't Gregory drink Dewar's?* he thought grudgingly. *Proves he's not really in the bloodline.* With a sigh, he settled himself on the comfortable leather couch and put his feet up on the coffee table. Who'd have thought he, of all people, wouldn't have been able to father a child. Damn rotten luck.

If he were his biological father, he could have passed along his brains to Gregory. It's not that the boy wasn't smart; he was. It's just that he didn't apply himself. He had a chance to join one of the most prestigious law firms in the Southeast, Pinckney & Walters, a firm Red had built from scratch, and he couldn't even pass the bar exam. Well, once he passed it and settled into the firm, things would be different. They might go back to hunting together, and fishing. Like the old days. Might change the name to Pinckney and Pinckney. That dang bar exam had just been making things a little tense around the house, but once Gregory had passed it…

"Got a minute, Daddy?" Gregory asked from the doorway to the den.

"Sure, of course, come on in. Pour yourself a Scotch."

"No thanks. Might have a beer though." Gregory opened the small refrigerator underneath the wet bar and pulled out a lite beer.

"How can you drink that stuff, son? If you won't have a Scotch, at least have a real beer."

"Claims to be made from Rocky Mountain spring water. Can't get realer than that." Gregory smiled and sat down in a nearby chair and took a chug of beer. A brief silence settled between them.

His father rattled the ice cubes in his glass, then took a large gulp. "Your mom's gone to her cocktail reception?"

"Yes, sir. She said Lily Ann would make us supper."

"The heck with that. Why don't we go down to Rusty's, get us a nice steak?"

"I think Lily Ann's already started cooking."

"She doesn't mind. She can eat it herself."

"No thanks."

"Suit yourself." Red hoisted himself up off the couch and went to pour himself another drink.

Gregory took a swig of beer, gave a deep sigh, and began. "Daddy, I've been thinking. Maybe it's time for me to go away for a little while, see a little bit more of this country."

"Why would you want to do that, when you're living right here in God's paradise?" He ambled back to the couch and sat down, swirling his ice cubes before taking a swallow.

"I'd like to get out of South Carolina for a little while."

"And go where?"

"I dunno. Up north, maybe — "

"Yankee land?! That lite beer's made you lightheaded!" Red chuckled.

"Oh come on, Daddy. It's the twenty-first century, there're no more Rebs and Yanks."

"There'll always be Rebs and Yanks, as long as there's a north and a south."

"Fine." Gregory took another swig of beer. This wasn't starting off well.

"What's all this talk about leaving about, Gregory? You always loved the South."

"I still love it, but…aw, heck, here." Gregory held out the letter from the Judicial Department. His father snatched it up and began to open it excitedly. "There's no hurry, Daddy. You're not going to like the results."

His father quickly scanned the letter, then crumpled it and threw it in the corner. "What in the heck's the matter with you, Gregory?! Why can't you pass the dang bar?"

"I don't know, Dad — "

"Any idiot with two cents worth of brains can pass this exam. I passed it and — "

"'Only studied for two weeks.'" Gregory finished a sentence he knew by heart. "I know, Daddy, but I'm just not you."

"I'm not asking you to be me, I'm just asking you to pass the durn bar exam!"

"I'm trying."

"No you're not. You're too smart to fail this exam three times. You just didn't study, that's all. Don't you see, son? Your future's all right here for the taking. Join the firm, get married, kids, nice place on the beach, leader of society. Heck, you could buy more of those horses you love so much, have a whole stable-full. What's wrong with you?!"

"Maybe I just don't want to be a lawyer!" Gregory snapped. "Did you ever think of that?!"

"Don't raise your voice to me!" Red slammed his drink down on the table.

"Sometimes that's the only way to get you to listen! Why is this so important to you? Why can't you just let me be who I want to be?"

"And who is that?"

"I don't know yet. I just want to find out."

"I want you to walk tall, walk proud — "

"Drink Dewar's." Usually Gregory could stop himself when the argument threatened to get out of hand, but tonight he didn't seem to be able to. Or want to. "Maybe I'm just a lite-beer drinker, Daddy!" He started for the door.

Red's anger had turned his face the color of his name. "I'm not through with you!"

"Maybe I'm through with you!" Gregory marched quickly out the door and ran up the stairs to his room.

"Get back here, Gregory! Get back here! I'm not chasing after you!" Red screamed at his retreating son. "Gregory!"

When Gregory did not return, Red turned to the bar and poured himself another Dewar's. This time he didn't bother with the ice; he just gulped it down straight. "That's my thanks for giving him a good home," he muttered angrily. He finished his drink and slammed out of the back door, shouting, "Lily Ann, forget about dinner!"

Up in his bedroom, Gregory grabbed the letter from the Department of Social Services.

Dear Mr. Pinckney:
In response to your inquiry, the Department of Social Services is not authorized to provide any information about your natural mother.

We regret that we cannot assist you with your inquiry.

Yours truly,

Belinda Smith

On the bottom of the letter Gregory had written down two names. The first was Elizabeth Hollins, a social worker who had handled his case and had retired shortly after he had been born. He'd found her through a friend who worked at the Department of Social Services. Gregory smiled at the thought of his meeting with Elizabeth at the Palmetto Manors assisted living facility. She was a slender, white-haired woman in her late eighties with a dentured smile that had immediately put Gregory at ease. As it happened, he had shown up right at the end of Happy Hour, which might have loosened Elizabeth's tongue a little.

"You're not a preacher, are you?" had been Elizabeth's first question upon meeting Gregory. Before he could answer, she had gone into quite a spiel. "The clergy stop by here occasionally. I got nothing against preachers, but I get the sense that they come by here not because they want to but because they think they should. Like checking the box. I checked too many boxes in my life, only got one left: died and gone to heaven."

She had finished the wine in her paper cup. "Would you mind getting me a little bit more of this stimulation, sonny? We're allowed one glass, and this is only my second." Gregory had laughed. He liked this lady.

When Gregory had answered her request, he took advantage of her pausing to drink to explain his mission.

"Lawd, sonny, I retired twenty-five years ago. I cain't remember every woman who put up her child for adoption."

Then Gregory had played his trump card. Showing her a baby quilt, he had asked, "Ms. Hollins, have you ever seen this?" It was a pattern of nine small squares, with a butterfly inside each of them.

Elizabeth had taken the quilt and slowly rubbed her fingers over it. She had closed her eyes. "My, my…yes, I remember. A pretty, brown-haired woman, said it was an Amish quilt, begged me to make sure it went along with the baby to his new home. I remember her because she was so strong, no tears or anything. And she was convinced that if this quilt went with the baby, everything would be all right. She convinced me, too, so I did it."

"Ms. Hollins, could you possibly remember her name or anything about her?" The odds had been long, but just maybe…

"Let's see…" Elizabeth had taken a long sip of the wine, again closing her eyes. "I met her a couple of times before the baby was born, and that was it. She was stayin' over at the Radcliffe's…Retired doctor, he was, from Pennsylvania." Gregory had waited patiently while she racked her brain. "Her name…seems like it was an odd one, one I'd never heard before…I thought it had something to do with yodeling at first, till she spelled it…Yoder! Yes, that was it! Mae Yoder! My grandmother's name was Mae is how I remember it!" Elizabeth had swallowed the last of her wine, proud of her memory.

"Thank you so much, Ms. Hollins!" Gregory actually had his mother's name! Yoder. But where was she from? If the doctor had been from Pennsylvania, maybe his mother had been, too. Gregory had a final inspiration. He had sneaked Elizabeth one more glass of wine before asking her to try to remember where his mother had been from.

"I remember she had this funny accent, spoke what she called Pennsylvania Dutch. Said she was Amish. Well, I'd never heard of such a thing. Dutch people in Pennsylvania? But then she'd explained it all to me."

Standing in his room, Gregory now looked down at the letter in his hand. *God bless you, Elizabeth Hollins! Yes, you gave me the clue I needed.* Underneath her name, Gregory had written another: Mae Yoder. And beside that was a location: Lancaster County, Pennsylvania.

He placed the letter back in the envelope and moved to the window. The sun was beginning to paint a beautiful picture over the lowlands, orange and gold. The alligator was gone, sunk deep into the swamp to await the new day. The breath of a breeze caused the tops of the marsh grasses to sway, like a tipsy alcoholic. A flock of ducks skimmed the horizon. A chorus of frogs started vocalizing as dusk lowered over the estate. Gregory heard the squeal of tires leaving the driveway. *Daddy's gone,* he thought. *Do I want to go, too? With so little to go on?*

He walked to his bureau, opened the bottom drawer, and carefully withdrew the quilt that Meredith, his adoptive mother, had given to him when he'd turned twelve. "It's from your biological mother," she'd said. "She left it with you when she put you up for adoption. I think you should have it."

Gregory had placed it in the drawer and forgotten about it. Then one day last spring, he'd seen it and pulled it out to look at. He'd thought, *My real mother made this. I wonder who she is?* And that simple question had rattled around inside his brain for months until, finally, he was ready to try to answer it.

Gregory looked around his room. Yes, there had been good years spent there. His adoptive mother?…Meredith had loved him as best she could. His adoptive father?…That was more complicated. But they had been good parents, all in all. He took out a sheet of paper and wrote:

Dear Mama and Daddy,

I am taking Bo and setting out on a little adventure. I have a clue as to where my biological mother might be located, and I'm going to try to find her. This has nothing to do with you, Mama. You have been a wonderful mother. And you, Daddy, though we've had our differences, I know you love me and only want the best for me. That is what this is all about: finding who I am.

I'll let you know where I land so you won't worry. Just give me a little time. Please try to understand that this is really what I need right now.

Love,

Gregory

Gregory looked at the letter. *Is there anything else to say?* No, he'd said all that was necessary. He pulled a suitcase from under the bed. The first thing he placed in it was the Amish baby quilt.

CHAPTER 3

Ivan Heminger slowly ran his fingers over the top of his bald scalp, an unconscious practice when he was thinking through a problem. He missed having the full head of black hair that had made him such an attractive younger man. *Another thing you gotta accept with age!* Ivan was fifty-nine, and he had the growing paunch to prove it. He also had the graying hair, at least what remained on the sides and back of his head. Ivan was a big man, tall at six foot two, with an oval face, piercing blue eyes, and thin lips that could easily morph into a charming smile or a tight, sinister line. These days, the charming smile was not as readily displayed as usual.

Stay calm, he reminded himself. He thought about having a shot of vodka to help, then glanced at the small clock on his desk. 2:17 p.m. A bit early, even for Ivan. Besides, he wanted to stay in control. Sometimes a shot of booze helped with that; sometimes it didn't. That was the unpredictable nature of alcohol. This time Ivan opted uncharacteristically to go with conventional wisdom and lay off the booze to help himself stay focused.

Seated at his large, mahogany desk, Ivan picked up a framed photograph of a beautiful young woman who was looking directly into the camera, holding the reins of a thoroughbred horse. She had a dazzling smile that revealed a row of perfect white teeth and luscious, blond hair that spilled about her shoulders. Wanda, his daughter, with her horse, Dandelion. At that moment she was probably back at Cedar Ridge Farm, riding Dandelion or grooming him.

Wanda came home as often as she could from summer school. It had already been almost five years since she started college, and next year, hopefully, she would finally graduate Penn State. Ivan smiled at the photograph as he returned it to his desk. He was glad to have Wanda around. She was practically the only reason Ivan had to smile.

Ivan rose and began to pace his office. He would love to have a cigarette, but he'd stopped smoking five years ago. Cleaning up his act. He'd stopped catting around years ago, too, deciding it was too much hassle. It had cost him his first marriage to Sheila, a plain-looking woman with plenty of smarts. "Smarts" was not what Ivan had been after in his youth. But he'd learned. That's why Shelly, the secretary now outside his office, was short, skinny, and fiftyish, instead of the usual well-built bimbo who could hardly type but who was good at other things. Ivan had remained mostly faithful to Liz, the secretary whom he had decided to "promote" to being his second wife — after she'd told him she was pregnant. That had been twenty-two years ago. But it was worth it, to have wonderful Wanda in his life.

He looked out the window. Downtown Lancaster, Pennsylvania. It wasn't much of a view. Even in the corner office of a premiere law firm, what was there to look at? Office buildings and stores. Not even good-quality stores. Those had moved out to Park City Mall years ago. No, Ivan hadn't missed going to this office. He preferred the one he had at home, on the farm, upstairs in the barn. That's where all his pictures hung. Here he'd kept the framed law-school diploma, the thank-you letter from the Salvation Army he'd helped out in a big way years ago, and several large photographs of nature he'd installed just so the walls wouldn't look so bare.

And the Bible on the desk. That was a nice touch, Ivan thought, since so many of his clients were Amish or Mennonite or Wenger Mennonite or Brethren or some of the other Plain People sects from Lancaster County and the surrounding area. But their number had declined significantly over the years, first when Ivan got divorced, then when he'd adopted a lavish lifestyle, and finally as he had spent more and more time on his passion: racehorses. That's when Ivan had placed the Bible on his desk. But Plain People weren't stupid. They knew when a Bible was just a Bible and not a testament of faith.

It took some time for Ivan's partners, all of whom were junior to him both in age and in their participation in the firm's profits, to tire of doing most of the work while Ivan took most of the profits. There had been some good years when Ivan's wealth had increased significantly. But finally, five years ago, his law partners had descended on him and given him a choice. They would either resign immediately and start their own practice, or there would be a new profit-sharing and management arrangement.

Neil Lewis had summarized the situation: "Ivan, we're not asking you to resign. You've already done that. We're just looking to make official what's already going on." So Ivan had taken the deal, reminding himself he never had liked Lewis and was sorry he'd ever hired him, even if he had gone to Harvard.

So, there he was in his downtown office. That's because he certainly hadn't wanted the visit he'd surely be receiving to take place at his home office. Liz or Wanda or Tommy the farmhand might notice and start asking questions. No, it would be much less suspicious if the visit took place here. The annoying Shelly would be curious, of course, and would try to glean whatever information she could, but Ivan could do what he always did with Shelly: stonewall her.

At that moment, the object of Ivan's thoughts knocked discreetly on the door, entered the office, and said, "Excuse me, Mr. Heminger. There's a Mr. Jenkins here. He says he's a friend of a Mr. Mancuso and that you're expecting him." Shelly leaned forward, close enough for Ivan to get a whiff of her cheap perfume, and whispered conspiratorially, "He doesn't have an appointment."

"Thanks, Shelly," Ivan responded calmly. "Send him in, please."

Shelly left and reappeared with a well-dressed, middle-aged man in a dark-gray suit, red-and-blue striped tie, and shiny black shoes. The suit wasn't tailor-made, like Ivan's, but it fit well and certainly wasn't cheap. It fit a little too well, as far as Ivan was concerned, since the visitor's neck and chest muscles were powerful and much bigger than those of an average man his age. He looked like a weightlifter or a professional fighter, but Ivan was glad that there was at least a chance that Shelly would take him for a normal businessman. "This is Mr. Jenkins," she said.

"Thank you, Shelly, that'll be all," Ivan said, crossing the room to Jenkins. Shelly hesitated just a moment to express her disappointment that she wouldn't be taking notes, then left. Ivan offered his outstretched hand. "I'm Ivan Heminger."

Jenkins gripped Ivan's hand powerfully, looked at him with cold, brown eyes, and said nothing. Ivan quickly shut the office door Shelly had purposefully left open. "May I offer you something to drink?"

"I don't drink," Jenkins said levelly.

"Please, have a — "

"Mr. Mancuso wanted me to pass along some information he has received," Jenkins interrupted. "He's heard that you owe a good deal of money to some rough characters who are running out of patience with you. Something about a deadline that passed a week ago."

Ivan tried to explain. "I know I'm late but — "

"I'm speaking here," Jenkins said forcefully. "As you know, Mr. Mancuso likes you. He is also concerned about you, and he asked me to tell you to be very careful. These kinds of people have been known to do terrible things to people who don't pay their debts."

Ivan was confused. "These kinds of people?" Mancuso was the guy Ivan owed. Why was Jenkins talking about "rough characters"? He decided not to pursue the question. "I've always been good for my debts."

"I don't know anything about that, Mr. Heminger," Jenkins replied.

For a thug he certainly speaks articulately, Ivan thought. *Maybe he isn't a thug, but then —*

"All I know is that Vinny the Snake will be following up with you," Jenkins continued. "He will probably call you here in a few days and ask to have a cup of coffee with him. It would be a good idea if you are in your office so you don't miss Vinny's call — unless, of course, you'd like Vinny to visit you at home."

Vinny the Snake?! Who's he? Whoever he was, Ivan didn't want him showing up at his home. "I understand," Ivan replied as calmly as possible. "Please tell Mr. Mancuso that I appreciate his concern and that I'll be here each morning for the rest of the week."

"Did I say he'd only be calling in the morning?" Jenkins asked pointedly, then turned and left without another word.

The visit had lasted less than two minutes, but it had felt like thirty. Ivan opened his bottom drawer, poured himself a shot of vodka, drank it off, then poured himself another one. He began to nurse it as he walked around his office, thinking. He knew that Mancuso had a reputation as being a decent guy, at least to the extent that someone who ran an illegal gambling operation could be thought of as decent. Mancuso wasn't the sort that would break someone's legs just because he could. Maybe he would be reasonable to deal with, despite the fact that Ivan had already missed two payment deadlines. But Mancuso also had a business to run and wouldn't hesitate to turn a pit bull like Jenkins loose if he thought it made sense.

Ivan looked out his window and saw Jenkins get into a Mercedes and pull away. Nice car, nice suit, altogether a professional meeting — if one could call it that. *Probably being prudent.* After all, Ivan might be recording the meeting. It's easy for almost anyone to record anything. From Mancuso's perspective, it's at least conceivable that Ivan was considering testifying and entering the witness protection program. *At fifty-nine? Relocate my whole family? Not likely.*

Ivan polished off the last of his vodka. The meeting hadn't gone as badly as he had feared. The eternal optimist, Ivan was confident that he'd somehow get past this particular problem. What he had more trouble getting past was that he'd have to spend all day every day sitting in his office, doing nothing but waiting for the call from Vinny the Snake. With you-know-who monitoring every call. *Maybe the bimbo secretaries were better,* thought Ivan as he muttered a quick good-bye to Shelly and headed home.

Shelly was a bit puzzled why Ivan spent so much time in the office that next week. She had a feeling that it had something to do with his earlier meeting with Mr. Jenkins, but she had learned absolutely nothing by Googling "Jenkins," "Mancuso," "Mankuzo," and a number of other variants of the names. When a Vincent Briganti called, she took a moment to Google his name before relaying the call to Ivan, but she found nothing.

"Hello," Ivan said.

The voice at the other end simply said, "Meet me at Randall's Diner in fifteen minutes," then the phone was abruptly hung up. Ivan poured himself a shot of vodka before making the five-minute drive to Randall's. It was early for a drink, only eleven, but the time didn't matter, only the circumstance.

As he entered the diner, Ivan had no problem recognizing Vincent Briganti. It was Jenkins! This time, however, Jenkins or Vincent or Vinny the Snake or whoever he was, sported a tee shirt and blue jeans. Tattoos spread out on each of his heavily muscled arms, and his thick neck rose like a trunk from the collar of the tee shirt. He was sitting in a booth with a cup of black coffee in front of him. When he saw Ivan he rose from his seat and greeted him with a bear hug that took his breath away. "Great to see you!"

Ivan looked confused.

"Pardon the greeting," Jenkins/Briganti said. "I needed to get a feel for your chest and hip. You're too smart to be wired, but it never hurts to make sure." He even smiled, but Ivan was too scared to return the smile.

"Why did you say your name was Vincent Briganti? Who are you, really?"

"That don't matter. What matters is, you owe me a half million dollars."

Ivan corrected him. "I owe Mr. Mancuso the money, and I will get it to him as soon as I can."

"Mancuso's no longer involved. I bought the debt from him at a discount."

"Then I owe you a half million dollars," Ivan responded as forcefully as he could. "And I'm good for it. I just need a little time."

"I don't think you understand. You owe me a half million *now*."

"Look, Mr. Jenkins, or Briganti, or whatever your name is."

"Call me Vinny. I like to be on a first-name basis with my clients." He smiled again, but it didn't feel all that friendly to Ivan. "Sit down."

Vinny sat and Ivan did, too. "I need ninety days," he said, as calmly as he could.

Vinny countered. "I borrow money to buy these loans, and money's not free. I'd break you in two right now, but Mancuso asked me to give you a chance to come through. Tell you what, you need ninety days, right?"

"I do," Ivan responded hopefully.

"And I need a little something, too. Something you might be able to help me with. Would you like to help me, Ivan?"

It didn't sound like a question. "Of course."

"You're racing Dandelion in two weeks, right?"

"That's right. My daughter's sure he's going to win. You want to bet on him?"

"Not exactly. I want Dandelion to lose. In fact, I don't want him to win, place, or show."

Ivan thought how devastated Wanda would be if Dandelion ran so poorly. "Why?"

"I usually don't answer stupid questions, but I'll make an exception. The more people bet on Dandelion, the more I collect when they lose. *Capisce?*" Ivan had watched enough television to know what that meant. He nodded that he understood. "Good. Dandelion's gotta race though. You can't scratch him." Ivan nodded again. "The horse race plus the money in ninety days, and we'll call it even."

Vinny rose. "Just one more thing. You don't come through on this, there are going to be some very angry people. I wouldn't want anything to happen to you because my half mil's unsecured, you know what I mean? I don't want anyone to find Ivan Heminger at the bottom of the Susquehanna. *Capisce?*"

Ivan didn't even bother to nod this time. He just numbly waited for the next command. It came after Vinny made a point of patting his pockets. "Do me a favor, Ivan. I don't got no small change. Leave the girl a ten." And with that, he turned and left the booth.

Ivan stared at his hands. They were trembling. His shirt was drenched with sweat. The waitress came over. "Can I get you anything else?" Ivan shook his head, and she tore the bill from her pad and put it on the table. "All right, thank you," she said as she turned to leave.

"Just a minute," Ivan said. He took out his wallet, fumbled for whatever bill he had in there, placed it on the table, and walked out of the diner. The waitress picked up the bill, stared at it, and called out, "Wait, don't you want your change?" Ivan just kept walking. The waitress looked again at the bill. *Fifty dollars!*

CHAPTER 4

Gregory smiled happily as he looked out the pickup truck's window at yet another beautiful Amish farm in the heart of Lancaster County's "Dutch Country." He could tell the farm was Amish because of the lack of electrical wires running from the roadside to the main house, as well as the presence of a tall windmill, which supplied the owner with power to draw water from the stream. He didn't know much about the Amish, but he knew that much. He wanted to learn more. Any people who could create such beautiful farms, with their large white barns, well-kept yards, perfectly groomed gardens, sturdy fences, and acres of thriving corn, must know something about living in harmony with the land. And harmony was something Gregory very much longed for.

His life had seemed out of tune for some time now. Being a lawyer had made no sense. It wasn't who he was. Failing to pass the bar exam — three times — had proved that to him, if not to his father. Yet who was he? Gregory had pondered this question for the past week as he'd wended his way toward Pennsylvania. Finding his mother, if indeed he could, might provide an answer.

But the farther Gregory drove from South Carolina, the less urgent he felt about finding her. Oh, he intended to do it. It's just that it might not be such a bad idea to find a place in this beautiful countryside to live for a while, stay put somewhere, and slowly begin the search. Yes, *slowly* was the key. He had been living too fast-paced a life; he could tell that now. Ever since he'd crossed the Pennsylvania border, he had felt himself slow down. He'd even gotten off Interstate 81 and taken back roads. Was there some sort of peace in the air here that calmed the spirit? Gregory didn't know, but he did know he'd like to breathe a lot more of it to find out.

He passed a sign for the Village of Honey Brook. Not much of a village, as far as he could tell. Perhaps a quarter of a mile of houses facing the main road, with one or two farms spanning the horizon behind them. A small sign reading "Post Office" hung outside someone's house. There was no store, no gas station, not even a fast-food place. *Could this be America?* Gregory thought with a smile. He parked and went inside the post office. When he emerged five minutes later, he had the address of a Zook farm, where the lady in the post office had said he might find a place to stay and maybe even somewhere to keep his horse.

Gregory drove slowly until he spotted a small road on his right. "Zook Lane," the sign read. He turned onto it, careful to swing wide so the horse trailer he was pulling would make the turn. He drove down an incline and rattled over a cattle bridge spanning a small creek. On the hill ahead rose a large white house with a wraparound porch, and a smaller house behind it. Across the lane stood a barn with several chicken houses stretched out behind it, and, down the hill near a creek, an old cottage. A windmill revolved slowly in the still morning breeze. Behind the house a woman was hanging clothes on a line. She was short and plump and had to stretch to reach some of the clothes.

"Hello!" called Gregory, slowing his car. The woman didn't answer, so he stopped and got out. "Excuse me for interrupting."

"That's all right. I interrupt a lot. My sister, Mabel, says it's one of my worst … what's that word she uses? Character something."

"Characteristics?" offered Gregory.

"That's it. I'm Hanna. Who're you?" She smiled crookedly at Gregory.

"My name is Gregory Pinckney. I wanted to ask — "

"We don't have any names called Gregory around here," interrupted Hanna. "No Pinckneys either."

"It's southern," explained Gregory.

"You from the South?"

"South Carolina."

"My Mennonite cousins go through there on the way to Pinecraft, in Florida." Not sure what to do with this information, Gregory nodded politely. "Is there a horse in that trailer?"

"Yes. His name's Bojangles. Bo for short."

"I don't like horses. I got thrown when I was a little girl, hit my head, made me a little slow, some say soft in the head. But my head doesn't feel any softer than anybody else's." Hanna gave her head a quick feel. "Lemme feel yours."

Gregory didn't quite know what to do. He'd never met anyone who'd asked to feel his head, certainly not after knowing her for all of thirty seconds. But Hanna's big smile on her plain, broad face made him feel as if it was a reasonable request, so he bent his head forward. Hanna felt it with her fingertips. Her hands were strong.

"Feel any soft spots?" asked Gregory.

"No, but you oughta cut your hair; it's too long. Now you feel my head."

Flummoxed by this command, Gregory paused for a moment. Hanna lowered her head toward him. What could he do? He placed his hands on Hanna's head and felt around with his fingers.

"Find any soft spots?" asked Hanna.

Gregory considered which might be the best answer, yes or no. "Yes" would confirm Hanna's self-description, but Gregory didn't want to accuse her of being soft in the head. On the other hand, he didn't want to contradict her. He decided on a diplomatic "maybe." This seemed to satisfy Hanna, and she raised her head.

Gregory tried again. "I'm trying to find a place to stay."

"We don't have no motel."

"I don't want a motel. For one thing, I need a place to board my horse."

"We got horses. Mules, too. But we don't have rooms."

"I was wondering about that cottage down by the creek."

"It's rundown." Hanna moved away, looking off toward the cottage, and frowned.

"Maybe I could fix it up. I'd be happy to pay rent."

"You mean, money?" Her frown changed into an expectant smile.

"That's usually the way it's paid. 'Course, if you'd rather I do chores — "

"Why not do both?"

Gregory paused a minute, as much to slow down the conversation as to think about how to respond. "Well, maybe…"

"How much?"

"How much do you want?"

"A thousand dollars."

"That seems like a lot — "

"A hundred then."

"A month?"

"That's what the last renter paid. But he couldn't afford much more." She looked at Gregory. "You look like you're rich. Make it $150 a month. And you'll have to pay for your horse's food. Can you pay me now?" Hanna stuck out her hand.

"Don't I get to see the cottage first?"

"After you pay me," demanded Hanna.

"That's not usually the way it's done."

"I'm an unusual person."

Gregory gave a small laugh. "That you are, Hanna, that you are." He reached into his jeans and pulled out his wallet. As he did so, a buggy rattled over the cattle bridge and came up toward the house. It was enclosed, so Gregory couldn't see who was inside.

"Hurry up," said Hanna. "That's Mabel and Becca. We don't want them messing in our business."

Gregory counted out one hundred and sixty dollars and gave it to Hanna. "Shake!" she requested, and Gregory shook her outstretched hand. He waited for his ten dollars in change. But Hanna simply tucked the money into her apron.

The buggy came to a stop outside the barn, and two women got out. One of them was around Hanna's age, small and wiry with an air of crispness about her. The other looked to be in her early twenties. She looked pretty, Gregory thought, and as they approached, he could see that he was right. She was tall, with strong cheekbones. A long neck supported an open face that was clean and bright. Her brown hair was gathered under a covering. Her eyes were a shade of green Gregory had never seen before, more blue than green, really, and soft, like the rest of her.

"This is Pinckney Gregory," said Hanna when the two women were within earshot. "He's our new tenant."

"Tenant? We don't rent out rooms," said Mabel, looking sternly at Hanna.

"Not a room, the cottage," Hanna explained.

Rebecca inhaled quickly. "The cottage?!"

"Yes," declared Hanna excitedly.

A small frown creased Rebecca's brow.

Mabel said, "I'm sorry, Mr. Gregory — "

"Actually, my name's Gregory Pinckney."

"We don't rent out places here. There's a bread and breakfast over to Leola; it's not far." Mabel gave him a weak smile of encouragement.

"Too late, he's already paid," said Hanna, waving the money.

"We'll just give him back the money, then," said Mabel. She reached for the money, but Hanna snatched it away. "It's mine!" she snapped.

"Hanna, give me that money," demanded Mabel.

"It's mine," replied Hanna defiantly. "Now I can buy an ice cream maker."

"Give it to me!" Mabel said more firmly.

"No!" said Hanna.

Gregory tried to intervene. "It's all right, Hanna, I can find somewhere else."

"A deal's a deal, Pinckney! We shook on it." She drew herself up to her full five feet two inches, raised her head, and thrust out her chin.

For a moment, no one seemed to know what to do. Gregory stood helplessly, his wallet still in his hand. Rebecca eyed him. He was dressed in jeans, a button-down shirt, and well-worn penny loafers that had seen better days. She guessed that he was not used to life on a farm and that she might be able to solve her problem with a little directness.

"You realize, Mr. Pinckney, there's no plumbing in the cottage." Rebecca eyed him steadily. "No bed, no bureau, nothing. It's just a room. And no electricity. No lights, no radio."

"No television," chimed in Hanna.

"Well, that does sound kind of harsh," Gregory said.

"I thought so," said Rebecca. "Hanna, please give Mr. Pinckney his money back."

"But I may need harsh," continued Gregory. "You see, Miss...?"

"Rebecca Zook. And this is my mother, Mabel. Hanna is my aunt."

"Nice to meet you." Gregory shook their hands and continued. "It may sound kind of crazy, but I've just come from a world of...well, you might call it luxury. I think it might be good for me to rough it for a while. That creek can probably provide me with all the bathing water I'll need. And a kerosene lamp's all I'll need for light, at least for now. I don't plan to spend much time inside; it's summer." Gregory eyed Rebecca, who stood motionless and unsmiling. "I guess what I'm saying is, why don't we just give it a try for a month, see how it goes? You're not using the cottage for anything else, are you?"

"Not really," Rebecca replied hesitatingly.

"Well, all right then."

"I'll show you around!" exclaimed Hanna.

Rebecca quickly interrupted. "No, I'll do it. You've got to finish hanging up the wash, don't you, Hanna?"

"And then you need to start helping me bake those cherry pies," said Mabel.

"I told him he's gotta pay for his horse feed," said Hanna.

"You have a horse," inquired Rebecca. "What kind?"

"A palomino," answered Gregory.

"Becca loves horses," said Hanna. "But she doesn't get to ride 'em."

"Hanna, get to that wash," insisted Mabel. "I guess we'll be seeing you around, Mr. Pinckney." She nodded curtly and moved off.

"Welcome to our farm, Mr. Gregory." Hanna smiled, then went back to her clothesline.

"Come along, Mr. Pinckney," Rebecca said, and she started down the lane.

She seems a little curt, thought Gregory, as he followed her. *Did I say something to offend her?*

When they'd reached the creek, they turned to follow a path that led alongside the water. Dandelions sprouted in the fields, and yellow cups and blue cornflowers claimed their territories wherever possible. In the distance a man with a straw hat and black pants worked a plow behind a team of mules. Cows meandered in another field. The blue sky stretched for miles around.

"This is a beautiful farm," Gregory said.

"Thank you," said Rebecca. Gregory waited a minute to see if she was going to add anything to her perfunctory reply. When she didn't, he decided to give up on conversation for the present.

Outside the cottage, Rebecca stopped. "Mr. Pinckney," she began, "I didn't tell you the complete truth back there. The cottage is being used for something else. I am sorry for misleading you.

"What's the complete truth, then?"

"The truth is, I am using the cottage for something. Something…personal." Gregory waited for Rebecca to go on, but she hesitated.

"What is it, Ms. Zook?" asked Gregory.

"I'd best just show you." Rebecca pushed open the cottage door and gestured for him to enter.

Inside was a rectangular room some fifty feet long by thirty feet wide, with a high ceiling. Given its appearance from the outside, Gregory was surprised to see how clean it was inside. Though the air was a trifle musty, there was hardly any dust. He saw a broom in one corner. But what really caught his eye was a small, rectangular frame in the center of the room, a chair pulled up beside it, and a kerosene lamp on a nearby table.

"What's that?" he asked.

"A quilting frame," Rebecca replied.

"Oh, I've always wondered what one looked like." Gregory approached the frame and examined it. A nearly completed quilt stretched across it. "That's a small quilt," Gregory opined.

"It's a wall hanging," Rebecca answered.

"I didn't know you used quilts for wall hangings."

"Not many people do, I suppose. But I like to make them."

"Are those saddles?"

"Yes."

Another one-word answer. She's not much of a conversationalist, thought Gregory. He tried again. "I've never seen saddles in a quilt design before. I like it."

Rebecca ignored the compliment. "Mr. Pinckney, since you have been rented this room, I shall remove my quilt."

"Are you sure that's necessary? I don't take up much room."

"It wouldn't be right for me to be here while you're in this place," Rebecca replied. "So I shall move my quilt."

Oh, so that's it. She doesn't want to be bothered changing her quilting operation. "Ms. Zook, I can see that me moving in here might present a problem. I'll gladly look for another place."

"That won't be necessary, Mr. Pinckney. I have a place I can move it. It will have to be tonight," said Rebecca.

"In the dark?"

"Yes."

"Why can't you do it in the daytime?"

"Because I prefer to do it at night," Rebecca answered, somewhat sharply. *This Englisher asks so many questions!*

"Suit yourself." Gregory was tired from having driven hundreds of miles and tired of the conversation. "I'll just get my things and let Bo out of the trailer, if you don't mind."

"Bo?"

"My horse."

"Oh, yes, I'm so glad you've got a horse!" Rebecca smiled for the first time.

Well, at least she likes one of us, thought Gregory.

"I'll move the quilt frame near the door so as not to disturb you. When I knock on the door, would you mind just handing it out to me?"

"Happy to oblige, Ms. Zook."

"Thank you. We can bring you some covers to use as a bed tonight, and tomorrow you can go to Howard's Auction to shop for a bed, bureau, and other things you might need."

"Thank you."

"One other thing. Don't drink the crick water. There's a pump out back for well water." Rebecca gave him a small nod and left the cottage.

Gregory watched her go. *At least she kept me from poisoning myself. So much for the vaunted Amish friendliness.*

Later that night, as he lay on the covers, his head resting on a pillow of crisp, white cotton, Gregory watched the moon slide silently past his open window. He inhaled, smelling a pleasant mixture of grass, earth, and animal. *How did I end up here? And why?*

He had left South Carolina in a huff and a hurry, but he'd decided along the way to slow down, to risk not trying so hard to control the focus of his life, but instead to let God take over. Gregory hadn't thought much about God in a long time. He'd been too busy. Now here he was on an Amish farm, resting on an Amish quilt, suddenly living among a quiet people with a strong faith. Some power had led him here.

He knew no one. A place of strangers. Yet Gregory felt curiously at home. *Maybe this is what they mean by God's country,* he thought as his eyelids slowly closed.

CHAPTER 5

Saturday night, after supper, when Rebecca had finished washing the dishes, she put on her purple dress and her nicest covering. The Amish aren't much for full mirrors, considering them another sign of vanity, but the Zooks did have a small one in a hall off the kitchen, and Rebecca, at the risk of seeming vain, allowed herself a look. She liked what she saw — the dress fit nicely, her twenty-two-year-old body was firm, her face was clear and smooth, and her eyes were shining with light. She liked to look into those eyes and ask, *Who is this woman? How did she come to be here in this time and place? Why did God put her here and what is His plan for her? See that dark-brown hair, those smallish ears, those thick eyebrows, that long neck? That's someone called Rebecca Zook. But who am I?*

"What are you looking at?" asked Hanna from behind her.

"Oh, Hanna, you scared me." Rebecca said as she turned away from the mirror.

"Better not let Mabel catch you looking in that mirror. I know why you are," Hanna said smugly.

Rebecca knew she shouldn't ask, but she couldn't stop herself. "Why?"

"Your boyfriend's coming to get you for the singing."

"Jacob is not my boyfriend."

"Your fancy, then." Hanna had a way of mangling some words to produce new ones.

"He is not my fiancé," Rebecca countered, feeling the smallest prick of foreboding. She moved on down the hallway, Hanna following. "I'll be back around ten or eleven," she said, and went out the door.

"Becca!" Hanna called after her. "You forgot your hymnal." Hanna held it in her hand in the doorway, and Rebecca came back to retrieve it. "Thinking about your fancy and forgot your hymnal!" Hanna crowed. Rebecca grabbed the book and playfully tapped Hanna on the top of her head. "Ow!"

"Serves you right."

Rebecca scurried away before Hanna could think of something else to say. Then she walked down to the end of the lane to wait for Jacob. The sun was beginning to set on the western horizon when she got there. Jacob was already waiting in his open-aired buggy. Traditionally, unmarrieds didn't ride in a enclosed buggy. The elders employed many rules to keep young people from kissing and other physical contact. But, like young people through the ages, Amish youngsters found a way to do it anyway.

"Prompt as usual, Jacob." Rebecca smiled at him as he jumped off the buggy and offered her a hand.

"I like to be on time," Jacob replied, as he climbed back onboard and clucked the horse into motion.

"It's a fine quality," Rebecca said, and she meant it. Jacob had many fine qualities. He was a hard worker, never shirking his responsibilities. He seemed to have an innate sense about farming: when to sow and when to harvest, how to rotate his crops to conserve the soil. He was good with animals, too. He didn't need to call the vet to deliver a calf or piglets. He treated his horses with care and kept them well-fed. Best of all, as the youngest son, he was guaranteed to inherit the farm, seventy acres of rich Pennsylvania soil with a dozen buildings. Jacob's future was secure, and it could be Rebecca's future, too. So why was she less than thrilled to be contemplating it?

"What did you think of Amos's sermon last Sunday?" he asked, as the horse trotted down the road to Fisher's farm for the singing. Jacob was deeply religious, and that was another thing Rebecca liked about him. They had had many a discussion about the Bible and God's purpose for his people.

Rebecca recalled the sermon. "'Be ye not unequally yoked together with unbelievers.'"

"'For what fellowship hath righteousness with unrighteousness? What communion hath light with darkness?'" finished Jacob. "Staying separate from the world is one of the basic tenets of our faith."

Rebecca smiled to herself. It seemed funny to hear a phrase like "basic tenets" coming from the tanned and serious face with the black hat atop its head. But then, Jacob was pretty well-read when it came to the Bible. "Frankly, Jacob, I always thought it was a bit harsh, to tell the truth," offered Rebecca.

"Harsh?"

"Yes. We have to live among the English, right? I just don't think it helps to keep thinking of them as unrighteous."

Jacob flicked the reins, and the horse moved more quickly. "But anyone who doesn't have faith and forsake the world is unrighteous."

"Why can't they just be different, and let's leave it at that? And light and dark not communing? As a matter of fact, I think they go well together, because you can't have one without the other." She looked at Jacob, but he kept his eyes on the road. "Like in quilting, it's sometimes the dark background that brings out the lighter blocks."

"Do you talk like this to your parents?"

"No, they wouldn't understand. Do you?" Rebecca looked at Jacob. His answer was important.

He was silent for a moment, considering. "Are you saying you'd like to join the English?"

"Of course not," Rebecca answered. "I'm Amish. But I sometimes wish things weren't so black and white in our world. I sometimes wish there were more room for gray."

"Better not let the elders hear you talking like that," cautioned Jacob.

Yes, thought Rebecca, *they wouldn't approve. Why does it seem that everything in life needs approval? That's why I like making my quilt in secret: no one needs to approve it.*

Rebecca looked at Jacob. He was a good man, steady, serious. But, like many Amish men, he could be rigid. She wondered how much she might be able to loosen him up if they were married.

They reached the Fisher farm, and Jacob pulled the buggy over and parked it beside one of the other buggies. The singing brought together young, single people from different Amish communities. That was one reason Rebecca enjoyed it. She got to mingle freely with people her age and talk to people she didn't see all the time. It made her life seem less ordinary. *What's going on with me?* she pondered. *I thought I'd sown my wild oats. I'm supposed to be ready for ordinary now.*

At twenty-two, Rebecca was one of the oldest people at the singing. Even Jacob was a year younger than she was. *That's how desperate people probably think I am to get married. Going out with a younger man!* But she didn't feel desperate. Her mother certainly did, however. "I got married at eighteen" was one of her favorite reminders to Rebecca. Hanna was pushing, too, calling Jacob her "fancy." It seemed everybody was worried about Rebecca becoming an old maid — except Rebecca.

Inside the barn, many of the participants were already seated at the long table, men and boys on one side, women and girls on the other. Rebecca took a seat next to Madie Lapp, a short, stout girl with a square, kind face. Madie was two years younger than Rebecca and flush with excitement about her upcoming wedding to Amos Yoder.

"We're getting married in November, after the crops are in. That'd be a good time for you and Jacob to get married, dontcha think?" asked Madie.

"I suppose," said Rebecca.

"Has he asked you yet?"

"Not yet."

"What's wrong with the man?" Madie said indignantly. "He'd best snatch you up before somebody else does."

Rebecca changed the subject. "How are you and Amos getting along?"

"He's so funny!" exclaimed Madie. "When we ride in the buggy, he lets his knee slip over and rest against my leg, pretends he doesn't know what he's doing. But he knows! And I know, too. We both know things without saying them. It's kind of a secret language."

"Sounds nice," said Rebecca. And she meant it. Jacob never let his knee slip next to hers when they rode. She wondered what she'd do if he did. Rebecca had the normal urges of any young woman, but she was also somewhat frightened of intimacy. It was a little confusing, so she was glad when Morris Beiler announced the first hymn, "Fling Wide the Gates."

Rebecca liked spirited hymns like this one, quite a bit different from the ones in the Ausbund hymnal they used in church on Sundays. She especially liked how the women sang "Fling wide the gates" in a long, melodic arc while the men repeated under them "Fling wide the gates" in a quicker, pulsating response. And, at the end, while the women sang, "King…come…in," the men fit in the words "King of glory come in" so they all finished together on "in." *Women and men go their separate ways but end up together at the "in"!* Rebecca allowed herself a small laugh at her unintended pun.

When it was her turn to pick a hymn, Rebecca chose "There's a Wideness in God's Mercy." She loved the idea that God's mercy is as wide as the sea, that His heart is "most wonderfully kind." And the last verse represented a kind of prayer for Rebecca:

> If our love were but more simple
> We should take Him at His word
> And our lives would be all sunshine
> In the sweetness of the Lord.

Yes, she prayed, *let me find a simple love.*

After the singing, they all sat and visited for a while. Women and men seemed to naturally separate into two groups. Rebecca talked with Priscilla Yost, an eighteen-year-old girl from Leola, who chattered on about her garden. "I've never seen so many green beans so early," she said brightly. "How's your garden growing?"

"Fine," Rebecca answered. She didn't seem able to muster the usual energy to engage in chitchat. "Excuse me, Priscilla. I'd like to get some air."

Rebecca drifted outside, where some of the men were tossing a baseball around by the bright light of the moon. The sight reminded her of Johnny Schmucker. Johnny had been Rebecca's "fling." She had met him three summers before at another singing. She couldn't help but notice the handsome, blue-eyed blond who had sung every hymn with such gusto. When the singing was over and the men had gone outside to throw baseballs, Rebecca had watched as Johnny dazzled everyone with how hard he threw. She remembered how flattered she'd been when he had approached her as the evening wound down.

"Gum?" Johnny had asked, offering her some Juicy Fruit. Rebecca didn't chew gum. Neither did most of the Amish she knew. But, as she was about to find out, Johnny wasn't like most Amish.

Rebecca had declined the gum, but by the end of the conversation, she had accepted Johnny's invitation to bring some friends and attend the next week's baseball game in Ephrata. Johnny had hit a homerun. After the game, he had handed Rebecca a baseball. "That's the home run ball I hit. Here." He had taken the ball, autographed it, and handed it back to her. "Might be worth something someday."

He's so cocky, Rebecca had thought. *But kinda charming.*

After ice cream that night, Johnny had walked Rebecca home and kissed her. Like the gum, like the autograph, like most things in Johnny's world, he had just done it. And what a kiss! Not a careful one — no, a headlong, grab-you-in-his-arms, full-out kiss! It had left Rebecca stirred.

That had been Madie's name for that certain feeling when Rebecca had risked telling her about Johnny later. "Did you feel the stirring?"

"Stirring?"

"Yes, a kind of electrical jolt inside. When Amos kisses me, I always feel the stirring."

"I felt something!" Rebecca had giggled.

Madie had laughed, too. "That's it!"

Many more ball games, ice creams, and walks home with Johnny followed. And many more kisses. He had begun to visit Rebecca at her home, until her mother spoke to her one day while they were hanging up the wash.

"Why are you seeing so much of Johnny?" she had asked.

"I like him, Mam. He's fun."

"Maybe too much fun. I don't like his family. His brothers and sisters have all left the church, and I'm sure Johnny will, too. I know for a fact that his father drinks beer in the tobacco shed. You need to find somebody nice. Nice is better than fun, to my way of thinking."

Rebecca had gotten the message, but still she hadn't been able to resist Johnny. Then he took the decision out of her hands. When February came, he had left for Florida to try out for the Pittsburg Pirates. "It's just something I have to do, Becky."

Rebecca had been devastated. And his long, final kiss had only made her feel worse.

"I said, are you ready?" Jacob's voice interrupted Rebecca's reverie. "What were you thinking about? I had to ask you a couple of times."

Rebecca didn't want to hurt his feelings, but she wasn't going to lie. "Baseball," she replied simply.

They both knew the emotions that lay wrapped up in that one word. Rebecca had been honest with Jacob about her feelings for Johnny when they had first met. He had always felt self-conscious that he couldn't throw a baseball very well. Baseball was a subject they were both happy to avoid.

"Ready to ride home now?" Rebecca nodded, and they walked together to the buggy and got in. She watched Madie get into Amos's buggy and wave. She waved back, and saw her slide over next to Amos as they rode off.

"Did you enjoy the singing?" asked Jacob on the way home.

"I did. Did you?"

"Yes."

"What's your favorite hymn, Jacob?" Rebecca asked impulsively.

"Never really thought about it."

"Well, do you like fast hymns or slow ones?"

"Never thought about that either."

This conversation isn't going anywhere!

Rebecca contented herself with picking out constellations in the sky, as the horse moved them slowly through the soft, Pennsylvania night.

At the end of the lane, Jacob stopped the buggy, and Rebecca started to get out. "Thank you, Jacob. I had a really good time."

"Would you wait a minute please, Rebecca?" asked Jacob. She slid back into the buggy and looked at him expectantly.

He took a gulp of air and began. "Rebecca, we've been seeing each other for about two years now. You know how much I care about you, and I think you care about me." He looked at her now, and she smiled back. "And, well, I was thinking that maybe it's time we got married."

You were "thinking"? It's supposed to be a proposal, not a description of what you've been thinking! But Rebecca held her thoughts. Instead, she said, "Why do you think it's time?"

"Well," started Jacob slowly. "For one thing, Mam and Dat said they're ready to move into the gross dawdy house if we're ready to get married. For another, I was thinking that you and I were the oldest people at the singing tonight, and I'm kind of tired of being around these young people."

That's kind of him. I'm the one who's oldest.

"And the *Farmer's Almanac* says it's going to be a good year with the crops, God willing, so we'd be starting off well."

Yes, the timing is probably pretty good. But isn't love supposed to come in here somewhere?

"My father is going to give me the farm," Jacob continued. "I think we could have a *gut* life together."

A gut life. Rebecca could picture it all. Pregnant all the time during the first fifteen years or so, having eight or more children. That was fine; she loved children. Cooking, cleaning, washing, taking care of people she loved. And community. Yes, community, the backbone of the Amish faith. The living of a life not just for self. The more-than-oneness of existence within the Amish faith. There was a lot to be said for marrying Jacob. He was a *gut* man. It would be a *gut* life.

Rebecca! she chastised herself angrily. *Why isn't "good" good enough? What is this "more" I keep dreaming about? I'm waiting for something, and I don't even know what it is!*

Jacob had stopped talking. It was time for Rebecca to say something. "Jacob," she began, "first of all, I am grateful that you would want me for your wife. You are right; we would have a good life together. You are a good man, and I do care about you." Rebecca took a deep breath. What were the words? "But I don't know if I'm ready to get married yet."

Jacob looked shocked. "But why wait? I thought you and I were…" He let the rest of the thought die in the silent, night air.

"We were!" answered Rebecca. "We are!" she corrected herself. "We…I…" Rebecca had never felt more at a loss for words. "Jacob, you surprised me. Do I have to decide tonight?"

"You want some time to think about it?" His confusion was palpable.

"Yes," she replied, relieved that there at least seem to be a solution at hand for the moment. "Let me think about it."

"How long?"

"Before the last crops are in," Rebecca promised.

"That's a long time."

"If I decide before then, I'll let you know."

"You'll let me know," said Jacob, discouraged.

He's right, it sounds like some sort of business deal. She reached over and took his hand. "Jacob, I care about you. I do. And I want to make you happy. I just…need some time. Please?"

"Sure," said Jacob. "Take your time."

His downcast eyes and shrunken spirit almost made Rebecca reconsider, but she didn't want to marry out of pity. "Thank you," she said. She kissed him on the cheek and jumped down from the buggy. As Jacob drove off, she waved at him. He didn't wave back.

Rebecca started toward her home. It was darker now. Everyone would be asleep. She walked confidently down the lane she had traveled thousands of times. As a child she had often been afraid, walking alone at night, but now, as the Bible said, she had put away childish things. The rustling in the cornfields or the crickets' incessant chorus no longer frightened her. Instead, she found reassurance in their familiarity. It made her know God was present.

As she crossed the small bridge over the crick, she paused and looked down. The moon was reflected in the water, a crescent moon, like a diamond on the hand of God. She remembered the hymn they'd sung that evening. *If our love were but more simple.* Simple love…Her love for God felt simple, in a good way. But love for another human being, especially a man, was anything but simple.

Her eye caught sight of the large stone standing in the middle of the crick — solid, stable, withstanding the water rushing past it. Her life with Jacob. Her life on an Amish farm. Her life. Solid as a stone. And as unmoving. She saw a twig pass, dancing on the water, swept away by the current. *Where is it going?* she wondered, as it bubbled out of sight. *Where is all this water going…? I don't know.* She sighed and looked back at the stone in the crick. *But somewhere….*

CHAPTER 6

"Hi, is Ivan around?" the nicely dressed man with almost jet-black hair and a pleasant smile asked politely, standing just outside Ivan's box at Lancaster Downs Race Track.

Wanda lowered her binoculars. "I think he went to place a bet. He should be right back. I'm Wanda Heminger."

"You must be Ivan's daughter. I'm Vinny."

"Nice to meet you." Wanda offered Vinny her hand. She noticed how firm his grip was and how his muscles bulged under his black silk shirt. *Why would anyone wear silk on a hot summer day?* she wondered. She also noticed the tattoo on his left arm. A snake wrapping itself around an American flag. *Daddy knows people with tattoos?!* "You a friend of my father's?"

"A recent acquaintance. I hear you're quite the horsewoman."

"Yes, I love horses. My horse, Dandelion, is running in the next race."

"He's favored to win, I believe."

"He is! Did you bet on him?"

"In a manner of speaking," Vinny replied. "Did you go to Penn State?" he asked, pointing to the beer mug with the familiar Nittany Lion logo.

"I go there. I'm in summer school now; I just came back for the race."

"No kiddin'. I went there, too."

"Really?" Wanda gasped delightedly.

"Yeah. Played a little ball for Joe Pa."

"You played football at Penn State? Wow!"

"Well, *play* is stretching it a bit. I was too big to be a linebacker and too small to be on the line. But I was on the roster. Just for two years though."

"I'm impressed." Wanda gave Vinny one of her dazzling smiles.

"Thank you, Wanda," Vinny replied, returning a smile of his own.

Ivan and Liz descended the stairs toward their box. When he saw Vinny, Ivan stopped. For a moment he felt sick, as if he'd been punched hard in the stomach.

"Mom, this is Mr. Vinny — I didn't catch your last name," Wanda said.

"Vinny will do."

"He's a friend of Daddy's."

"Nice to meet you," Liz said, as she sidled past Vinny and sat in the box. She was wearing a yellow summer dress and a big white hat that tilted fashionably. "We placed the bets," she said to her daughter.

"Great!" said Wanda.

"To win, place, or show," replied Liz. "Just to be sure." She took out the racing program and began reading.

"My Dandy's gonna win!" Wanda shouted, raising her fist. "Isn't he, Daddy?"

"Of course." Ivan tried to muster as much enthusiasm as he could.

"Hello, Ivan," Vinny said. "Great to see you! Just came by to wish you luck on the race."

"Thanks, Vinny, that's nice of you," Ivan managed to say, with at least a touch of friendliness.

"You know I'm on your side," Vinny added. "By the way, your daughter and I have something in common. I'm a Nittany Lion, too. Did I ever mention that?"

Of course you never mentioned it, thought Ivan. *I've only spent ten of the worst minutes of my life with you.*

"Hey, Vinny, why don't you join us?" Wanda suddenly asked. If Ivan had felt sick before, this qesture made him think he might vomit on the spot. "We've got room."

Vinny paused and seemed to consider the proposition. He looked at Ivan, drawing out the moment. There was actually a twinkle in his normally cold eyes. "I'd like to," he finally said, "But I need to get back to my group." Ivan relaxed a touch, and the knot in his stomach loosened.

"All right," Wanda said. "But if you're ever out near Cedar Ridge Farm, please drop by. I'd love to show you around."

"I just might take you up on that, Wanda. It all depends." Vinny smiled, not at Wanda, but at Ivan. The knot in Ivan's stomach reasserted itself. "Good-bye. May the best horse win."

"Dandelion!" Wanda shouted. Vinny smiled and moved up the stairs. "He's a nice man, Daddy. Where'd you meet him?"

"Just around," Ivan said. He moved into the box and sat down next to his wife.

"I'm going to get a beer," Wanda said. She glanced at the big clock in the infield. "Just ten minutes to the race! I'm so excited! Aren't you, Daddy?"

Ivan forced himself to look at his daughter, the daughter he loved so much, the one he had just spent the last week making sure would suffer a terrible blow. Talk about a punch in the gut. And delivered by her own father. "Really excited, honey!" he managed.

"Can I get you anything?"

"No thanks."

"Mother?"

"No thanks, Wanda."

"You sure? You look a little peakish."

"I'm sure. Hurry back. Don't want to miss the race," Liz said.

"No way!' Wanda ran up the stairs. Ivan relaxed his shoulders for the first time in five minutes.

"No wonder I look peakish," Liz said. "Dandelion's going to lose this race."

Ivan had a panicked moment. Did Liz know what he'd done? But how could she? There weren't any clues. Ivan had simply fired the farmhand so he would be in control of feeding Dandelion. It hadn't been hard to do. Knowing how prickly Tommy was, Ivan had simply complained about the way the horses looked, especially Dandelion. As predicted, Tommy had gotten angry. "If you don't like the way I do things, hire someone else," he'd blurted out. So Ivan had fired him on the spot and taken over feeding the horses.

He fed Beauty just fine. But Beauty wasn't racing. Dandelion was, and he'd made sure that, for the last week, Dandelion hadn't gotten nearly enough to eat or drink. The plan had been to sap his energy, but in a way no one would notice. Ivan was about to find out if his plan would work. But what was his wife talking about?

"How do you know?" he asked anxiously.

"Paula told me," Liz responded, and Ivan breathed, relieved. Paula was a psychic Liz went to religiously. She practically ran her life based on what Paula said. Liz had even made Ivan go with her to Paula's house before she would agree to marry him. Ivan had fought like crazy not to have to go. The whole thing was stupid, as far as he was concerned. Another bimbo idea from his bimbo secretary. But Liz had insisted, threatening to never see Ivan again. One look at her had convinced him he hadn't wanted that to happen, so he had agreed.

Paula Psychic, as she called herself, lived in a small suburban house on the outskirts of Lancaster. It was a normal-looking house, but what went on inside was anything but normal. Leading Liz and Ivan to a dimly lit back room, Paula had placed them in two chairs and then had seated herself on a couch, lying down. For a few moments, she had breathed deeply. Silence prevailed. And then she had murmured, "I am with you, Liz. What is it you seek?"

Liz had then peppered Paula with questions about her impending wedding: if the Oak Grove Chapel was the right spot, if she should invite her estranged father, if the June 21 date was appropriate, and, finally, if Ivan Heminger was the man Liz should marry. Though he had scoffed at what he considered ridiculous goings-on, at that moment he had been riveted. His fate was in Paula's hands. Whatever the source of her knowledge, or even if there was a source, Liz had taken her answer seriously. "Ivan will look after you," Paula had whispered.

Ivan had smiled, and Liz had clapped her hands in delight. But a curious thing had happened when they had been about to leave the room. "Wait," Paula had said. "Something else is coming through." Liz had grabbed Ivan's arm and they had stopped, waiting. "Something for Ivan," Paula had continued. A long pause had ensued, and then Paula had spoken: "If you can prove you have the will, / A dandy death can cure your ill. / But nothing can be done at all / When your son shall cause your fall."

"What the heck's that mean?" Ivan had demanded. "I don't even have a son."

"All I do is allow the spirit to come through," Paula had said.

"Fine. Thanks. Let's go." He'd grabbed Liz's arm and hustled her out the door before any more "spirits" started talking through Paula.

On the ride home, Ivan had scolded Liz for believing in that "voodoo," as he'd called it. "What's a dandy death, anyway?" he'd asked, scornfully. "A happy one?!" But Liz had been furious, so Ivan had dropped the subject. After all, what did he care? He'd received the psychic seal of approval to marry Liz, and that's all that mattered.

And now, apparently, she had consulted Paula again, this time about Dandelion's chances in today's race. "You went to see Paula *again*?"

"She told me Dandelion was going to lose. That's why I tried to stop you from betting so much money on him."

"Did she tell it to you in rhyming couplets?" Ivan asked. As for the money, he planned to show Wanda the bunch of tickets he had bet on her horse.

"Very funny," Liz responded, coldly.

Ivan knew this was a touchy subject, so he asked seriously, "Did she say why he'd lose?"

"Kinda. She said something about Dandelion's not having a bellyful." Despite himself, Ivan caught his breath. "Do you know what that might mean?"

"I have no idea," Ivan said firmly. *This stupid psychic might actually know something.*

"It's not going to make that much difference to me. But I know how disappointed Wanda's gonna be. Don't tell her about Paula, okay?"

"Of course not," Ivan said, at the same time wondering if he might be able to blame Dandelion's loss on the psychic.

Wanda returned with her beer just as the bugle was calling the horses to post for the next race. "There's Dandy!" She pointed to her horse, being led toward the gate with her jockey, Vacero, walking gently beside him.

"Vacero told me he felt a little sluggish this morning, but he looks fine now," she said.

Ivan had to agree. Dandelion was striding confidently, his powerful body hardly straining. What if he hadn't starved him enough? Even if Dandelion came in third, Ivan was sunk. "There are going to be a lot of angry people," Vinny had said. Ivan gulped. He knew what the rest of the picture Vinny had painted looked like.

He suddenly thought of Rex Smith, his former trainer. Rex would have known what to do. Rex always knew what to do. Ivan thought back to their first meeting, almost thirty years before, at a horse auction.

"Meester, I wouldn't buy that horse," a swarthy, grungy little man had said to Ivan as he watched a chestnut mare being led around the corral.

"Why not? He did great in his last race, and the owner's only selling him because he needs to raise money."

"Look at the horse's back right hip," Rex had said. "You see how it's higher than the left one. There's also something going on with his back. I could patch him up, but it would take half a year, and you won't make no money during that time."

"You can fix up a horse that's not doing well?" Ivan had thought of his trainers' bills, with little result to show from them.

"I can fix any horse. I can train any horse. You need someone. I'm your man. My name's Rex Smith."

Ivan had almost laughed. The man had a strong Mexican accent, but his name was Rex Smith. Still, he had followed Rex's advice and hadn't bought the chestnut. And a few weeks later he'd heard that the man who had bought him was out a lot of money when the horse came up lame.

So Ivan had hired Rex. And he had proved to be an excellent hire. Part chiropractor, part trainer, part psychologist, and, importantly, part pharmacist, Rex had seemed to know exactly what a horse needed. He could make any horse reach its potential, and if a horse needed a little pharmaceutical help to reach it, Rex had a seemingly endless supply of what he called his "leetle concoctions" to give the horse a boost.

In those days, horses were often raced even if they should have been rested, and in those cases, it was important to give them something to mask the pain. The problem, however, was that the substances that masked the pain often had the disadvantage of hindering the horse's performance. But not Rex's concoctions. They seemed to take care of the pain without much of a drop off in performance.

Yes, Rex had been a wonderful partner, until…

Looking at Dandelion at Lancaster Downs, Ivan wondered what "leetle concoction" Rex might have come up with that would have slowed

Dandelion enough to lose the race without having the drugs discovered. Nowadays, horses were tested a lot more thoroughly, just like athletes. *Rex would have come up with something.* But Rex hadn't been around for almost twenty years, so Ivan had had to come up with something on his own.

"And they're off!" The bell and the caller's urgent shout brought everyone to their feet.

"Run, Dandy, run!" Wanda shouted as the crowd erupted in noise.

And Dandelion ran. "It's Dandelion ahead by a length and a half!" the caller announced. "Followed by Brinsloe and Red Rocket! As they enter the first turn, Dandelion is running hard at the post. Buffalo Bob is coming up fast on the outside…"

"Go Dandy!" Wanda yelled.

"Go, Dandelion, go!" Liz echoed.

"Daddy, why aren't you yelling?" Wanda asked.

So Ivan yelled. "Gooooooooo Dandelion!" What else could he do?

"They're at the halfway in forty-four and four," the announcer called. "The pace is wicked! Crescent Moon has now taken third, Flyaway has moved into second, but Dandelion is maintaining his lead."

Slow up, slow up! Ivan thought to himself. But out loud he shouted, "Run, Dandelion!" Wanda and Liz began to jump up and down. "Run!" they screamed.

"To the backstretch, Dandelion holds by a length," the caller announced. The crowd's energy was surging now, the noise building and building. "Fleet Count is coming up on the outside. He seems to be making his move.

Make it! Make it! urged Ivan silently.

"Heading for the three-quarters, Fleet Count has moved into third, followed by Make My Day, Goldenrod, and Star-Spangled Girl. Flyaway's tiring, fading to fourth. Fleet Count is closing the gap on Dandelion."

Close that gap!

"They're heading for the homestretch."

"Run, Dandelion, run!" chorused Wanda, Ivan, and Liz together.

For a split moment, Ivan was actually excited at the prospect of a Dandelion victory. Then he remembered the cost of victory. *Stumble, Dandelion, stumble!*

"Into the stretch now. Vacero has gone to the whip. Might be a sign that Dandelion is tiring. Fleet Count is neck and neck with Dandelion. Vacero is whipping hard! Fleet Count surges ahead!" The crowd roared as Fleet Count took over the lead. Ivan roared with them.

For a frozen moment, Wanda looked at her father wonderingly. Why was he cheering? But then her eyes flew back to the race. "You can do it, Dandy! You can do it!"

But Dandelion was now in third place. "Less than a sixteenth to go," the announcer called. "Fleet Count ahead by a length, Make My Day second, Dandelion third. Here comes Goldenrod!"

Come on, Goldenrod! Come on!

"Run hard, Dandelion!" Wanda screamed.

The crowd screamed, too, as Fleet Count crossed the finish line, two strides ahead of Make My Day. But Ivan wasn't watching who won. He was praying for Dandelion not to show.

"Third place is going to be tight!" the announcer shouted. "It's neck and neck, and it's…!" Ivan had been holding his breath so long he thought he might explode. "Goldenrod by a hair!"

Ivan breathed. The cheers of the crowd died down as the final horses crossed the line. Wanda stood, deflated, like a sad rag doll. Liz glanced at Ivan with a knowing look. He looked at Wanda. "Too bad, honey," he said. "I'm so sorry."

"Oh, Daddy!" Wanda broke into tears and ran into his arms. She sobbed. Ivan held her — and tried not to think how he had just broken his daughter's heart.

CHAPTER 7

After a week at the Zook farm, Gregory was beginning to feel more at home. Home, in this instance, was a great deal different from what he was used to. Rebecca, as promised, had told him how to drive to Howard's Auction, and Gregory had purchased a bed, bureau, chair, desk, and bench. He had never seen a store like Howard's, a warehouse filled to the brim with antique castaways, everything from hand-carved bureaus to a wooden magazine rack with deer legs that Gregory hadn't been able to resist. For a wicked moment, he had contemplated sending it to his mother.

Instead, he had called her and told her he was fine. When she'd asked where he was, Gregory had demurred. "I'd rather not say right now, Mama, if you don't mind." She had minded, of course, but Gregory had insisted. He wasn't sure why, except that it would be just like his mother to come looking for him, and he didn't want anything to disturb this new sense of home that was growing inside him.

Gregory had settled in, more or less. He had been able to pump water into a bucket and heat it in a pot on the wooden stove in the cottage to make coffee. For his meals, he usually drove to Miller's Dairy, the nearby ice cream shop with restaurant that was popular with the locals. Walking to the outhouse was inconvenient, of course, as was reading by the light of a kerosene lantern. But, all in all, Gregory had to admit, there was a lot to be said for the Amish way of life.

Each day Gregory felt himself relax more and more, as he remained cut off from the constant hustle and bustle of the world of the English. It amused Gregory to think of himself as "English," but that was what the Amish called anyone who was not Amish. It made him want to speak with a British accent every time he heard it. He had tried it once, with Hanna, but she had simply asked, in her inimitably direct manner, "Why're you talking so dumb?" Clearly Gregory would have to adapt his sense of humor to Amish life as well.

He had placed his bench just outside the cottage door, and one of his favorite things was to sit and contemplate the thousands of stars in the sky. Without the presence of electric lighting, the night skies in this part of the world were spectacular. At first, Gregory had enjoyed trying to find the Big Dipper or Orion's Belt, but after a few nights he had abandoned this drive to accomplish something, even if it were only the naming of a constellation. Instead, he slowly learned to just sit in the dark, and be. Yes, the simple life had its appeal.

If he felt bad about anything — and *bad* was too strong a word — it was about Bo. The Zooks had a stable for their horses and mules, but the only room for Bo was a makeshift stall Gregory had created at the end of the stable. It was cramped compared to the stable Bo had enjoyed in South Carolina. Fortunately, it was summer, so Bo was able to spend most of the time in the meadow. Still, it was definitely different to have his beautiful palomino crammed in among the mules. But different was what Gregory was looking for, and Bo didn't seem to mind.

There weren't that many places to ride either. He couldn't just ride in the fields where the crops were growing. And even the vacant fields were planted with alfalfa or left fallow to reinvigorate themselves for the next season of crops. There was nothing but farm after farm after farm. After the freedom he'd had in South Carolina to ride all over the countryside, Gregory felt somewhat constricted. He contented himself with riding Bo up and down the various lanes that framed the fields, but, to be truly content, he hoped he'd find larger stretches of open field or longer trails soon.

It was after one of his early morning rides on Bo that Gregory had looked up to see Rebecca approaching him outside the barn. He hadn't spoken much with her since he'd moved in. The Zooks worked hard, and Gregory had learned that Rebecca had a side job in a quilt shop in town. So there hadn't been much occasion to get to know her. And her seeming annoyance at his having forced her out of her quilting room had made Gregory reluctant to even try. So he was surprised to find her walking purposefully toward him as he loosened the saddle and swung it onto a nearby fence.

"Hello, Mr. Pinckney," Rebecca said.

"Hello, Ms. Zook," Gregory answered. There followed an awkward pause, which Gregory filled by offering, "Nice day."

"Yes, it is," said Rebecca.

Another pause ensued. Then both spoke at once.

"Mr. Pinckney." "Ms. Zook."

Gregory quickly said, "Please, go ahead."

But Rebecca insisted, "No, you go. What were you going to say?"

"Well," Gregory began hesitantly. "I was going to ask if it would be all right if you called me Gregory. 'Mr. Pinckney' makes me feel so old."

"All right," Rebecca said. "And you may call me Rebecca."

"Agreed," answered Gregory with a smile. "Well, now that we've dispensed with the formalities, did you want something?"

Rebecca stammered a little. "Well…Gregory…I wondered if…" She looked down at the ground.

Gregory tried to help. "Yes?" he asked.

There was a long pause, during which Rebecca seemed to undergo some internal struggle. Then she suddenly burst out, "I wondered if I could brush down Bo?"

Gregory was caught a little off guard. "Bo?"

"Yes, Bojangles." Rebecca waited. Then she added, "Your horse."

Gregory recovered somewhat. "Oh, yes, of course, Bo, my horse." But then he couldn't remember what she'd asked. "What about him?"

"I'd like to brush him down, if you don't mind," said Rebecca, a bit impatiently.

"When?"

"Now. This is when he needs it, right?" *This Englisher asks so many pointless questions!* "Haven't you just finished riding him?

"Yes, yes, of course," Gregory answered. "Just a minute." He disappeared inside the barn and returned with a brush, which he handed to Rebecca. "Do you know how to do it?"

Rebecca tried not to be insulted. "I brush down our workhorses occasionally. I guess it's the same thing."

"I'm sure it is."

Rebecca approached Bo, saying soothingly, "Hi, Bo. You are such a beautiful horse. Did you know that?" She rubbed his forehead gently. Bo tried to nuzzle her hand. "Would you mind if I groomed you a little? You have such fine hair. All right, here we go." And she began to brush Bojangles's mane, firmly but gently.

Gregory could see that Rebecca was not afraid of horses. He could also see that she and Bo seemed to understand each other, the way horse and human sometimes do. They had that connection, that ineffable chemistry. Not everybody connects with a horse in that deep way. Plenty of people own horses, ride them, take care of them, treat them well. But only a few have a real understanding of the animal, almost a spiritual connection. Maybe *mystical* is the better word. Whatever the word, it was clear to Gregory that Rebecca and Bojangles connected.

He ventured further conversation. "That first day we met, what did Hanna mean when she said you wouldn't ride my horse?" asked Gregory.

"My mother was always afraid of horses. She'd heard too many awful stories about accidents. And then, when Hanna got hurt, well…"

Rebecca spoke with a sadness that prompted Gregory to continue. "So you never liked riding?"

"Oh, no, I always wanted to ride. I used to sit on top of a horse inside the stable, just to have the sensation of riding. I convinced Mother that was safe enough." She brushed Bo silently for a few moments. Gregory noted the care she took, and her gentle way with Bo.

Then he had an inspiration. "Rebecca, why don't you go for a ride on Bo sometime?"

"Ride Bo?" Rebecca looked startled. "Oh, no, I couldn't."

"Just one little ride?"

"I have too many chores to do."

"No time for horsing around, huh?" Gregory joked. But Rebecca didn't laugh. *So much for a sense of humor*, he thought.

"Thank you, anyway. Here." She handed him the brush.

"Okay," Gregory assented.

She turned her attention to Bo. "There. You look even more beautiful." She and Bo looked in each other's eyes. "Yes, I know you appreciate it. You're welcome." She gave Bo a hug, patting his neck. "Good old Bo."

"You did a beautiful job. Thank you."

"You're welcome."

Again, a silence arose between them. *Why can't I think of anything to say to her?* Gregory chastised himself. *It's like I'm thirteen years old or something.* Finally he ventured, "I think Bo likes you. You may brush him as often as you want."

Rebecca responded happily, "I would like that very much."

Another pause. Gregory opted for the old standby. "What are you doing today?"

"I'm going to work at the quilt shop. And you?"

"I'm going down to the county records office," Gregory said.

"What for?"

"I'm trying to find someone."

"Find someone? Who?"

"It's a long story," Gregory replied. "I'll tell you if I find her."

"Okay., well, good luck." Rebecca started to leave.

"I'm sorry if moving into the cottage caused you any problems," Gregory suddenly said. "I'll try to find my own place soon."

"That's not necessary. I moved my quilts to a spare room at the quilt shop, so there's no problem at all. We're glad to have you here."

"You are?" Gregory eyed her. "All of you?"

"Of course. Have a nice day, Gregory."

"You, too, Rebecca." They exchanged smiles, and Rebecca walked away toward her house.

Gregory led Bo toward the pasture. "You get along with her fine, dontcha? Maybe you can teach me. And maybe we'll get her to ride you someday. Whattaya say, Big Boy?" He opened the gate, slapped Bojangles on the rear, and watched him gallop happily into the pasture.

Several hours later Gregory found himself poring over birth records at the Lancaster County Courthouse, looking for a baby girl named Mae Yoder, who was born about forty-four or forty-five years ago. There weren't that many Maes born in Lancaster County in that time frame, but Yoder was a very popular last name. After hours of doing research, checking and crosschecking, Gregory had a list of nine Mae Yoders, one of whom might be his mother.

The problem was, most of these women had probably married, and Yoder had been their maiden name. *Well, maybe some of them stayed single,* Gregory thought. *At least the Amish don't move around much. The address on the birth certificate is probably where they still live.*

Using the GPS system in his Ford pickup, Gregory was able to find the first home of a Mae Yoder. He drove down a long lane of the farm, past a sign that read, "Yoder's Turkey Farm." When he knocked on the door of the main house, however, he learned that Yoder was not her maiden name. The next two homes provided similar results. The fourth home had no Mae living there at all, and the owners were of no help. Maybe the farm had been sold to another family. Who knew where this particular Mae Yoder was now? *What if she'd moved away, perhaps to another state? And what if she's the one who is my mother?* Gregory was a little discouraged. This was going to be much harder than he'd imagined.

At the fifth home, he had better luck. As he parked in the lane, a group of small children scattered and ran toward a woman who was picking beans from her garden. Gregory approached cautiously.

"Hello," he called when he was near enough. "I don't want to bother you, but I have a question I hope you can answer. My name is Gregory Pinckney. I'm staying at the Zooks' farm," he continued, hoping the fact that he was living with an Amish family might improve his image in the eyes of the obviously suspicious woman.

"Which Zook?" she asked, warily.

"Elam Zook. His wife is Mabel. Live over in Honey Brook."

"Yes, I know them."

"Excuse me, but is your name Mae Yoder?"

"It is."

"You have lovely children." The children snuggled closer to their mother, a little afraid of this Englisher.

"What can I do for you? Are you a tourist, or are you the new turkey inspector?" At the word *inspector*, the children drew a little closer to their mother.

"No, no, nothing like that," Gregory answered quickly. "I'm just a…" *Well,* what *am I?* He decided to forego a description. "I'm trying to find someone named Mae Yoder, I mean, someone who's maiden name is Mae Yoder. I don't want to bother you, but I thought maybe you might know her."

The woman stood silently, pondering the request. Gregory shuffled from one foot to the other. It really was awkward trying to state his reasons for asking. He couldn't just come right out and say, "Are you my mother?

Did you give birth to a baby boy years ago in South Carolina? Were you an unwed mother?" He stammered toward the truth. "I was adopted. I'm twenty-seven years old, and I was raised in South Carolina. I learned that my mother's name is Mae Yoder and that she was from somewhere in Lancaster County. I'm trying to find her."

"Are you saying I'm your mother?" the woman asked somewhat testily.

"I'm not saying, I'm just asking." Gregory began to perspire.

"I don't go birthing babies without being married!" Mae Yoder was clearly annoyed and anxious to end the conversation to get back to her gardening. "I don't know how I can help you."

"Sure, I understand. I'm sorry. I didn't mean to bother you."

The woman said nothing.

"Okay, have a nice day."

Gregory gave a halfhearted wave, backed away, and walked quickly toward his truck. As he got in, he looked back at the woman he'd accused of being his mother. *Accused?* It wasn't like she was a criminal. He'd *hoped* she might be his mother. Was that the right word? Watching her staring at him defiantly, arms akimbo, one or two children still clinging to her skirt, Gregory had a final thought. *I'm glad* she's *not my mother!*

Gregory decided to forego any further investigation and return to the Zook farm. It had been a discouraging day. He'd found some names, sure, but there didn't seem to be a way to track them down without awkward situations arising. No doubt, word would soon be spreading about this strange Englisher who was bothering the whole neighborhood with questions about his mother. *"Isn't that just like an Englisher, not to even know who his mother is?" "And what makes him think she's Amish? That's an insult!" "We Amish are not the kind to go off and get pregnant and then travel all the way to South Carolina to birth the baby!"*

As usual when he felt upset, Gregory saddled up Bo and went for a ride. The steady sound of the hooves, the wind in his face, and the smell of the earth soon had him feeling a bit better. He didn't really watch where he was going, didn't really care. He just let Bo lead the way.

Gregory thought about the meeting he'd had with Rebecca that morning. For the first time since he'd arrived at the Zooks' farm, he'd enjoyed her company. She hadn't been exactly effusive, but then neither had he. And with Bo, Rebecca had really relaxed. *Too bad she can't ride him. It'd be fun to have someone to ride with, even double-mounted. Maybe we can find another horse, and I could ride him while she rides Bo. Anyway, I've got to find him some company.*

When Gregory finally looked up, he realized he didn't know where he was. Bo was walking him slowly down a lane he'd never seen before. It curved alongside some woods, an unusual feature in this landscape filled with farm fields. At the end of the woods, he pulled Bo to a stop. Stretching before him on the other side of a white fence was a meadow filled with beautiful green grass.

I bet Bo would like to nibble some of that. Maybe I could just ease him up and let him chomp awhile. I'm sure the owner wouldn't miss a few blades of grass. He sidled Bo up to the fence and loosened the reins. Bo immediately bent his head, raised his upper lip, and began tearing off grass with his teeth, chewing contentedly.

Suddenly a horse and rider came galloping over a rise in the meadow. Gregory could see that the horse was a thoroughbred, the way it streaked over the earth. He could also tell that the rider knew what he was doing, crouched low over the horse's neck, knees gripping the sides, horse and rider bouncing in perfect rhythm. Bo raised his head and let out a whinny at the sight of the other horse.

The rider looked at Gregory and Bo, then shifted his path and headed toward them. As they slowed, Gregory could see long, blond hair spreading out beneath the riding helmet. *Not a man after all.* The rider pulled back on the reins and approached the fence. "Hello," she said, coming to a halt. Her horse and Bojangles immediately began sniffing each other about the face. "Are you lost?"

"I reckon I am," answered Gregory.

"You *reckon*? Where're you from, — not from around here?"

"I'm from South Carolina."

"You're a long way from home. Hope you didn't ride all the way up here!" The woman smiled at Gregory brightly, revealing a set of perfectly white, straight teeth.

"No, 'course not," Gregory answered, smiling back. "Hope you don't mind Bojangles borrowing some of your grass."

"Borrowing?" she replied. "I hope he's not planning on giving it back." Gregory laughed. "Bojangles, you just help yourself. Well, now that I know the name of your horse, what's your name?"

"Oh, pardon me. I'm Gregory Pinckney."

"Nice to meet you. I'm Wanda Heminger, and this is Dandelion."

"Dandelion. That's an unusual name for a horse. Why'd you pick that?"

"Because a dandelion is wild and free. Like me," Wanda said with a knowing smile. "It looks like Bojangles is running out of grass. Would you like to bring him over here?"

"Yes, thanks, Bo'd appreciate that."

"The gate's down here." Wanda began riding down the fence, Gregory following on his side. When they reached the gate, Wanda jumped off, opened it, and Bo walked through. Gregory also dismounted and let Bo happily munch the grass alongside Dandelion.

Wanda removed her helmet, and her blond hair cascaded around her shoulders. She was a beautiful woman, in her early twenties, with deep, blue eyes and smooth, tanned skin. Her riding clothes fit her perfectly, showing off a resplendent body.

After the stress of the morning's activities, Gregory was delighted to be in such pleasant company. "Dandelion's a beautiful horse, Wanda," he said.

"Thank you. He's a racehorse." She bent down and picked a dandelion and placed it charmingly behind her ear.

"I can tell."

"Only he lost his last race."

"What happened?"

"I don't know. It's like he ran out of energy or something. But he'll be ready for the September Sweepstakes. Bojangles is quite a horse, too, by the looks of him."

"Thank you."

"You brought him all the way up from South Carolina?"

"Yeah. We're staying over at the Zooks' farm."

"Elam Zook?"

"You know them?"

"Elam made this saddle." She took Dandelion's reins and led him to Gregory. He examined the saddle.

"It's beautiful. I didn't know Elam did such work."

"It's his hobby, I think. He makes harnesses, saddles, all sorts of leather goods. My daddy buys lots of 'em." She let go of the reins, and Dandelion moved off to find some other grass. "This is our farm. Cedar Ridge."

"Well, if the rest of it's like this meadow, it must be beautiful."

"It is. You should come see it sometime."

"I'd love to. And Bo would love to, too. Things are kind of cramped at the Zooks' place."

"Anytime." Then she said, suddenly, "Hey, you must know something about horses, right, Gregory?"

"I know a fair amount. Been riding 'em all my life."

"Perfect! How'd you like to stable Bojangles at our farm? We've got great facilities, and he could have the run of the place. He and Dandy could race together. It would give Dandy someone to compete against."

"And it would give Bojangles some company. Thanks, Wanda, I just might do that. How much would it cost?"

"Nothing!"

"No, I'd have to pay you."

"You will, Gregory. Daddy fired our stable boy — I never did find out why. Anyway, we need someone to take care of the stables, look after Dandelion… and Bo! We'd pay *you*!"

"A job?"

"Not a hard one. You and I could ride together. It'd be fun!" She smiled her beautiful smile at Gregory.

"I could use some money. And it would be fun — for Bo and for me." He grinned at Wanda. "Let me think about it, all right?"

"You can think about it all the way back to the barn."

"Yes. Nice meeting — "

"Our barn," Wanda said. She mounted Dandelion in one swift, graceful move. "Where you and I are racing to. And then you're going to stay for supper. My daddy makes a mean steak, and you look hungry." She smiled her dazzling smile. "Are you hungry, Gregory?"

Gregory laughed. "I am!"

"Then come on!" Wanda said.

Gregory ran to Bo and jumped in the saddle. He swung Bo alongside Wanda and Dandelion. She let out a cry as she kicked Dandy's flanks. "Yeeeiiiiiiii!" Wanda and Dandelion sped off over the meadow at full gallop. Gregory leapt to the challenge.

"Come on, Bo!" he cried, and the chase was on.

CHAPTER 8

Two weeks later, as she walked to Mrs. Ansbacher's quilt shop for her afternoon stint, Rebecca thought over the changes in her life. They weren't many, but they felt significant. For one, Jacob hadn't popped in to say hello when the quilting bee had met at Lydie's house, and he hadn't invited her to go with him to the next singing either. When she examined her feelings, Rebecca found that she didn't mind not having Jacob be such a presence in her life for a while.

She had used the extra hours to work on her quilted wall hangings, and now she was halfway through finishing another one. That would give her six, all on the theme of horses: saddles, heads of horses (she had two of those), bridles, riding hats, riding crops, and full-size horses from a side view. Mrs. Ansbacher had finally persuaded Rebecca to let her display one wall hanging for sale, the one with the saddles. It hadn't sold, but it had caused quite a bit of curiosity, with many customers asking who had created such an interesting quilt. As per their agreement, Mrs. Ansbacher had always answered, "The artist wishes to remain anonymous."

The artist! Rebecca didn't really think of herself as an artist. In fact, she blushed a little if she was in the shop when someone inquired about her wall hanging. If the "someone" was Amish, the woman would sometimes cluck her disapproval of Rebecca's work. "Why would she want to go making a quilt like that? Why doesn't she stick to the way we were taught?" Or, "Saddles, for goodness sake! I like the old Amish patterns." That's just what Mabel would have said, and that's why Rebecca was glad she'd decided to make the wall hangings in secret. She supposed her mother would have to find out someday, but by then maybe a wall hanging or two would have sold. Then her mother wouldn't be so critical. Where money was concerned, the Amish were always practical.

Another change was the presence of Gregory on their farm. Rebecca didn't see him that often; she was too busy. But he did allow her to brush Bojangles whenever it was convenient, and they had talked while she did it. Gregory had told her a little about his life in South Carolina, even about failing the bar exam. And she had answered his questions about the Amish. "Why don't they use zippers, only hook and eye?" "Why not belts, only suspenders?" "Don't you ever take off your covering except to sleep?" "What is the difference between an open-air buggy and an enclosed one with a roof?" *So many questions!*

"You sure have a lot of rules," Gregory had concluded. Rebecca had never thought much about it, but now that she did, she could see what he meant.

Gregory made Rebecca think in ways she'd never thought before, and she found she liked that. She took to timing her comings and goings around the end of Gregory's daily ride so she could be with Bojangles more often. At least she told herself that was the reason.

Lately, however, Gregory hadn't been around much. He'd begun riding Bojangles over to Cedar Ridge Farm and spending the whole day there. Wanda's father had offered him a job, taking care of Dandelion and Beauty, a chestnut stallion. Gregory had told Rebecca that it was better to ride there than to ride up and down lanes near the farm. The Cedar Ridge fields were green and lush, acres and acres of open space where Gregory could ride to his — and Bo's — heart's content. There was a beautiful barn and a fully equipped tack room with the finest brushes, saddle soap — all the implements necessary for keeping a horse groomed. And happy.

Wanda had even begun to teach Gregory how to jump Bo a little. "It's fun to learn something new," Gregory had said to Rebecca.

"Is Wanda a good teacher?"

"She knows a lot about horses."

"I've seen her this summer in town. She's pretty." Rebecca had been so mad at herself for saying that, but she had not been able to stop.

"Yes, she is."

This conversation had caused a different kind of stirring in Rebecca, one she wished she hadn't had.

Rebecca was glad to turn right on Center Street finally and see the quilt shop at the end of the block. She'd soon be busy and wouldn't have time for unsettling thoughts about Gregory and Wanda. When she entered the shop, Mrs. Ansbacher approached her quickly. "Oh, Rebecca, there was man in here, and he was asking all sorts of questions about your quilt."

"Who?"

"Someone from New York!" Mrs. Ansbacher spoke in an excited whisper. "He says he owns a gallery in some place called SoHo. Those New Yorkers have the craziest names for things!" The craziness of New Yorkers was one of Mrs. Ansbacher's favorite themes. She got quite a few tourists from New York coming into the shop, especially in summer, and she claimed she could always tell someone from New York. "They're louder," she'd declare. "And they're always in a hurry. One day one of them knocked over a whole display, rushing around." Rebecca was afraid Mrs. Ansbacher was going to launch into this story again today, even though she'd heard it a thousand times. But this time she didn't.

"What kind of gallery?" asked Rebecca, smoothing down the apron over her dress to get ready for customers.

"One for paintings and such not, I 'spect."

"I see he didn't buy it."

"No, but he said he'd be back, so maybe he will." Mrs. Ansbacher liked Rebecca and thought she had talent. In fact, she tried to get Rebecca to try her hand at painting, but she demurred, saying that the Amish had no time to be artists. They did practical things.

Rebecca went about her work. Plenty of people said they'd "be back for sure," and plenty of them she never saw again. That was the nature of the business. She straightened a few quilts, including her wall hanging. The man must have taken it down to examine it more carefully. *I hope he appreciated the stitching,* Rebecca thought, then chastised herself for feeling proud.

The door opened, and someone she knew walked in. He was carrying a small book bag. "May I help you?" Mrs. Ansbacher inquired.

"Thank you, I just came in to look around. And to say hello to Rebecca. Hi," Gregory said, giving Rebecca a friendly smile.

"Hello, Gregory," said Rebecca, unconsciously giving her apron another smoothing.

"You two know each other?" asked Mrs. Ansbacher.

"This is the man who is boarding at our place this summer, remember?" Rebecca said.

"Ah, yes, from South Carolina, right? Nice to meet you."

"Nice to meet you, Mrs. Ansbacher. I'm Gregory Pinckney." He shook her hand. "I've heard about your shop. Rebecca really likes working here."

"And I like having her work here," replied Mrs. Ansbacher.

"What are you doing, Gregory?" asked Rebecca.

"I've been meaning to come by and see where you work. So this is it?"

"Yes."

"Aren't you going to show me around?" asked Gregory.

"Oh, well..." Rebecca, who could be quite loquacious in the barn while brushing Bojangles, suddenly found herself at a loss for words. Fortunately, at that moment, another customer came through the door. "Excuse me," said Rebecca, moving away.

"I'll take care of Mrs. King," said Mrs. Ansbacher. She turned to the woman. "How are you, Lydie?

"Hello, Elizabeth," Lydie King replied. "Hello, Rebecca."

"Hello, Lydie," Rebecca answered.

"I thought I'd see what kind of swatches you have, something I might use for a flower basket," Lydie said to Rebecca.

"Rebecca's got a customer," said Mrs. Ansbacher. "But I can help you, Lydie. Come this way." She led her to another part of the shop, leaving Gregory and Rebecca alone.

"Well?" asked Gregory.

"There's not much to show," said Rebecca.

"Maybe you could explain quilting to me."

"Are you planning to make a quilt?"

"I'd like to someday." He noticed her hesitate. "What's wrong?"

"Nothing. It's just that I don't think I've ever heard a man say he'd like to make a quilt."

"Well, now you have. Do these patterns have names?"

"Some of them do."

"What's this one?" He pointed to a quilt. It had eight white-tipped stars, with a smaller white star in the middle, all of them pointing toward a blue border. Pieces of colored fabric surrounded the inner star.

"It's called Evening Star. Each of the stars in the quilt is a diamond-shaped, nine-patch block."

"I'm not sure what that means," Gregory said, genially. "But it sure is beautiful."

"Look at the way the colors radiate from the center and appear to pulse with light."

Gregory looked more closely. "You're right, Rebecca! You have the eye of an artist."

Rebecca was pleased Gregory thought that, but she felt compelled to deny it. "I don't think so." She pointed to another quilt. "This pattern is Log Cabin. It's one of our more popular ones. And this is Shoofly."

"They're all so different!"

"The mistakes are what make them truly different."

"Mistakes?"

She showed him hand stitches. "A machine would make all these stitches exactly alike. But you can see here, they're a little crooked. No two quilts are ever alike, even when it's the same pattern."

"Like snowflakes."

"Yes." Rebecca had never thought of it like that before.

"And, like the work of any artist," said Gregory, "totally unique. Have you ever heard of Piet Mondrian?"

"Who's that?"

"A painter. He liked to paint geometric shapes in bold colors. These Amish quilts remind me a little of him. Of course, he wouldn't make things so ordered."

"Have you seen his paintings?"

"Yes, at MoMA."

"Momma?"

"The Museum of Modern Art," Gregory explained. "In New York City."

"Oh," said Rebecca. She couldn't keep the disappointment out of her voice. Amish never went to museums. *I wonder if they have any quilts at MoMA,* she thought. *Rebecca, watch your pride!*

"Hey, I recognize that!" Gregory suddenly exclaimed. "That's yours!" He pointed to Rebecca's wall hanging displayed on a wall. "Are you selling it?"

"Mrs. Ansbacher wants me to. I haven't decided yet. Of course, I could always use the money."

Gregory squinted at the price tag. "Two hundred ninety-five. Not bad."

"I told her to make it high, because I'm not sure I want to sell it."

"Well, now that I'm making money, maybe I'll buy it."

Despite herself, Rebecca felt pleased. That pesky feeling of pride again! "That's okay, you don't have to."

"Maybe I want to. That reminds me; there's something I want to ask you." Gregory withdrew his baby quilt from the book bag. "Do you recognize this pattern?"

Rebecca looked at the small quilt. "Nine squares, using a nine-patch to make each square." She considered for a moment. "I don't think that's a particular pattern."

"I think someone up here made it."

At that moment, Lydie King approached them. "We'll see you at the quilting bee in a few days, won't we, Rebecca?"

"Yes, Lydie."

Gregory's quilt suddenly caught Lydie's eye. "Where'd you get that, Rebecca?" she exclaimed.

"It belongs to Gregory. I don't think you've met. Lydie King, this is Gregory Pinckney."

"How do you do, Mrs. King," Gregory said, offering his hand.

Lydie took it, but her eyes remained focused on the quilt. "This is yours?" she asked.

"Yes, ma'am," Gregory replied.

"Where'd you get it?"

"I brought it up here from South Carolina."

"You're from South Carolina?"

"Yes, ma'am." Gregory smiled.

Lydie looked at him for a long moment, intently scanning his face. "Welcome to Honey Brook," she said finally, then turned to Mrs. Ansbacher. "May I pay, please, Elizabeth?"

"Of course." She led the way to the counter, Lydie following with the blue and yellow swatches she'd found for her Flower Basket quilt.

"I'd better let you get back to work," said Gregory. "Thanks for the tour, Rebecca."

"You're welcome, Gregory."

Gregory made his way past the women at the counter, saying good-bye. Lydie watched him disappear out the door and walk down the street.

"You've got the most beautiful name," Mrs. Ansbacher said, holding up the check Lydie had just signed. "Lydia Mae. That's what we used to call you when we were little. "

"Lydie is so much simpler," she responded, picking up her goods.

"Well, that's pretty, too," said Mrs. Ansbacher pleasantly.

"Thank you, Elizabeth." Lydie smiled vaguely and left the shop. Mrs. Ansbacher entered the amount in her books and placed the check in a drawer.

Rebecca looked at her wall hanging. *So there are real artists who also use geometric shapes? I wonder what this Mondrian's paintings look like.* She felt a momentary glimmer of kinship with him. *Fellow artists.* Rebecca couldn't help laughing at herself. *Listen to me! I'm not an artist!* But she remembered how she'd felt when Gregory had called her one.

And now he was off to Wanda's, probably to go riding and share thoughts with her. *Why are you thinking like this? Stop it!* The door opened, and another customer walked in, much to Rebecca's relief. "Good afternoon, she said.

"Hello," the man answered, in a polished, somewhat aristocratic tone. He was about forty-five, of medium height, with thick, curly, black hair and piercing brown eyes. He wore sleek jeans and a crisply ironed shirt — dark blue with bold, white vertical stripes. "I was here earlier."

Ah, the New Yorker. If the clothes didn't give him away, the accent did.

"Is Mrs. Ansbacher here?"

Rebecca looked around and saw no one. "She must have slipped out to the back of the shop. I'll get her."

"That's all right. I just came to buy something. Do you work here?"

"Yes," Rebecca said. "How may I help you?"

The man walked over to Rebecca's wall hanging and removed it from the wall. "I want to buy this." Rebecca was a bit taken aback and did not reply. "I said I'd like to buy this," the man said again. "It is for sale, isn't it?"

"I don't know," Rebecca blurted out.

"You don't know? It has a price tag on it, doesn't it?" When Rebecca just stood there, not answering, he continued testily. "Maybe you *should* get Mrs. Ansbacher."

"We have other wall hangings," Rebecca offered, trying to collect her thoughts.

"I can see that, but this is the one I want to buy." He moved toward the counter and called into the back room. "Mrs. Ansbacher!"

Mrs. Ansbacher appeared immediately. "Oh, Mr. Goldfarb, you came back!"

"I said I would. I'd like to buy that wall hanging we talked about earlier, but I'm having trouble getting her to sell it to me." He nodded toward Rebecca.

"Oh," replied Mrs. Ansbacher. Seeing Rebecca standing there hesitantly, she understood the situation. "I see," she said, vaguely. She understood, but she didn't know what to do about it. A long moment of silence prevailed.

"If you don't mind, I need to get going," Mr. Goldfarb said. "May I pay by credit card?"

"Mr. Goldfarb," Mrs. Ansbacher began, swallowing, "I told the artist I would ask her permission before I sold that."

"Why?"

"Well, she's not sure she wants to part with it." Mrs. Ansbacher looked beseechingly at Rebecca, but it seemed the proverbial cat had gotten her tongue.

"Then why would you display it with a price tag?"

"To see if it would sell," she replied, realizing she wasn't making much sense.

"And it has!" Mr. Goldfarb was losing patience. "Look, can you call the woman who made this and ask her right now? I can't believe making a simple purchase would be such a hassle!"

Rebecca continued to stand there silently. It was one of those surreal situations, where people are talking about you and you're right there, but it's as if you aren't.

"I can't call her; she doesn't have a phone," Mrs. Ansbacher explained.

"Doesn't have a phone in this day and age?"

"But I can contact her."

"Then please do."

"She's right here," Mrs. Ansbacher said, pointing at Rebecca.

Mr. Goldfarb looked at Rebecca, incredulously. "You?" he practically shouted.

Mrs. Ansbacher saw that she needed to do some fence mending. "Mr. Goldfarb, this is Rebecca Zook. She wasn't sure about selling the quilt, because it's not really Amish. That is, it *is* Amish, because Rebecca's Amish, but the pattern isn't Amish." Mrs. Ansbacher wasn't sure how much mending she had accomplished, but Mr. Goldfarb seemed to switch gears suddenly.

"Very nice to meet you, Ms. Zook," he said. He shook her hand warmly. "I really, really like your work."

"Thank you," was all that Rebecca could muster.

"I've never seen a quilt with saddles before. And I love the way you've arranged them around the horse's head, drawing our eyes to the center." Mr. Goldfarb seemed to warm to his subject matter. "And each saddle is unique, just a little bit different, but you have to look carefully to notice it. A saddle horn here. A straight line here, instead of curved. Very original. And the colors of the patches are marvelous. That dark brown, there, with purple. I don't usually like purple and brown — it's too boring. But the colors you've chosen work well together, not boring at all."

Rebecca couldn't believe it. He sounded as if he were lecturing about something. Only the something was her wall hanging. She managed another "Thank you."

Mrs. Ansbacher came to the rescue. "I agree with you, Mr. Goldfarb. I keep telling Rebecca she's got real talent. Maybe now you'll believe me, dear," she said to Rebecca. "Mr. Goldfarb owns that gallery, remember, in that 'Ho place in New York City?"

"SoHo," Mr. Goldfarb corrected her. "Yes, and I have an exhibit coming up in the next few weeks. I thought I would display this quilt, maybe frame it to look like a painting. That is, if someone would kindly sell it to me," he added, smiling. He could turn on the charm when necessary. "Is the price the problem? I'd be glad to pay more."

Rebecca finally came to her senses. "Oh, no, it's not the price, Mr. Goldfarb. I'm glad that you like my quilt. And I'd be happy to sell it to you."

"Wonderful!" said Mrs. Ansbacher.

"The reason I hesitated," Rebecca continued, "is that I'm trying something new, and it's not really an Amish pattern in the traditional sense, and I'm not sure I want my family and neighbors to know about it. Not that they would do anything, exactly, but people would know. And then they'd talk."

"The Amish are quite modest, Mr. Goldfarb," Mrs. Ansbacher explained. "They don't like to draw attention to themselves. It's the sin of pride."

"Well, that's hard," Mr. Goldfarb began, sympathetically. "For an artist not to be able to be proud of her work is hard. It's tough enough just to do it."

"It's just a quilt," replied Rebecca. "I'm not sure it's art."

"Well, I am," said Mr. Goldfarb. "Tell you what, you come to my exhibit and eavesdrop. I bet you'll hear plenty of people exclaiming over your work."

"Oh, yes!" cried Mrs. Ansbacher delightedly.

"In fact, you won't have to eavesdrop. We can make it a meet-the-artist moment, and you can hear the compliments first-hand."

"Wouldn't that be wonderful?!" Mrs. Ansbacher looked at Rebecca happily.

"I'm afraid I couldn't do that, Mr. Goldfarb," said Rebecca.

"Why not?"

"For one thing, I have too much work here."

"I'll let you off, Rebecca," Mrs. Ansbacher offered.

"I mean, work on the farm, too," clarified Rebecca.

"You could drive to New York and back in one day," said Mr. Goldfarb.

"I don't drive," said Rebecca.

"Take the train then, or the bus."

"No, thank you, I really can't. My parents would never approve," Rebecca said firmly. "But if you really want to buy the wall hanging, I'll sell it to you. I can't believe you'd want to show it in your gallery, but once it's yours, I suppose you can do whatever you want with it."

"All right, then," replied Mr. Goldfarb, a bit disappointed. "I'll send you an invitation anyway, in case you change your mind. So, Mrs. Ansbacher, here's my credit card."

While Mrs. Ansbacher rang up the sale, Rebecca wrapped the wall hanging and placed it in a bag. *Someone just bought my quilt. My quilt! God surely works wonders.*

"Here you are, Mr. Goldfarb." Rebecca handed him the bag.

"Thank you, Ms. Zook. I hope you'll change your mind and work things out so that you can come to New York. Good-bye, Mrs. Ansbacher. Nice meeting you both." He waved and left the shop.

"Oh, Rebecca, can you believe it?" Mrs. Ansbacher shouted as soon as he'd disappeared.

No, thought Rebecca, *I truly can't.*

"You sold your quilt!" Mrs. Ansbacher gave Rebecca a big hug. "I told you that you had talent!"

My goodness, Rebecca thought. *Maybe I do.*

CHAPTER 9

It was hot. As Ivan sweated in his office upstairs in the barn, he cursed himself for having decided not to put in air-conditioning. He hadn't actually thought he'd be in the office all that much. But he had to be there now. He didn't want anyone overhearing this phone call.

Ivan had realized that he needed to get going. He had mistakenly thought that the due date was ninety days from the race, but Vinny had recently reminded him that the clock started ticking at the diner. Ivan wasn't worried though. He remembered the start-up company he'd invested in years ago, instead of taking his legal fee. The company, CompuTech, manufactured an important computer component and had somehow managed not to go bust when the dot-com bubble burst. Recently, the CEO had written the investors saying the company was in the process of being sold.

Ivan, who hadn't paid much attention to his investment over the years, was pleasantly surprised to discover it had multiplied so much that he would walk away with a low seven-figure payday when the deal went through. That would cover his debt and leave him a little extra for…what? Normally the answer would have been betting on horses, but this latest episode with Vinny had definitely curbed his enthusiasm for that. The CFO had promised to call Ivan after the meeting that day with the potential buyer and tell him whether the deal had been signed.

Ivan was his usual optimistic self, but it was approaching seven o'clock in the evening, and he had heard nothing. The slightest bit of worry was beginning to invade Ivan's mind. He suppressed it as he often did, by mixing another vodka. "Mixing" was probably not the right word, since Ivan took his vodka on ice with only a couple of lime twists. Once in a while, as a joke, he would whisper the word *tonic* over the top of the glass, and consider it mixed. Mixed or not, the bottle was nearing empty after several hours of steady drinking on Ivan's part. That's why he was happy when he heard Gregory stirring around in the stables below, putting up Bojangles after a ride. Ivan could use some distraction.

He decided to take Gregory a drink, to finish off the bottle. He'd liked Gregory the minute he'd met him, when Wanda had brought him over and proposed hiring him to look after the horses. He could tell he was smart, and Ivan always liked smart people. So he'd hired him, and Gregory had been around quite a lot in the past two weeks.

Ivan also had begun to have this crazy idea that Gregory and Wanda might make a pair. He loved his daughter, but he realized she took more after her mother in the brains department. Fortunately, she took after her in the looks department, too, and looks could go a long way toward getting a man's fantasies fired up, and those kinds of fantasies often ended up in the reality of a marriage. Just ask Ivan. So maybe the idea of having a smart son-in-law wasn't such a crazy idea after all.

Ivan filled a glass with ice from the small refrigerator, tossed in a couple of lime twists, poured the remainder of the vodka into the glass, and set off down the stairs. He found Gregory putting feed into the trough for Bo. Wanda and Dandelion weren't around. *Probably out riding or jumping,* thought Ivan. *Good. We'll have a little man-to-man.*

"Hello, Gregory," Ivan said cheerily.

"Hello, Mr. Heminger."

"Please, call me Ivan. You Southerners are so polite. I like that. Wanda around?"

"No, sir, she's out riding."

"Good. How about a drink?" Ivan held out the glass of vodka. "I took the liberty of pouring you a little vodka."

"Here?"

"Why not? We both like stables, don't we?"

Gregory shrugged. "Okay, why not? Thanks," he said, taking the glass. "Anything in this?"

"Just fun," said Ivan, chuckling.

"Here's to fun, then," said Gregory, lifting his glass.

Ivan raised his. "To fun!" he said, and they both drank. Ivan sat down on a bench backed up against a stable wall, and gestured for Gregory to sit down on another one nearby. "Ah," he said, "good to get off my feet."

"You been working in your office?"

"Yeah. Gotta a deal coming through." Ivan took a swallow. "You enjoying your work here?"

"Oh, yes, sir. I love taking care of horses."

"How're you and Wanda getting along?"

"Fine. She's a nice girl. Good rider. I hope racing Dandelion against Bojangles is helping her tune up for the Sweepstakes."

"Yes, she'd love to win that race."

"I was sorry to hear about the last race."

"Yes. Never can tell what'll happen in a horse race," Ivan replied. This was not his favorite subject. "Wanda'll be graduating Penn State after this year. I wonder what she'll do then. She say anything to you?"

"No, sir."

"Tell you the truth, Gregory, horses seem to be the only thing that interests her, and I'm not sure how far that can take her in life. What do you think she should do?"

"I haven't really thought about it, Mr. Hem−... Ivan."

"Well, do me a favor, son. Think about it some, will you? Maybe you can be a kind of mentor for Wanda. I think you're a clear thinker. I think your advice would be good for her."

"What kind of advice?"

"Nothing specific. Just whatever comes up. Take her out for a drink sometime, maybe to a picture. Yeah, take her to the theater in Lancaster. Tell her what your thoughts are on life, art, anything. Just talk to her. Would you do that for me?" Ivan smiled warmly at Gregory.

"I guess so." Gregory wasn't sure what to say. He enjoyed Wanda's company, but he'd never considered having more of it.

"That is, if you don't have anything else planned. Or if you don't have anyone else you're spending time with," Ivan added.

"No, I've got time."

"You've got to admit, she's not exactly hard on the eyes," Ivan said, winking at Gregory.

"Wanda is very beautiful. It will be a pleasure to spend more time with her."

"Good, good." He polished off his drink and rose. "Just leave the empty glass on the stairs when you're finished. I'll get it on my way down."

"Just a minute." Gregory took a long drink and finished his vodka.

"Well, I like a man who can drink," said Ivan. "No lite beer for you, eh?"

Gregory had an instant thought of his father and their last conversation. He wondered if he'd changed all that much. "No, sir," he said.

"Let's do it again," Ivan said genially. He put his arm around Gregory affectionately. "Only next time, on the veranda. Deal?"

"Deal."

Ivan heard his phone ringing upstairs. "There's my call. Gotta go." And he dashed off, leaving Gregory holding his glass. Gregory placed an ice cube in his hand and held it out for Bo. Bo swallowed it enthusiastically. "You like vodka, too, eh, boy? Well, I guess another one won't make you an alcoholic." He held out another ice cube, and Bo took care of it in the same manner. Gregory laughed. "I'm not so sure!"

Upstairs, Ivan opened the door to his office and ran quickly to the phone. "Hello?" he said. "Yeah, hiya, Billy." Ivan paused, listening. His eyes went slack. "What do you mean, no deal?!" He shifted the phone to his other ear and listened more intently. "Are you sure? What happened?" Ivan took a deep breath and listened. Billy went on for a while about how the buyer had gotten cold feet at the last minute. Ivan half listened. "Yeah, sure, let me know if anything changes, Billy." He hung up the phone and stared blankly into space.

Ivan decided he needed another drink, so he filled his glass with ice and pulled another bottle of vodka from the cabinet. He poured himself a full glass and sat heavily at his desk. He swallowed a big gulp. It stung as it went down, but he hardly felt it. He shook his head hard, trying to clear his mind. Glancing at the calendar on his desk, he noticed he still had more than sixty days until October 1, the due date. But he had been counting on the deal going through, and he couldn't think of any more options.

Then he thought of one. Sheila. She'd received $2 million from Ivan in the divorce settlement. Given the stock market's rise in the eighties and nineties, she'd no doubt parlayed that into many millions more. Sheila certainly had the cash. He'd go to her, hat in hand, and tell her she'd been right, tell her he never should have gotten into the horses. He'd say how sorry he was that he'd left her, how sorry he was that he'd cheated on her, how he'd promise to pay her back just as soon as — *Who am I kidding?! She'll laugh right in my face. I* cannot *go to Sheila.*

That thought depressed Ivan a little. He had traded his smart, but aging, wife for a beautiful blonde with a body that wouldn't quit, but brains that did. If he hadn't been so reckless, he probably wouldn't be in the fix he was in now. But that was the past. He had to solve the future. And he'd better do it fast.

Ivan gulped some more vodka and walked to the window. Looking down into the courtyard in front of the barn, he saw Wanda ride up on Dandelion. Gregory walked out to greet her. Ivan could hear their voices faintly, and, on an impulse, he opened the window wide so he could hear them better.

"Have a good ride, Wanda?" Gregory asked. He helped her dismount.

Did he hold her waist just a little bit longer? Ivan pondered.

"The best!" Wanda replied.

"How's Dandelion?"

"Wonderful," Wanda said. "Dandelion is dandy!"

Gregory laughed, but Ivan hardly heard him. *Dandy? Dandy? Why does that word stick in my mind?* He moved away from the window, thinking intently. *I know that word! I mean, of course I know it, but it means something to me. Something different...something special...What?!* He went for the vodka bottle on his desk, reached for it desperately, started to pour, and then he stopped. He had it: *If you prove to have the will, / A dandy death will cure your ill.*

Paula Psychic! She'd said that, and since it had seemed like an oracle, Ivan had written it down. It was probably in his desk somewhere. Something about a son. But he didn't care about the rest of her prediction, just the first part, which had popped into his head just that instant. *A dandy death! Not a happy death, not a wonderful death! The death of a horse named Dandy!*

Ivan poured the drink and drank it down. *The death of Dandelion? But how will that help?* Even as he said it, Ivan knew the answer. It was right there in Rex's freezer, where it had been for twenty years.

It had been Rex Smith's idea. Rex the Fixer, Rex who had a solution for everything. A solution that usually came in a vial. He had certainly put his pharmaceutical education to clever use, Rex had. Ivan thought back to the last time his reckless gambling had gotten him into trouble and he'd needed money fast.

"Kill some horses," Rex had suggested.

"What?!"

"Sure, for the insurance. I've got a leetle concoction that'll work, and no one will be the wiser — least of all the insurance adjusters. Trust me. You'll have your money in sixty days."

You'll have your money in sixty days. Ivan turned the sentence over and over in his head. *Sixty days. Sixty days.* He looked at the calendar again. There was time.

CHAPTER 10

As he was returning to the Zook farm that same day, a rumble of far-off thunder caused Gregory to look up at the sky. It had darkened considerably since he'd begun his afternoon run on Bojangles. "Looks like rain, Bo. Quite a lot of it, too. Best get you back home." He clucked his tongue, tapped his heels into Bo's flanks, and off they galloped.

As they sped down the lane, the first splattering of drops began to speckle the earth. Gregory could see a fair amount of activity on the Zook farm as he approached. Elam and Henry were shouting to each other as they hastened to beat the impending downpour. Mabel and Hanna were gathering in the clothes. Rebecca and her brother rolled out the hay wagon, while Elam frantically brought out the mules. They were just hitching them up when Gregory rode into the yard outside the barn.

"What's going on?" he called.

"Big storm coming," Elam shouted back. "Might be hail, from the looks of it."

"Then hadn't you better be getting inside?" asked Gregory.

"Have to protect the rest of the tobacco crop!" called Elam.

"How're you gonna do that?" Gregory had dismounted and was leading Bo toward the barn.

"Harvest it!" shouted Henry. "Thank goodness most of it's in, but we still have a few rows to go." He jumped up onto the wagon and took up the reins. Rebecca climbed up beside him. They moved to pick up Elam and then headed out to the tobacco fields as fast as the mules could go. After they'd deposited the clothes inside, Mabel and Hanna burst from the house and began running toward the fields.

Bo pranced about anxiously. "Whoa there, big fella. I know, I know, you aren't any fonder of rain than I am. Let's get you inside." Gregory slid open the barn door and led Bojangles into his stall. He closed the barn door to protect against the rain, then filled Bo's bucket with feed. Bo began to happily munch.

Gregory took off the saddle and blanket and slung them on top of the stable wall. He slipped the bridle off and hung it up. He grabbed the brush and began brushing Bo's hair. Outside, streaks of lightning exploded in the turbulent clouds. Seconds later, the bang of thunder roared across the fields. Gregory went to the door and opened it slightly.

Wouldn't like to be out in this. The Amish are always at the mercy of the weather. Gregory was glad to be inside, dry and warm. Yet he also felt a little guilty.

But I don't know anything about harvesting tobacco. He stood for a moment in the middle of the barn, undecided. *Heck, how hard can it be? I oughta be able to help somehow.* And with that, he opened the barn door further, stepped outside, closed the door behind him, and ran in the direction of the Zooks.

When he stopped, he could see that the wagon was already filling with plucked tobacco leaves. Elam and Henry was each racing down between two rows of tobacco, using a trimmer to clip the tobacco stalks at the bottom, letting them fall to the ground. Hanna and Mabel followed behind, picking up the stalks and putting them on a lathe, which Rebecca then placed in the wagon, being careful not to harm the leaves. Gregory stood motionless for a minute, not knowing what to do. "How can I help?" he called out.

"Stack 'em," Mabel called back, offering him a lathe full of stalks. Gregory took the lathe and walked quickly to the back of the wagon. Rebecca was just placing some tobacco on the wagon bed. She shielded her eyes and called out, "Thank you, Gregory! Please be careful."

"Oh, I'm all right," Gregory replied.

"I meant, the tobacco," Rebecca said. "Try not to bruise the leaves."

"Oh, yes, of course," Gregory mumbled. Rebecca headed back for more tobacco, leaving Gregory feeling a bit foolish for thinking of himself over the tobacco.

He didn't have time to ponder such thoughts, however. The rain had started coming down in spurts, big drops of it plopping in the dusty barnyard and wetting the tobacco. Then came some relief, as the dark cloud moved swiftly toward the east, but a bigger cloud loomed close. Henry jumped into the wagon and moved it down the rows, and Gregory ran to gather another lathe and place it carefully in the back of the wagon. He and the Zooks worked together for nearly an hour, cutting, spearing, and piling, until the last of the stalks was laid in the wagon. Then Henry beckoned for his mother and aunt to get in beside him, and he drove the wagon to the tobacco shed.

Elam, Rebecca, and Gregory ran toward the shed. The rain began in earnest, but Henry would get the wagon to the tobacco shed before the tobacco could get too much wet. Gregory felt almost exhilarated as he ran. He'd enjoyed the intense work. He felt part of a team. He could sense the psychological benefits of the Amish way of life, that sense of community that pervaded every aspect of their existence.

Gregory also enjoyed working side by side with Rebecca. Something about the way her covering had slipped to the side of her hair, the way her dark curls had matted to her forehead, and the graceful way she had wiped raindrops from her face with the back of her hand had caught his attention. *Why am I noticing these details? And why am I thinking how pretty Rebecca is?*

Henry drove the wagon into the shed. Once safely inside, everyone began to relax. The rain changed to hail, pounding on the roof, but nobody cared. A sense of triumph pervaded. There was silence, as each person caught a breath, then Henry and Elam began to hang the tobacco. "We can handle things from here on, Gregory," Elam said. "Really appreciate your help though. Why don't you join us for supper?"

"I'd love to," Gregory responded. Did he notice a small smile on Rebecca's lips at his answer?

"*Gut*," said Hanna. "We need to fatten you up, don't we, Becca?"

Rebecca was caught off guard. "I don't know, Hanna. He looks all right to me."

"*Denke!*" Gregory smiled, happy to use the Amish word. Was that a blush that suddenly colored Rebecca's cheek?

"I didn't mean...," she stammered. "I mean, your weight seems...Oh, Hanna!" Rebecca quickly exited the tobacco shed, saying, "I'd better get supper started."

"I'll come with you. We need to rett up first." Mabel followed her daughter out the door.

"I'll help with the cleaning up, then I'll dig some new potatoes," added Hanna, as she also moved out the door toward the house.

Gregory suddenly found himself standing alone in the middle of the shed. Henry stood on a ladder, receiving stalks from Elam and hanging them from the rafters. Outside, the storm began to abate. "What does rett up mean?" he asked.

"Clean," Henry replied.

"Oh." Gregory mentally added it to his growing list of Amish expressions. "Well, I'll get into some dry clothes, if you don't need me."

"Don't take too long," said Elam. "Supper's at four thirty."

Some forty-five minutes later, Gregory found himself looking at plates and bowls piled with egg noodles with browned butter, boiled potatoes, corn, and chowchow, a dish Gregory had never heard of. It was chock full of cauliflower, carrots, green and yellow beans, and cabbage, soaked in a watery concoction of vinegar, sugar, salt, and pepper. Gregory had never seen so much food served at a simple supper, but it seemed a normal meal to the Zooks.

Everyone bowed their heads without prompting, and Gregory followed suit. He waited for someone to say a prayer, but they sat in silence for what seemed an eternity. He kept peeking, the smell of all that food stirring his stomach. Finally Elam raised his head and began passing a platter of roasted chicken around the table.

"I rung that chicken's neck myself," Hanna announced proudly.

"Hanna, nobody cares about that," Mabel said.

"Says who? Do you care, Gregory?" Hanna looked at him with her mischievous brown eyes.

Gregory didn't know quite how to respond. He'd never been asked if he cared about who killed the chicken he was eating. As far as he was concerned, chicken came wrapped in cellophane in the supermarket. But here among the Amish, there was a connection between the food on your plate and the people who put it there. Simple. Direct. The way most things Amish seemed to be.

"I'm glad you rang its neck; it's delicious," Gregory heard himself say, thinking that was one of the most bizarre sentences he'd ever uttered. To turn the conversation in a direction he could more easily handle, he announced, "I'm going to move Bojangles over to Cedar Ridge Farm, Elam."

"Oh!" Rebecca exclaimed, despite herself.

"Why is that, Gregory?" asked Elam.

"I appreciate your generosity, all of you," Gregory said. "But there's a lot more room for Bo to run at the horse farm, plus other animals for him to ride with."

"You mean, Wanda to go riding with, right?" winked Henry.

"Please pass the potatoes," Rebecca said quickly. Mabel passed them along, and Rebecca busied herself putting potatoes on her plate.

"As a matter of fact, it has been nice to have someone to ride with," Gregory answered. Wanda's a good horsewoman. She's teaching me how to jump Bo, just for fun."

"When will you move him?" asked Rebecca.

"I thought I might as well do it tomorrow," said Gregory. Rebecca ducked her head and ate a bite of potatoes to hide her disappointment.

"Go right ahead," said Elam. "You're working over there anyway, so it makes sense. Now, I have some news myself."

"What's that?" inquired Mabel.

"You know how Aaron Weaver sold his farm last winter?"

"To that developer?" said Henry.

"That's right."

"And now we've got ten ugly houses where we used to have green, open fields," chimed in Mabel.

"That may be," said Elam. "But Aaron put a lot of money in his bank account in exchange."

"Some exchange," said Henry. "Now he can't farm anymore."

"That's the point," said Elam.

"Dat, what are you talking about?" asked Rebecca with concern in her voice.

"I'm thinking about selling the farm."

The table exploded with anguished cries. "What?" "You can't be serious, Pa!" "Sell the farm? Why?" "Where would we live?" "What would we do?" "Don't talk crazy, Elam!"

"Now hear me out," said Elam. "I'm not sure I want to spend the rest of my life worrying about what'll happen if we don't get the tobacco crop in out of the hailstorm. Or what'll happen if there's a bumper crop of corn and the price drops. Or whether the barn burns down, a mule kicks somebody, or the cows get loose and trample the garden."

"But that's our way of life!" exclaimed Mabel. "It's all we know."

"Well, not really, Mabel. I know how to make saddles. Harnesses, too. All kinds of leather goods."

"You mean, do that for a living?!"

"Why not? Look at the price I got for Wanda's saddle."

"That's one saddle," argued Mabel.

"That's right. Just imagine how many more I could make if I did it full time. I think I could make a good living with a leather shop."

"But what about me?" Henry suddenly interjected. "What am I gonna do, Dat? The farm is supposed to come to me!"

"Are you saying it's your farm?" Elam shot back.

Gregory suddenly wished he were somewhere else. What was he doing in the middle of this family argument? He cast a glance at Rebecca. She was watching wide-eyed, not believing what she was hearing.

"No, Dat," Henry said meekly. "I'm just saying farming's all I know."

"You could learn the leather trade, too," said his father.

"But I like farming. I like the smell of the earth, the feel of an ear of corn's silky hair, the wail of a new calf, the taste of a tomato fresh off the vine. I want to farm."

"I know you do, son. But maybe it's time we took a different look at the future. There's less and less land. More and more Amish are going into trades: woodworking, cabinet making, carpentry."

"Because they have to!" cried Henry. "They'd farm if they could."

"I'm not so sure, son," said Elam. "I hear more and more talk about how tired people are of farming."

"That's just the usual complaints, Elam," said Mabel. "Just talk. That doesn't mean they want to change their lives completely."

"It wouldn't be completely, Mabel. We'd still live here in this house. We'd keep enough land to have a nice yard and a big garden. I'd convert the tobacco shed into a nice leather shop. You wouldn't have to get up at four thirty every morning to milk the cows. And help harvest the tobacco after working all day in the house, because it has to be done right away. Cleaning out the manure, painting the barn — there are so many things I wouldn't miss at all."

"People will talk," said Mabel. "You don't sell your land to a developer."

"I'll do my best to make sure it's not a developer."

"Let's try it!" said Hanna. "I could make pies to sell. I make good pies."

Rebecca decided this was a good opportunity to move the conversation away from this news that threatened to divide her family. "Yes, Hanna, you do make good pies. Let's try some right now." She got up from the table and started clearing away the main dishes.

Hanna joined her. "I've made peach and cherry."

"Which do you want?" asked Rebecca.

"Both," said Hanna. "Would you like both, Gregory?"

"Why not?" he answered.

Mabel also began clearing away dishes. Rebecca refilled everyone's water glass. Elam and Henry sat silently. The women neglected their usual chatter. For a while, the only noise was the sound of clanking dishes and the soft, sputtering rain.

Gregory managed to get through his two pieces of pie. He would indeed fatten up if he had many more Amish meals. Further conversation began, somewhat furtively. Hanna discoursed on the quality of that season's peaches. Elam mused on what might have happened if they hadn't gotten the tobacco in on time. Mabel asked Rebecca to help her fold clothes after supper. Only Henry said nothing, and he excused himself as soon as the closing prayer had concluded.

Lying in his bed later that evening, Gregory pondered the fate of the Zook family. He couldn't blame Elam for no longer wanting to farm, but it still seemed sad to think their way of life might be coming to an end. Elam would probably do well in the leather trade. He'd shown Gregory some of the harnesses and saddles he had made in his spare time, and they were superbly crafted. Hanna and Mabel could supplement the family income by getting jobs cleaning other people's houses, a job many Amish women seemed to prefer later in life. They didn't maintain a lavish lifestyle, so it wouldn't take much to sustain them. Maybe Hanna could realize her dream of having a bakeshop. Henry really seemed to love the land, to love farming. What if he didn't take to the leather trade? What if he couldn't find something he enjoyed doing? It would be a shame to waste a life forcing someone to work at a job he didn't enjoy. That is the future that had awaited Gregory in law, and that is why he had left home. Henry could always leave home, but the Amish were so much about family and about being people of the soil. They never thought of their livelihood as being a *job*. Selling the farm didn't seem right.

And what about Rebecca? She'd probably get married and start her own family.

The thought of her marrying had a curiously disturbing effect on Gregory. He jumped off his bed and looked out his window. The storm had completely passed. A three-quarters moon was rising, casting a warm light over the Zook farmstead. In this light, Gregory saw a figure crossing the barnyard. He recognized her immediately.

A few minutes later, Gregory slipped inside the barn to find Rebecca brushing Bojangles. "Did you know you were leaving?" she asked the horse. "Going to a much nicer stable, Bo. I know you'll really love it. Lots of people to brush you, too." She patted Bo's cheek. "Probably much better at it than I am."

"I doubt that." Gregory's voice startled Rebecca.

"Oh!"

"Sorry. Didn't mean to frighten you." He crossed the space between them.

"That's all right. I was just telling Bojangles good-bye."

"It's not like he's moving to Alaska. He'll still be nearby. Maybe you can come visit him at Cedar Ridge."

"I don't think so." Rebecca put away the brush.

"Hello, Big Fella," Gregory said to his horse. "Not used to so many visitors so late at night, are you?"

Rebecca faced Gregory squarely. "I'm sorry you had to be a witness to what happened tonight."

"A family quarrel? That's nothing, you should see the way my family fights!" But Rebecca was in no mood for joking. "Sorry. I know it upset you."

"I just feel so bad for Henry, if Dat really sells the farm. He loves this place."

"Don't you?"

"I do," Rebecca said. "But lately the Amish way of life hasn't seemed…" She paused. She wanted so much to talk to someone about all that was going on in her heart. *What makes me think I can talk to Gregory? He doesn't know anything about the Amish life and what we cherish.* She looked at him, standing there, looking at her with smiling eyes. *I just can't do it.* "I'd better go." Rebecca started to leave the stable.

"Wait a minute, Rebecca." He reached out and gently grabbed her arm. Rebecca stopped, and Gregory dropped his hand. "I just wanted to tell you, nobody has brushed Bo like you do."

"What do you mean?" Rebecca looked at Gregory with those blue-green eyes, now forlorn, brimming with tears. Not for the first time, he noticed the small freckle in her left eye. Like a tiny star. It added to the allure.

"I mean, there is, I don't know, a tenderness between you and Bo, yet a firmness, too. And Bo stands perfectly still. He doesn't even do that for me. I can tell he really enjoys it. I see it in his eyes."

"His eyes?" Rebecca's own eyes brightened. "Can you really see things in Bo's eyes?"

"Of course."

"I think he has the most expressive eyes. It's like he talks with his eyes. I suppose that's dumb." Rebecca's enthusiasm was replaced with embarrassment.

"Not at all. People can talk with their eyes. Why not horses?"

"Do you really think people can talk with their eyes?"

"Don't you?"

"Yes, I do. But I always thought I was being a little, I don't know…silly." She slipped behind Bo, patting his rump and stroking his side.

"I hope not."

"What do you mean?"

"That would mean I'm being silly, too."

"Oh, I didn't mean — "

"I was teasing!" Gregory could tell she was embarrassed. "Your family doesn't tease much, does it?" He came into the stable on the opposite side of Bo from Rebecca.

"I don't know. I've never thought about it." The stable began to feel too small for Rebecca, with all three of them in it. It wasn't an uncomfortable feeling. More like a growing excitement she wasn't ready to experience quite yet. "Good night, Gregory," she said.

"Wait a minute!" She stopped, turned, and looked at Gregory. *Those eyes again!* He knew he'd stopped her for no particular reason, just because he was enjoying her company. She waited expectantly. "Don't you want to say goodnight to Bo?"

Rebecca smiled. She took Bo's face in her hands and looked deep into his eyes. "Good night, Bojangles," she said softly. "Sweet dreams." Bo was still, and they looked at each other for a long moment. Rebecca relaxed, her smile brightened, and she nuzzled the horse affectionately. She turned to Gregory. "Have a good night, Gregory."

"Goodnight, Rebecca. Don't worry; I'll bring Bo back often." Rebecca nodded and left the barn.

Gregory patted Bo's face. "You'd like that, wouldn't you, boy?" He looked directly into Bo's eyes. "But you and I know I wouldn't be doing it just for you, right?" He gave his horse a loving pat on the cheek and headed for the cottage and, he hoped, sweet dreams, too.

CHAPTER 11

"Rebecca, Mr. Goldfarb called for you!" Mrs. Ansbacher greeted Rebecca with this announcement when arrived at work.

"What did he want?" asked Rebecca.

It had been a week since Gregory had moved Bojangles over to Cedar Ridge Farm. Despite his promise, Gregory had yet to bring Bo back to visit. *Probably too busy.* Rebecca tried to give Gregory this excuse, but she still missed seeing Bo. She hadn't even seen Gregory that much. He spent most of his time at Cedar Ridge. *Probably with Wanda.* That thought stirred Rebecca in a way she recognized, but was loathe to name. She tried to convince herself that it was Bo she missed, not Gregory. But when she was honest with herself, she had to admit it was both.

"He didn't say what he wanted," replied Mrs. Ansbacher, "except that he wanted you to call him. Here's the number." She gave Rebecca a yellow sticky note with the number 212-629-5758 penned in Mrs. Ansbacher's neat hand. Rebecca folded the paper and put it in her pocket. "Well, aren't you going to phone him?"

"This is a New York area code, isn't it?"

"Yes."

"That's long-distance. I'll have to get some money from my drawer at home and use the phone at the end of the lane."

"You'll do no such thing, Rebecca Zook," said Mrs. Ansbacher firmly. "You'll use my phone."

"But — "

"And no buts about it. It's not that expensive to phone New York from here. Unless you plan on talking for a long time," she added with a twinkle.

"Goodness, no, I plan on making it very brief."

"Here." Mrs. Ansbacher turned the counter phone toward Rebecca.

Why won't a customer come in? Rebecca wanted someone or something to distract Mrs. Ansbacher, so she could gather her thoughts. Why would Mr. Goldfarb be calling her? Maybe he wanted to order another wall hanging. Maybe he'd sold her saddles wall hanging. But there was no reason to call her to tell her this.

No one came into the shop, however, and Mrs. Ansbacher just stood there, behind the phone, smiling patiently. Rebecca dialed the number.

"Goldfarb Gallery," a man's voice answered on the other end. "How may I help you?"

"Is Mr. Goldfarb in?" inquired Rebecca.

"Speaking."

Rebecca swallowed. "This is Rebecca Zook."

"Rebecca!" Mr. Goldfarb answered excitedly. "I'm so glad you called. That exhibition I mentioned is opening Friday, a week from today. Many of my clients will be here. And I found the perfect gold-leaf frame for your quilt. It looks even more beautiful now. You must come see it! I'll be happy to pay your way here and back, and put you up in a nice hotel."

Rebecca was stunned. Go to New York? To a gallery? "As I said, Mr. Goldfarb, I can't go to New York. But thank you again for inviting me."

"I was hoping your parents might let you come for this special occasion."

"I'm sure they wouldn't let me come," Rebecca said. "There's too much to do around the farm." Even if there weren't a lot to do around the farm, Rebecca couldn't imagine her mother allowing her to go to New York City. The Amish tried to keep their children away from the world. To her mother, New York City was Sin City.

"All right, Rebecca," Mr. Goldfarb said, disappointedly. "Just thought I'd try one more time. If you change your mind, you have my phone number."

"Yes. I hope your showing, or whatever it's called, goes off very well. Thank you again."

"My pleasure. And please do think about coming. Good-bye."

"Good-bye." Mr. Goldfarb hung up the phone, and so did Rebecca.

Mrs. Ansbacher pounced. "What was it all about?"

"That exhibition he mentioned when he was here." Rebecca said. "He wanted me to come.

"And you said no?!"

"I'm too busy."

Rebecca began to settle into her work routine behind the counter, but Mrs. Ansbacher still pursued. "Don't you want to go, Rebecca?

"I can't go on the bus by myself. And who'd go with me? Mother and Hanna are busy themselves."

For a moment Mrs. Ansbacher was stumped. For Mabel, Hanna, and Rebecca to take the bus might be too expensive. But if they could get a ride…"Gregory!" Mrs. Ansbacher suddenly shouted. "Gregory could take you. I know Amish folk don't drive, but the church lets you ride with hired drivers, doesn't it?"

"Yes. But why would Gregory want to waste a whole day driving us to New York and back?" asked Rebecca.

"You told me about that museum you two talked about. Maybe he'd like to go see it. Might take you, too."

MoMA. I would like to see that, thought Rebecca.

"Not every Amish girl gets an invitation to go to New York to see her quilt on display," Mrs. Ansbacher said pointedly.

"To think like that is prideful. Besides, can you see Mam agreeing to let me go?" Rebecca looked directly at Mrs. Ansbacher.

"No, I can't, truthfully, Rebecca."

"Then that's the end of that." Rebecca decided a change of subject was best. "Did you have any sales yesterday?"

"They're in the drawer," Mrs. Ansbacher said. Rebecca pulled out the sales slips and began to update the accounts. *Your mother would never agree,* thought Mrs. Ansbacher. *But I know someone who might.*

Despite herself, Rebecca spent a good deal of the rest of the afternoon thinking about New York. *I wonder what an art gallery looks like...? My wall hanging will be on display...! Now, Rebecca, stop that; you mustn't be proud.* Rebecca could force her thoughts elsewhere for a while, but the idea of New York always seemed to creep back in eventually. And along with it came the idea of Gregory and the Museum of Modern Art.

That night Rebecca somehow managed to get through supper without showing her excitement. She desperately wanted to ask her mother if she could go, but she knew what the answer would be. So she ate her meal in silence while the usual chitchat went on aimlessly about her. She was just washing up the dishes when a knock came on the door. Hanna opened it, and there stood Mrs. Ansbacher.

"Hello, 'Lizbeth. How are you?"

"I'm fine, Hanna. How are you?"

"I'm good. This is a surprise. What brings you here?"

"Hanna, don't let her just stand there, invite her in," instructed Mabel. "Hello, Elizabeth. Please come in." Mrs. Ansbacher crossed the threshold. "Can we get you something to eat?"

"No, thank you, Mabel. We just finished dinner. Hello, Rebecca."

"Hello, Mrs. Ansbacher," Rebecca replied, washing a dish and setting it in the drainer. Mrs. Ansbacher almost never dropped by, so Rebecca had a suspicion why she'd come.

"I hope I'm not disturbing you," Mrs. Ansbacher continued. "I'm looking for Elam."

"He's in the barn," said Hanna. "Want me to get him?"

"No, that's all right," said Mrs. Ansbacher. "I might just mosey out there to find him."

"Whatcha want with him?" asked Hanna in her blunt manner.

"Got a question I want to ask him. Well, maybe it's more of a request." Mrs. Ansbacher smiled at Rebecca, who shifted her feet uncomfortably and picked up another dish to wash. "I won't bother you anymore. Good night."

"Good to see you, Elizabeth," Mabel said, moving quickly to open the door for her. When Mrs. Ansbacher had disappeared, Mabel turned to Rebecca. "I wonder what she wants with Elam. Do you know, Rebecca?"

Rebecca's conscience engaged in a mini-debate before she answered. *Well, I don't actually* know, she decided. "No, Mam, I'm not sure why Mrs. Ansbacher wants Dat." Which was true: she wasn't *sure*. She just had a strong suspicion.

Mrs. Ansbacher found Elam sitting on a bench outside the barn. "Evenin', Elam."

Elam looked up, surprised. "Elizabeth! Hello. What brings you over this way?"

"Got something I want to talk to you about."

"Have a seat," he replied, moving over on the bench.

"Don't mind if I do," said Mrs. Ansbacher, sitting down next to Elam. She got right to the point. "I wanted to share some news with you. It's about Rebecca."

"What about her?"

"I don't know if she told you, but she sold one of her quilted wall hangings."

"I didn't even know she was making any. A wall hanging?" Elam folded his arms and waited for Mrs. Ansbacher to proceed.

"She's come up with a design that has to do with saddles, Elam."

"Is that so?"

"She's got sort of a theme going about horses. It's not your usual Amish quilt pattern. Maybe that's why she hasn't mentioned it." Of course, Mrs. Ansbacher knew that that was precisely why Rebecca hadn't mentioned it. After all, she was the one who had provided her with a room where she could continue to work unnoticed. But she didn't want to get distracted with that part of the story.

"The point is, a man from New York bought Rebecca's quilt. He owns an art gallery. And he called the shop today and invited Rebecca to come to New York for an opening he's having at his gallery, an opening that'll feature Rebecca's wall hanging."

"Feature? How do you mean?" asked Elam. He uncrossed his arms and sat up.

"He's hanging it there on his gallery wall, alongside the work of other artists. He thinks Rebecca's work is as good as that of real artists, people who make art for a living."

"You say he invited her to come to New York?"

"He did. A week from Friday. And I came to ask you to let her go." Mrs. Ansbacher looked directly at Elam, who paused for a moment.

"Did you ask her mother, Elizabeth?"

"No, Elam, I came straight to you. I think we both know what Mabel will think. And I understand why she wouldn't let Rebecca go to New York by herself. But I don't think she has to go by herself. Mabel and Hanna could go with her."

"What about the all the work to do here?" asked Elam.

"Rebecca told me she'd picked the last of the beans. And I believe it's the time of year when the gardening work is slowing down, and it's not time to begin slaughtering hogs yet. The way I figure it, the three of them can go to New York and back in a single day."

"That would depend on the bus or train schedule, wouldn't it?" inquired Elam.

"Not if they go in a car."

"A car!"

Mrs. Ansbacher hurried on before Elam could protest. "Gregory could take them."

"Gregory? Why would Gregory want to drive them to New York City?"

"To be nice. To pay you back some for your hospitality. And because he wants to go to New York himself.

"How do you know?'

"'Because I asked him."

"You asked him? When?" Elam was amazed at her audacity.

"This evening, before coming over here."

Elam gave her a long look, then broke into a smile. "Why, Elizabeth Ansbacher! You've been busy, haven't you? "

"Rebecca is so creative, Elam. She could do all sorts of art, if she'd let herself go. I'm sure of it. I think seeing other paintings and being with other artists would inspire her."

"To be an artist?" Elam shook his head, uncomfortable with the thought.

"Well, maybe not full time. But just to express herself. You express yourself with your leather, don't you? You know how happy it makes you feel. Rebecca can settle down, live the Amish life if she wants. That's fine. But wouldn't it be something if she had been to New York City and seen her artwork hanging in a real gallery? She'd carry that memory the rest of her days."

"To make her think big of herself?" Elam frowned.

"Pride? Well, maybe there are times when pride is all right. I'm not Amish, so I don't know exactly how you feel," Mrs. Ansbacher continued, with some fervor. "But isn't it possible to use the talents God gave you, not to show off, not to draw attention to yourself, but as, I don't know, as a kind of gift back to God."

Elam rose and moved away, looking out over his farm. *I'm thinking of giving up farming, abandoning the very thing Amish have been doing for three centuries. I am happy when I do something fine with my leather. And when we all get together and raise a barn, aren't we glad we've built such a good, sturdy barn? That's not pride, necessarily. Not boastful pride, anyway. Maybe Elizabeth's right. Maybe it's a God-inspired pride, to use the gifts He gives to you.*

He walked back to Mrs. Ansbacher, still sitting on the bench. "I can see why your shop is such a success, Elizabeth. You're a good saleswoman."

"Maybe, Elam, maybe," said Mrs. Ansbacher, rising. "But I've found that I'm really most effective when I sell the customer something he wanted all along." They both laughed.

"Now, how'd you like to go convince my wife?" he asked, with a twinkle in his eye.

"Oh, I'm not *that* good at sales! But I have a sneaky suspicion you are."

"I'd better be!" Elam replied and shared another laugh with his old friend.

Walking home later that night, Mrs. Ansbacher felt excited about the day's events. Rebecca, whom she loved like a daughter, might be on her way to New York to exhibit her work. And she had helped make it happen. She felt a touch of pride. *Well, why not? God has His own plan, but there's nothing wrong with helping Him out if I can. And if Rebecca is successful in New York, that can only help* my *plan.* She continued on, humming contentedly beneath the starry sky, thinking surely, at least for that moment, all was indeed right in God's beautiful world.

CHAPTER 12

Ten days later, Mabel, Hanna, Rebecca, and Gregory found themselves standing at Rockefeller Center, staring up at the skyscraper before them. Gregory had driven them, and quite the ride it had been. Hanna had kept up a constant chatter, continually surprised at the world. "Oh, look, a 'musement park! Crazy people, riding them rolly coasters!" Then, "Look at all these cars? Where's everybody going?"

As they had sped along the New Jersey Turnpike, Mabel had kept telling Gregory to slow down. Nearing Newark airport, Hanna had suddenly shouted, "Look out! Airplane's gonna hit us!" as a low-flying Delta jet made its usual landing near the road.

The sight of the New York City skyline had induced a kind of awe. "Oh, my!" Mabel had murmured quietly.

"Goodness, Mabel, look at all them buildings!" Hanna said.

And Mabel had asked, "How can there be so many people in one place?"

But what had really scared them and had amused Gregory the most, had been the Lincoln Tunnel. Hanna had tried her best to talk Gregory out of going through it. "It goes under the river? What keeps the water out? Don't do it, Gregory!" All the way through the tunnel she'd kept her feet up off the floor, as if water might seep in at any minute.

For once, Mabel had allowed Hanna's observations to go uncontradicted. She, too, had been scared, and not for the first time on the trip. She'd spent the ride gripping the door handle of Gregory's pickup truck and hanging on silently. Rebecca hadn't been very talkative either, just staring out the window. Gregory had allowed her her thoughts, contenting himself with answering Hanna's questions, or thinking what a strange twist his life had taken, driving three Amish women into New York City.

And now there they were, staring at the skyscraper looming over them.

"What holds it up?" Hanna asked.

"Engineers know how to build it with steel beams and solid footings in bedrock, so it doesn't fall over," Gregory said. "But I couldn't tell you how they do it."

"Wouldn't catch me living in there," commented Mabel.

"They don't live there, Mam; they just work there," Rebecca said.

"They can fall out, just the same," replied Mabel. "Or get caught in a fire, like that terrible day with the terrorists. I don't like high things."

"Then you probably won't like New York," Gregory added.

"You didn't have to drag me all the way here to convince me of that."

"He didn't drag you, Mam. You said you wanted to come."

"I said Elam wanted me to come," Mabel responded. "And look at all of the trash. No wonder they have mice and roaches and goodness knows what else. They need to rett up."

The walk up Fifth Avenue was a cornucopia of astonishments for the women. Jews, Hispanics, Arabs, Koreans, blacks, homeless people strewn on the steps of St Patrick's Cathedral — an ethnic smorgasbord that dazzled the eyes of these homogeneous Amish. People with pierced ears, lips, eyebrows, tongues — "How do they eat?" Hanna asked. "Don't they get food stuck on it?"

"Don't even look at them," Mabel advised, disgusted.

But even she couldn't ignore who now passed before them, as they stood at the top of the ice-skating rink below 30 Rockefeller Plaza: a woman in skintight, red-leather shorts, gold boots, and tattoos over her entire body. Hanna and Mabel's jaws dropped. "What's this world coming to?" Mabel asked.

Of course, the three women attracted a few stares, too. Apparently even worldly New Yorkers didn't have much occasion to see Amish on their streets. But Mabel and Hanna were not intimidated. "They're looking at us like we're the strange ones," Hanna whispered to Mabel.

"My word!" replied Mabel, clucking her tongue in disbelief.

When they turned away from the ice rink, a nearby window display caught their eye: sculptures of three nude women, cavorting. "The Three Graces," the label said.

"Naked butts!" Hanna exclaimed.

"Look the other way, Hanna. You don't want to see that!" Mabel implored. They both turned their heads, as if avoiding a horror show.

Realizing that all the noise and newness might be overwhelming, Gregory tried to distract them by leading them to the shop window of Teuscher Chocolates. "How'd you like to work in this store, Hanna?" he asked.

"Bet I could sell a lot of chocolate!"

"Bet you could eat a lot, too. Rebecca, Mabel, come inside and pick yourself out some chocolate."

"Come on, Mam, it's our day in New York!" Rebecca said. She hooked her arm through Mabel's, and they walked into the store, Gregory following.

The tiny store was crammed with chocolates. White, mint, lemon, Mandarin, chocolate with pink pepper, truffles chocolate, mocha chocolate, even chocolate golf balls. Chocolate cows with red-chocolate tongues, chocolate ladybugs, penguins, giraffes, dogs, rabbits, fish, owls, bears, cats, dogs. Orange marzipan, dark hazelnut, nougat, almond, caramel, champagne truffles. "Oh, goody!" exclaimed Hanna, her face breaking into a huge smile.

"Oh, my!" said Mabel, her eyes wide.

What else is there to say? Gregory smiled.

They picked out a large bag of different chocolates. The bill came to eighty-four dollars.

"Oh, Gregory, we can't let you pay that much," Rebecca admonished. "Let's put some of it back."

"Not on your life!" Gregory said, fishing out his credit card. "I'm not going to stint on our day in New York." He handed the card to the clerk, and she rang up the bill and handed Gregory the slip to sign.

"I know the perfect place to eat this," Gregory announced when they had exited the store. "Follow me." He led them across the street to the steps of St. Patrick's Cathedral and opened the bag for them.

Hanna grabbed a fistful of chocolates and began chewing happily.

"Don't be greedy, Hanna!" Mabel said sharply.

"I'm not," replied Hanna, grabbing some more chocolate.

"There's plenty," said Gregory.

Rebecca took a truffle. "Thank you, Gregory." She placed it delicately in her mouth. Mabel followed suit, and for a moment no one said anything, as they savored their treats.

"What a church!" Mabel finally exclaimed. "It's like those churches in Europe; I've seen pictures of them in magazines."

"This is St. Patrick's Cathedral," Gregory explained.

"I don't know how people can worship in a place like this," Rebecca said.

"It's supposed to instill awe in you," Gregory replied. "When you're inside and look to the ceiling, you feel the awesome power of God."

"I know God is all-powerful," Rebecca replied. "But I like our church services in someone's home. I want to feel God's power *inside* me. I don't want to be afraid of God; I want to feel His spirit right there in that little farmhouse room with me." Rebecca had spoken simply, but fervently. She seemed to shine with a light within, Gregory noticed. This radiance only enhanced her beauty. He noticed that, too.

Gregory led the way through the heavy oak doors and into the interior. As usual, the place was bustling with tourists, moving silently up and down the aisles. A few parishioners were scattered throughout the pews, praying. Hanna saw an older woman in a green summer dress light a candle. She moved to light one herself.

"You're supposed to drop an offering into that box," whispered Gregory.

"What kind of offering?" asked Hanna in her full voice. One or two people gave her a quick glance.

"Money," whispered Gregory. "It's to worship God."

"You have to pay to worship God!" Hanna's voice seemed to boom in the tremendous silence of the cathedral. She put the candle back down.

"Hanna, *sei still!*" Mabel said in a low voice.

"I am being quiet," Hanna said loudly.

"I'll wait outside. It's too big, too dark." Mabel quickly exited the cathedral.

"Hanna, let's walk around, but try to keep your voice low," said Rebecca. She smiled at Gregory, suggesting he lead the way.

They went slowly down a side aisle. As they wandered, Gregory considered the trip so far. *New York can be overwhelming. And for Amish women?* He glanced at Hanna. *She's fine; she basically delights in everything. Don't know about Mabel though. And Rebecca?* He looked over his shoulder. Rebecca was walking slowly, looking into the chapels as she passed them, but not stopping to really look. *We need a break*, Gregory concluded.

When they left the cathedral, Gregory mentioned that it was time for the trip to the museum. Mabel and Hanna demurred. "What's the point in looking at pictures hanging on a wall?" demanded Mabel.

Gregory knew better than to attempt an explanation because he could see that it was a legitimate question. What *was* the point? Being inspired by beauty, he might answer. But Mabel and Hanna probably wouldn't find the artwork in the Museum of Modern Art beautiful. So he and Rebecca escorted them to a nearby restaurant, ordered coffee to revive their spirits, and established them in a cozy corner looking out onto the street, so they could watch the people passing by. Since there were bound to be some tattooed teens, scantily dressed women, and buff men walking hand in hand, Gregory felt sure the two Amish women would have plenty to chat about, and that would keep them happy. Meanwhile, he and Rebecca would visit the MoMA.

The museum was featuring an exhibit on the surrealists: Picasso, Dali, Miro, Magritte, and Pollack. Gregory and Rebecca strolled through it, silently joining the crowd. The idea of sharing modern painters with Rebecca had excited Gregory before, but as he looked at the cubist rendering of one of Picasso's guitars, or the squiggly lines of Miro, he began to wonder what in the world he had been thinking. That he was going to discuss fractured perspective with Rebecca, or the coloring scheme of Picasso's *Blue Period*? What was this Amish farm girl supposed to make of the melted watch draped over a tree limb in a Dali landscape? Or the spontaneous paint splatterings of a Jackson Pollack? What would be her thoughts about Magritte's *The Great War*, depicting a bowler-hatted man with a green apple painted full in his face? Or her feelings when staring at Picasso's *Girl Before a Mirror*, with her protuberant belly and circular breasts?

As they toured the exhibit, Gregory found himself moving faster and faster, barely pausing in front of the final paintings before hurrying Rebecca to the street outside.

"Rebecca, I'm sorry," he said as soon as he had the chance. She did seem somewhat dazed. "I was crazy to think this art would appeal to you. Your Amish art has patterns, but they are comprehensible patterns, understandable. The world in those paintings makes no sense, does it?"

"Not to me," Rebecca admitted quietly. "I'm sorry, Gregory. I wanted to like them, but I guess I'm just not sophisticated enough." She looked down at the sidewalk.

Gregory suddenly felt angry. "If sophistication means deep understanding, you're plenty sophisticated. Maybe simplicity is sophistication!" His own head was whirling now. "Oh, I don't know!"

Suddenly he had an idea. "Come on!" He grabbed Rebecca's arm and took her to the restaurant. Once outside, he said, "Wait here," and rushed inside. A minute later he appeared with Mabel and Hanna in tow. He hailed a cab, and a bright-yellow Ford screeched to a stop. "Get in, please."

"Where are we going?" asked Hanna.

"Central Park," he told the driver. They took off.

"How was the museum?" asked Mabel.

"It was…" Rebecca began, but didn't know what to say.

"Too New Yorky," Gregory finished for her.

"Tall?" asked Mabel.

"Too many people?" asked Hanna.

"Something like that," Gregory answered.

They drove in silence through the leafy park until Gregory said, "Here." The cab pulled over. The women got out as Gregory, in the front seat, paid the cabby and climbed out himself. "Follow me," he said, trying not to be giving commands, but also feeling a certain urgency. They trooped over green grass, past people lying about on blankets and others eating or reading. In a far corner, two youngsters tossed a Frisbee. Finally, Gregory said, "This is good."

They had arrived at what New Yorkers call the Sheep Meadow. It really had been full of sheep, back in the day. Now it was a large, open field of mostly green grass. There were very few people about.

Gregory took a deep breath. It was city air, true, but it was mitigated by the surrounding greenery. He took another breath. Mabel, Hanna, and Rebecca seemed to sense why he had brought them there. They, too, took deep breaths and began to relax. They turned around, silently looking at the trees, bushes, and grass of Central Park. It was far from the tranquility of their farm. They could still hear the traffic noise from beyond the trees, but it was at a distance. And at least they were somewhat surrounded by nature.

"I wanted to show you that New York isn't only noise and trash and people," said Gregory. "Frederick Law Olmstead, who built this park, knew people would need to escape."

"I'm glad you brought us here," said Rebecca, closing her eyes and turning her face to the sun.

"There's a nice patch of grass," said Hanna, pointing just ahead. She decided to sit on it. "Pretty good grass, too."

"Hanna!" protested Mabel.

"Why don't we all sit down, Mam?" said Rebecca. "I could use a rest."

So they settled down on the grass. Everyone was too tired to talk. Gregory stretched out. The lingering sun felt good on his face. He closed his eyes and tried to let his mind go blank. The sounds of the traffic seemed to fade away. After a moment, he felt a tug at his sleeve. It was Rebecca. "May I talk to you for a minute?"

"Sure." Gregory sat up. He noticed that Mabel and Hanna were sitting with their eyes closed. "What is it?"

"It's about this gallery exhibition. I'm afraid to go." She looked down at the grass.

"Why?"

"The people who'll be there. We'll stick out like sore thumbs."

"I told Mr. Goldfarb we'd be coming." Gregory wiped a line of sweat from his brow with the back of his hand. "He sounds like a nice man."

"He is. But the other art will probably be modern. My poor little wall hanging will be laughable next to it."

"Mr. Goldfarb wouldn't have hung it up if he thought it was laughable." Gregory looked at Rebecca intently. "It's not laughable, Rebecca."

"It's not that I care what people think," she began. "Well, maybe I do. But the three of us, with our plain dresses and our hair tucked under our coverings. Everyone will be wondering who in the world we are."

"And Mr. Goldfarb will explain to them that you are the artist and they are your Amish family." He took a deep breath. "I understand, Rebecca. But we told Mr. Goldfarb we'd be there, and we've come all this way. It'd be a shame not to at least see what your wall hanging looks like, beautifully framed and hanging in an art gallery. Wouldn't your dad be disappointed if we didn't go?"

Rebecca drew her hand to her throat, delicately. She paused. "Maybe...he might."

"I promise we won't stay long. We'll just pop in, look at your work, say hello to Mr. Goldfarb, and shake a few hands, then leave. All right?"

"All right." Rebecca gave him a small smile. "Thank you, Gregory."

"For what?"

"Taking us here, showing us around, being kind."

"Being kind to you is not exactly the hardest thing in the world to do, Rebecca." He hesitated. He reached out and squeezed her hand, then released it gently. "Let's go take the New York art world by storm!" He jumped up and pulled Rebecca to her feet. They joined Mabel and Hanna. "Time for the grand finale of our trip to New York!" Gregory helped each of the women to her feet and led them away to find a cab to take them to the Goldfarb Gallery.

The gallery was on Prince Street in Lower Manhattan. The buildings were much smaller there, former warehouses with converted lofts on top, small stores selling jewelry or books — all in all much more peaceful than the hectic midtown hustle and bustle. Silence prevailed in the cab ride south, each person pondering the day's events or wondering how the next one would unfold.

By the time they arrived and stood looking through the large glass windows at the crowd gathered inside, the party seemed to be in full swing. "A lot of people," mumbled Mabel.

"Look at that woman — she's wearing shorts!" exclaimed Hanna. "And there's a man in purple jeans, and — what's the undertaker doing here?!" she asked, pointing to a man in a tuxedo.

Gregory couldn't help laughing. *A New York party!* he thought. He'd always wanted to attend one. "We don't have to stay long," he told Hanna and Mabel. "Just say hello to Mr. Goldfarb, look at Rebecca's quilt, and leave. In fact, there's a café across the street; you two could wait for Rebecca and me there, if you'd be more comfortable."

"No, looks like they have ginger ale," said Hanna, pointing to a tall blonde holding a glass of champagne. "I'm thirsty."

"I want to see Rebecca's quilt," said Mabel. "Imagine, it's hanging in a gallery right here in New York!" Gregory glanced at Rebecca. She seemed surprised at her mother's insistence, and maybe a little touched that she might be proud of her daughter's work.

They entered the gallery. Fifty or so people stood in a large room intersected by two large, round columns supporting the ceiling. On the eggshell white walls hung various works of art, paintings mostly, with a sculpture or two standing on platforms. "Which one is Goldfarb?" Gregory asked Rebecca.

She scanned the crowd. "I don't see him."

"Well, let's find your piece, and maybe he'll find us." He set off through the crowd, turning sideways to inch his way forward. Rebecca followed, then Mabel, then Hanna.

A waiter passed Hanna, serving champagne. "Can I have some ginger ale?" she asked, and took a glass of champagne. The waiter gave her a curious look, then raised his tray high and made his way through the crowd. By the time Hanna looked back toward Mabel, several people in the way had cut her off from following her. She took a sip of champagne. The taste startled her. *Sharp ginger ale!* She took another sip. *I really like it.* Another sip — this time more of a big swallow that polished off the glass.

Mabel had receded so far into the crowd that Hanna could barely see her. *I'm not going into that crowd.* Hanna turned and wandered toward the other side of the room, where there seemed to be fewer people. Another waiter passed her, offering hors d'oeuvres. "Why are the hot dogs so little and short?" Hanna asked him.

He gave her a queer look, made even queerer when he noticed her long, light-purple dress, covered with her cape and apron — a lot of clothing for a hot summer day. "They're called pigs in a blanket," he said curtly.

"We just call 'em hot dogs," Hanna replied, taking one. She took a bite. "Yes, it's a hot dog." The waiter looked at her quizzically, then backed away. Another waiter took his place, carrying champagne. Hanna put her empty glass on the tray and took another one. "This is good ginger ale," she said, cheerily. The waiter laughed at her presumed joke and moved away. *Funny sense of humor,* thought Hanna, sipping her champagne. "Boy, this hits the spot!" she declared to a tuxedoed man with an orange stripe down his hair.

"It's French," he responded.

"I didn't know they made French ginger ale," Hanna answered. The man gave her an odd look and turned away. *Not very friendly,* thought Hanna. But, after all the "ginger ale," she found she didn't much care.

Gregory, Rebecca, and Mabel had managed to wend their way through the crowd to a relatively quiet corner in the back of the gallery. There, hanging on the wall, was Rebecca's quilt, framed in a beautiful gold frame. "There it is!" Gregory shouted. "Look, Rebecca."

"I see," Rebecca replied quietly. She stood still, staring at her work. "Do you like it, Mam?" Rebecca knew her mother had probably never seen a quilt quite like it, and certainly not framed.

"It's a beautiful frame," Mabel answered. Rebecca held her breath. "And the quilt? I like the colors; that's a pretty dark blue. Saddles?" Mabel pondered. "Why saddles?"

"I like their shape, Mam. The curves, the way the saddle horn thrusts up suddenly. I don't know, it just came to me — saddles! So I did it." Rebecca hoped she didn't sound defensive.

"I love it," said Gregory. "I think the dark-brown and purple go great together, especially with that black diamond border. It's intriguing, but it's also just, I don't know, evocative."

"Evocative?" Mabel asked.

"I agree," a man's voice behind them affirmed. They turned to find a well-dressed man of some forty years, wearing a crisp, white shirt, open in front. His light-blond hair was close-cropped, with a little gray beginning to peek in around the edges. A diamond stud sparkled from one earlobe. High-end Armani glasses rested delicately on his nose, and a snakeskin belt with a large, gold alligator buckle held up an expensive pair of tight blue jeans. "I collect quilts, but I don't have anything like this. Lots of patterns, of course, and appliquéd flowers or birds and whatnot, but interestingly enough, never a quilt with a horse theme. And I really like horses."

"So do I!" Gregory said. "I'm Gregory Pinckney." Gregory held out his hand.

The man shook it and said, "Ted Snow, nice to meet you."

"And this is Mabel Zook," Gregory continued, gesturing to Mabel. Ted nodded. "And this is the artist, Rebecca Zook," Gregory finished proudly.

"You quilted this?" Ted asked.

"Yes," Rebecca answered softly, struggling to make eye contact.

"Well, it's really good to meet you. I admire your work very much."

"Thank you. I'm not sure I qualify as having *work*," she continued modestly.

"Is this your only piece?" asked Ted.

"Well, actually, I do have a few more with this horse theme."

"I must see them!"

"Must see what?" Mr. Goldfarb joined the group, looking very dapper in a blue seersucker suit. A linen shirt with a faint hint of pink added just the right artistic touch. "Hello, Rebecca. I am delighted you decided to come."

"It's nice to see you, Mr. Goldfarb. Thank you for displaying my wall hanging."

"I'm pleased to do so" he replied.

"This is my mother, Mr. Goldfarb, and my friend, Gregory Pinckney." Rebecca stepped back to allow her mother to come forward.

"So nice to meet you, Mrs. Zook." Mr. Goldfarb took Mabel's hand and covered it warmly with his other hand. "You must be very proud of Rebecca."

"She's a good girl," Mabel managed.

"I bet she learned how to quilt from you," Mr. Goldfarb continued smoothly. "Maybe you have some quilts I might look at next time I'm in Honey Brook."

"Oh, no, I just make quilts for beddings. You wouldn't want to see any of mine."

"I just might," Mr. Goldfarb added.

Rebecca could see her mother was charmed, despite herself. "Mam makes beautiful quilts."

"Oh, now, Rebecca…" Mabel said, caught between enjoying all the attention and trying to deflect it.

"And how do you do, Mr. Pinckney." Mr. Goldfarb turned to Gregory and offered his hand.

Gregory took it assertively. "Nice to meet you, Mr. Goldfarb.

"Thank you for bringing them."

"Where are you from?" asked Ted, rejoining the conversation.

"Rebecca is from Lancaster County, Pennsylvania, Ted," Mr. Goldfarb said. "She's Amish."

"Really?" Ted said, surprised. "The genuine article, eh? All the better." He turned to Mr. Goldfarb. "Stephen, I'd like to buy Ms. Zook's wall hanging." Rebecca's mouth dropped open, and her eyes widened.

"Wonderful, Ted! I'm delighted to sell it to you!" Mr. Goldfarb answered, shaking Ted's hand warmly. "You've made an excellent choice."

"I know. Rebecca, would you mind signing the back of the frame for me?" He pulled out a silver pen and offered it to Rebecca. She took it as Mr. Goldfarb pulled the wall hanging down and turned it over. Gregory beamed at Rebecca, and a small smile played at the corner of Mabel's mouth as Rebecca carefully signed her name.

"There you go, Ted," said Mr. Goldfarb. "Autographed by the artist. I'm going to miss it."

"She has more quilts, Stephen!" said Ted.

Mr. Goldfarb turned to Rebecca. "You do?"

"I have a few more, Mr. Goldfarb."

"Then I must see them. I'll make a trip to Honey Brook as soon as I can."

"And you are welcomed to have supper with us," Mabel inserted, smiling at Mr. Goldfarb. "Have you ever had an Amish meal?"

"I don't believe I have, Mrs. Zook."

"We'll make a good one for you, and bake a schnitzel pie, too," Mabel pronounced with a proud, satisfied smile.

Hanna suddenly appeared, balancing a plate of pigs in a blanket in one hand and a glass of champagne in the other. "Mabel, you have to taste some of this ginger ale," she said, her voice rising in pitch and volume. "It's the best I've ever had." Hanna wavered slightly, and Gregory took her arm to offer support. "These little hot dogs are good, too."

"Hanna, not so loud," Mabel instructed.

"I'm not being loud, Mabel!" Hanna snapped.

Rebecca hastened to settle things down, gently relieving Hanna of her plate. "Mr. Goldfarb, Mr. Snow, this is my aunt, Hanna."

"How do you do, Mrs. Zook," Mr. Goldfarb offered his hand.

"Stoltzfus," Hanna corrected him. "I'm not married. Are you?"

"Hanna!" Mabel interjected.

"What?" Hanna asked, her eyes narrowing.

Mr. Goldfarb had recovered. "I beg your pardon, Ms. Stoltzfus. And, yes, I am married."

"Where's your wife?" Hanna asked, her usual direct manner somewhat enhanced by the champagne.

"My spouse is out of town," Mr. Goldfarb answered, delicately avoiding a situation he knew might not appeal to Amish. But Gregory understood, and a look at Rebecca showed that she did, too. This time Mabel stepped in to steer the conversation.

"This nice man, Mr. Goldfarb, is coming to supper someday, Hanna. He's the one who took Rebecca's quilt here for exhibiting. This is his party."

"It's a good party, Mr. Goldfart," Hanna answered, mispronouncing his name. Ted stifled a small laugh as best he could, and Rebecca blushed. "I like it."

Mabel seemed not to notice. "And guess what? This man here just bought Rebecca's quilt hanging!"

"He did!" Hanna turned to Rebecca. "How much did it fetch, Becca?"

"Hanna, it's not polite to talk about money in public, you know that," Rebecca said, lowering her voice.

"This isn't public, this is New York," her aunt shot back. "You can say anything in New York." She steadied herself. "All right, whisper it to me." She leaned forward, inclining an ear.

This movement, however, caused her to stumble. Mr. Goldfarb caught her in his arms, but not before Hanna had accidentally thrown the remainder of her champagne onto his linen shirt.

"Hanna!" Rebecca cried.

"Vas ist letz mit dich?!" cried her mother.

"Nothing's wrong with me," Hanna said.

Gregory retrieved Hanna from Mr. Goldfarb's arms. He released her and stepped back, pulling out a handkerchief and futilely dabbing at the champagne blotch now prominent in the middle of his shirt.

Ted surreptitiously pulled his newly purchased wall hanging from Mr. Goldfarb's other hand, silently offering a prayer that it had avoided the champagne shower.

"I'm so sorry, Mr. Goldfarb!" Rebecca said. "So sorry." She relieved Hanna of her empty champagne glass.

"I'm slorry, too, Mr. Goldfart," Hanna slurred. "Let me help you." She reached out and tried to grab his handkerchief. Gregory steadied her this time as Mr. Goldfarb quickly avoided her hand.

"That's quite all right," Mr. Goldfarb reassured Hanna. "It'll wash right out."

"I'll wash it," Hanna announced. "Take it off and give it to me. I'll wash it and iron it. I'm a good cleaner." She stood proudly, if a bit wobbly.

"That's all right, Hanna." Rebecca handed the glass to a passing waiter and turned to Mr. Goldfarb. "Of course we'll be glad to pay for the cleaning."

"Totally unnecessary, Rebecca. I take shirts to the dry cleaners all the time. This'll come right out. Now, where were we?"

There was a pause, as everyone tried to gather themselves to resume normal conversation. Gregory suggested delicately, "I think it might be time for us to be leaving. We've got a long drive."

Rebecca seized the opportunity immediately. "Oh, yes, we must go. Thank you so much, Mr. Goldfarb."

"If you feel you must — " Mr. Goldfarb began.

"Oh, yes, we've got cows to milk at four thirty in the morning," Mabel added helpfully. "Now, don't you forget to come to supper," she said to Mr. Goldfarb. "And bring an empty stomach."

"I'll make peanut butter pie," Hanna said, loud enough that one or two passing guests turned their heads at this unusual announcement. "I'm a good cook."

"I'm sure you are, Ms. Stoltzfus," Mr. Goldfarb answered. "I very much look forward to seeing you all again. And seeing more of your work," he said to Rebecca.

"You must show it to me first, Stephen," Ted said. "Now that I've bought this, I've got first dibs. Isn't that right, Ms. Zook?"

Rebecca stammered, "Well, I...I...I don't know how these things work." She turned to Gregory for help.

"I think we'll just let Mr. Goldfarb decide," Gregory said. "He'll be representing Rebecca, I presume."

"Of course," Mr. Goldfarb confirmed.

"Represent?" asked Rebecca.

"Be your agent," Gregory told her.

Rebecca looked shocked. "Oh!" she managed.

"Mabel, could we go to the bathroom before we leave?" Hanna tried to whisper to her sister, but, of course, everyone heard.

"The restroom is just down this hallway. Let me show you." Mr. Goldfarb started off.

"I'll go with you," Rebecca chimed in, following her mother and aunt down the hallway.

For a moment, the sounds of the party were all that Ted and Gregory could hear as they stood together. "I've always wanted to meet Amish people," Ted offered, smiling.

"This was far from typical," Gregory responded.

"Not much on drink, I assume?"

"I think pretty much forbidden. At least frowned upon."

"Well," Ted said, holding out his wall hanging. "At least she missed this when she tossed the champagne." They looked at it together for a moment, exchanging a chuckle.

"I'm glad it found a good home," Gregory said. "Enjoy the rest of your party."

They shook hands. Ted went back into the crowd, and Gregory headed for the front door. The party had thinned out. He looked over the remaining crowd in their expensive clothes, the women tall, thin, and beautiful, the men with well-toned bodies and perfectly coiffed hair, all of them buzzing with excited chatter. Gregory knew his charges were tired, and it would be a long ride home. No doubt Hanna and Mabel would fall asleep.

Good, that will give me time to talk to Rebecca alone. She must be excited. I'm happy for her. Gregory paused in his thoughts. *What if she were able to sell quilt work in New York? Would she give up being Amish? Would she move?* Gregory couldn't imagine either possibility, but he knew that life was never predictable. After all, here he was, standing in a New York art gallery, when only a month ago he had been on a South Carolina beach.

He thought of Rebecca's blue-green eyes: kind, intelligent, trustful. *Would I want her to move or to stay?* And then a new thought entered his mind for the first time. *Stay. With me.*

CHAPTER 13

The lamp cast a circle of light onto Ivan's desk. It was the only light in the room on this cloudy, moonless August night. Ivan sat behind his desk, slowly turning a glass of vodka. He was thinking hard, trying to focus, but he'd already had so much to drink that focusing was becoming a problem. Not enough of one, though, that he didn't stop turning the glass and take a large swallow.

The object of Ivan's focus sat just inside the circle of light. A vial full of one of Rex's "leetle concoctions." The liquid was a dull orange. Ivan had removed the vial from the freezer section of the small refrigerator in his office a couple of hours before. The compound had just become liquid. Next to the vial was a syringe. The instruments of Rex's trade.

Not all of Rex's concoctions had been for the horses. Ivan remembered the time Rex had given him a little bottle with an ounce or two of yellow liquid in it. "Meester Heminger, you have been very good to me, and I have special gift for you."

"What might that be, Rex?" Ivan had asked.

"Eet's my love medicine. You put a leetle of this in any woman's drink, and you can do whatever you want with her."

Ivan had taken the bottle, never intending to use it. He hadn't needed any help when it came to having his way with the ladies. But then there had come that one woman who wouldn't respond to Ivan's charms. So he had used Rex's love medicine. And it had worked. All too well.

Ivan shook his head violently to clear it. This was not the time to be remembering those kinds of histories. He had to stay focused on the present. Do what he had to do now, and the future would take care of itself.

Ivan got up from behind his desk. *I gotta stop thinking about this and just do it!* He sighed, polished off the last of the vodka in his glass, grabbed the vial and the syringe, and left his office before he lost his nerve. He flicked on a light switch at the top of the stairs, filled the syringe with Rex's concoction, and descended into the barn below.

Beauty's and Dandy's stalls were opposite each other. Ivan decided to start with Beauty. He needed to kill her, too, since Dandelion's insurance wouldn't cover the full half a million he owed Vinny. "Good girl," he said softly, stroking Beauty's mane. "Just relax. Everything's going to be okay." Ivan moved his hands over the horse's middle-neck, patting it quickly to prepare it for the syringe.

Once the horse seemed settled, he pulled the syringe from his shirt pocket, closed his eyes for courage, pushed the needle into Beauty's neck, and squeezed the plunger. He had seen Rex perform a similar injection many times, so he knew to do it quickly and get out of the way, in case the horse got angry. Beauty flinched, but stayed calm. Ivan stroked her. "That's all right, Beauty. That's all right, girl. You'll be fine soon. Just relax."

Ivan left and crossed to Dandelion's stall. He dreaded this. He knew that a small stable owner, such as himself, is fortunate to ever have a horse like Dandy. One might be in the business for a hundred years and never own such a horse. She was special, and, given an opportunity, she might have shown the world just how special she was. And she was Wanda's horse. He might complain about her spending habits, and he might wish she'd get married and settle down, but Ivan loved his daughter very much. And now he was about to kill her horse.

Dandelion gazed at Ivan as he walked into the stall. "Why are you doing this to me?" he seemed to ask. "Next year could be a breakout year for me. With a little luck and some better training, I could be running in the Derby."

"I don't know," Ivan said out loud. "I'm just doing what I have to do." *Whoa, I must have had too much to drink. Now I'm talking to horses!* Ivan took several deep breaths to steady his nerves.

His hands were shaking as he injected the solution into Dandy's neck. The horse reacted stoically, jerking only a bit as the needle penetrated his skin, and staying quiet. Ivan would never forget those huge brown eyes as he looked into them for the last time.

That took care of the insurance coverage. All he needed to do was file the claim and then turn over the proceeds to Vinny before October first. But he had to take care of the suspicion of foul play. For that, he needed Bojangles to die, too.

Ivan looked at the vial. He had no idea if the remaining liquid would be enough to kill Bo, but he wasn't about to go back to his office, take out another vial, and wait for it to defrost. He was feeling creepy enough in the silence of the barn on this very dark night. He wanted to get this over with and go to bed.

The horse neighed loudly as Ivan entered his stall. He reluctantly allowed Ivan to stroke his face. "That's a good boy," Ivan said. "Now let me give you a special treat."

Try as he might, however, Ivan could not get Bo to stand still long enough for the injection. The stall was big enough for him to keep turning so that he was facing Ivan. "Stand still!" Ivan commanded, but Bo would not obey. He began to neigh loudly. "Shut up!" Ivan yelled. He knew no one but Liz was around to possibly hear Bo, and she would be involved in her television show. But the neighing rattled him. It was almost as if Bo knew Ivan was up to no good.

After about three minutes of maneuvering, Ivan, desperate, aimed the syringe at Bojangles' neck and plunged. It stuck. Bo jerked wildly, rose up on his hind legs, and shook his neck violently. The syringe came loose and dropped to the barn floor. "Dammit!" Ivan exploded. He fell to his knees as Bojangles continued to rear and neigh loudly. Ivan could see the syringe near Bo's rear hooves. *I've gotta get that syringe!* He rose and left the stall. This seemed to calm Bojangles, and he stopped rearing up. *How am I gonna get that syringe?!*

Then Ivan had an idea. He went to Dandelion's stall and brought him out, leading him to Bo. Ivan knew they loved to race together. They were always near each other in the pasture. *Maybe Dandelion will distract Bo.* He pulled Dandy's face up near Bo's. They began to nuzzle each other. Ivan took advantage of this moment to walk quickly to the back of the stall, grab the syringe, and leave.

For a moment he watched the two horses gazing at each other. *Maybe this will be a moment of peace they will remember after...* Despite all the trauma of the evening, Ivan almost laughed. *Watch it, Heminger, you're turning into a sentimentalist.*

He led Dandelion back to his stall, then left the stable. *It's done*, he thought, heading for what he knew would be a sleepless night. But if he couldn't sleep, at least that meant he wouldn't have nightmares.

CHAPTER 14

Gregory lay in his bed and watched the sunlight slowly creep over the windowsill. Even though they had gotten back from New York after midnight the night before, he still woke up early. Habit. It was about five thirty, he estimated. He didn't tell time by his watch anymore, letting nature tell him. It was simpler that way. Simple. The Amish way. Without realizing it, their way of life was slowly penetrating his own, transforming it in many ways. His need to know the exact time, for instance. "About" five thirty would do.

As he sat up to stretch and watch the sunlight more intently, Gregory pondered how "about" his life had become. It was free of the burden of an exact schedule that had dominated his life before. Classes had begun at an exact time. Trains had departed at a certain minute. Stores had opened and closed at the same time every day. His mother even had insisted that supper begin at six sharp. Now, he realized, he hadn't had the anxious feeling that he was running late in a long time. There was no such thing as "running late" on an Amish farm. You did this chore first, then the next chore, and so on. Supper was when the dinner bell rang, calling you in from the field. You went to sleep at dark and woke up at first light.

Gregory sat in bed and relaxed his shoulders. Then he rolled them. They felt loose. He swiveled his head around a couple of times, releasing the tension. There wasn't much. He could definitely tell the difference. He'd even cut back on drinking coffee without realizing it. He used to need two cups of strong coffee to get going in the morning. Now he barely finished one. And it never even occurred to him to have any more during the day. He didn't need it. Whatever energy he received from a deep breath of God's pure air was enough. By slowing the pace of his life, Gregory had never felt more alive.

That was what had astonished him about his trip to New York. The energy of the place had been palpable. The noise, the people everywhere, the lights, the heights, the smells. New York had so much of everything. *Too much. And not enough of the things that matter to me.* Sitting in the sheep meadow had reminded him of that. It was a respite, a chance to get away from it all. *That's the difference. I don't want to get away from "it all" here. "It all" — the bright sun, the blue sky, the land lush with corn, the earthy smell of animals — "it all" is where I want to be.*

Where I want to be. Gregory thought about that a moment. He had come in search of his mother in hopes that, if he found her, it would somehow help him find himself. But as time had gone on, this goal had been replaced by a feeling of "at home." *Where I want to be.* If he were going to be there for a while, there would be plenty of time to search for his birth mother.

He got out of bed and went to the window to look out. The first thing that caught his eye was Rebecca coming out of the hen house with her basket of eggs. She was wearing her usual soft peach dress and plain black shoes. Even at this distance, Gregory could see the bright forehead, the round cheeks brushed with pink, the full lips, perfect in their symmetry. *What am I thinking? I can't see them at this distance. I'm imagining them! I'm imagining them because I know them so well. I know them so well, because I've looked at them so often. I've looked at them so often because I —*

A sudden rush of feeling caused Gregory to gasp. "Rebecca!" he cried out, impulsively. She stopped and turned toward him. She smiled. That he didn't imagine. It brought a smile to his own lips. "Wait!" He wrestled into his jeans, threw on a shirt, and walked quickly across the yard to her.

"Good morning, Gregory," she said brightly as he approached.

"Good morning, Rebecca," he responded, turning to tuck in his shirt. When he turned back, a moment of silence settled between them, gentle and warm as the sun.

"Did you want me?" she asked.

Yes, he had wanted her, but why? Now that he was standing there, he realized he had had no other reason than just to be with her. This thought staggered him slightly, so he could only stutter, "I...I was just wondering...how many eggs did you get this morning?"

She looked at him curiously for a moment, but answered as if it were the most natural thing in the world for Gregory to rush up to her to find out how many eggs she'd gathered. "I don't know. I didn't count them. Let's see..." She began touching the many eggs piled in her basket. "One, two, three, four, five, six, seven..."

Gregory watched her hand move over the eggs, fingers not long, thin, and elegant, but short and firm. A farm girl's hands. *Hands I'd like to hold.*

"...Twenty-one," Rebecca finished. "But I may have missed some."

"That's all right," Gregory said, wondering how he'd gotten into a conversation about eggs and wishing to end it. "Looks like it's going to be a beautiful day."

"Yes, I think so." She looked out over the land and took a deep breath. "Don't you just love the early morning air?"

"I really do." He took his own deep breath and closed his eyes. He could sense her near him. The feeling made him giddy, so he quickly opened them again. But still he could not think of anything to say. He had covered eggs and the weather. Now what? "Did you sleep all right?"

"Yes. I was tired!"

"Me, too."

"New York!" they both exclaimed, simultaneously, then laughed.

Gregory asked, seriously, "Did you have a good time, Rebecca?"

"I did, all in all. But I'm glad to be home."

"Me, too," Gregory said. *Home.*

"Off to feed Bo?" she asked. She had missed Bo since Gregory had moved him to Cedar Ridge Farm. And no matter how many times Gregory had brought Bo by in hopes of finding Rebecca out in a field, so she could rub Bo's neck and coo soft words into his ear, he still felt bad that he had taken him away from her.

"Yes, and Dandelion and Beauty. I was too tired to look in on them last night."

"How does Wanda like the saddle Dat made her?" Rebecca asked, then immediately regretted it. Why did she feel compelled to bring up Wanda? Was she jealous of all the time Wanda got to spend with Bo? Or was it the time Wanda spent with someone else that provoked Rebecca?

"She loves it," Gregory said enthusiastically. "Your father is a real craftsman." As soon as he'd mentioned Elam, he was sorry. He remembered the angry scene at the Zooks' supper table a few days ago.

It was a topic Rebecca didn't want to discuss either. "Better get these eggs inside. People'll be wanting their breakfast. Have a blessed day, Gregory."

"You, too, Rebecca." Gregory watched her stride purposefully across the yard toward the house, enjoying the sight of her swaying hips and strong back. Her dark hair peaked out a little from under her covering. Not for the first time Gregory thought how he'd love to see all of Rebecca's hair, spilling down silky-soft around her shoulders. He had only seen it tucked up under her covering. *Someday,* he hoped.

By the time Gregory had finished cooking his own breakfast and driven his pickup down the lane and out onto the highway toward Cedar Ridge Farm, it was, he estimated, almost six thirty. But he felt no need to hurry. The horses might be a little hungry, but not that much. It was too fine a morning to hurry. *That's not the Amish way, remember?* Instead, Gregory idled along, enjoying the view.

Farms stretched to the horizon on each side of the road. Gregory loved the symmetry of an Amish farm. The straight lanes, rarely curving, bisecting the fields. The three or four houses, always painted white, standing calm and firm. The clotheslines hung with black pants and dresses of purple, blue, peach, and pink. The smell of freshly cut hay, the golden fields of wheat. The corn marching row after row after row, thousands of stalks of it, so green and tall. Yes, Amish country was ripe with life.

It was with happy thoughts like these that Gregory parked his truck near the barn and got out. Had he been less focused on how fine he felt that morning, he might have noticed the peculiar silence emanating from the barn. No whinnying, no sound of tails swatting at flies, no stomping of hooves. Just stillness.

When he entered the barn, he was shocked by the scene before him. Lying on his side in his stall was Dandelion. His eyes were closed, and his tongue was hanging out. Gregory immediately knelt by his side. "Dandy, what's wrong?!" He placed his hand on the horse's side, feeling the rib bones beneath. What he didn't feel was the rise and fall of the horse's breathing. "Dandelion!" Gregory frantically pried open one of Dandy's eyelids. It revealed an eyeball staring vacantly. Gregory released the eyelid and gasped. Dandelion was dead.

For a moment, he didn't know what to do. He knelt there, trying to make sense of it all. Just yesterday morning Dandelion had been galloping around the track at full speed. And now? He looked down at the horse, then slowly rose and looked across the aisle. Where was Beauty? Her head should have been sticking over the stall door. He ran to her stall. There she was, lying on her side, just like Dandelion. *What's going on?*

With a panic that almost knocked him over, Gregory bolted from Beauty's stall. *Bo!* He hadn't heard Bo's distinctive whinny, which welcomed Gregory each morning. *Bo! Bo! Please!*

Gregory tore into the last stall. Bojangles lay stretched out on the hay. Gregory knelt beside him, touching his neck. "Bo! Bojangles!" At least his tongue wasn't hanging out. When he raised one of Bo's eyelids, the eye was cloudy, the gaze dull, but there was a gaze. Placing his hands on Bo's side, Gregory tried to still his own heart so he could sense the rise and fall of Bo's breath. It was there! Rising with difficulty, but rising all the same. Gregory hugged his horse. "Bo, don't die! You can't die!"

He felt his pockets desperately. *Where is my phone? The truck!* He sprinted outside, yanked open his truck door, grabbed his cell phone. *I've got to call a vet!* But Gregory didn't know any vets, and he couldn't waste time trying to find one. He punched 911 into his phone. A dispatcher answered. "911. What's your emergency?"

"I found some dead — " Gregory stopped himself. He couldn't report dead horses to 911; they'd tell him to call a vet. "Dead bodies," Gregory shouted.

"Where?" the dispatcher asked.

"Cedar Ridge Farm, off Horseshoe Pike, between — "

"I know where it is," said the dispatcher. "Ivan Heminger's place. Is one of them Ivan?"

"No," Gregory responded. "Send the police and an ambulance. Hurry!"

"What's your name?"

"Gregory Pinckney."

"How do you spell it?"

Gregory took a deep breath to calm himself. He needed to stay calm for Bo. "P-I-N-C-K-N-E-Y," he spelled.

"Ten minutes, police and an EMS will be there," the dispatcher said and hung up.

Ten minutes! Gregory rushed back inside the barn to Bo. He took off his shirt, dipped it into Bo's watering trough, and put it on Bo's forehead. He couldn't think of anything else to do, so he placed his hand on Bo's side, closed his eyes, and tried to breathe with his horse. *If I keep breathing, maybe he will.*

Somehow the ten minutes passed, and Gregory heard a police car screech to a stop. The barn door opened, and two Honey Brook Township policemen approached the stall. "Don't move! Keep your hands where I can see them," ordered the first cop, a slightly built, short man with an officious manner about him. "Are there any other people here?"

"Just me," Gregory said, rising with his hands in the air.

"Is that your truck outside?"

"Yes."

"We have a report of dead bodies and request for an ambulance."

"Here's one of the bodies," Gregory said, stepping aside and showing them Bojangles.

"Is this some kind of joke?" the first officer asked.

"I'm sorry, officer, but I don't know any vets in the area, and my horse is almost dead."

"This is not a job for the police," the officer responded.

"Please, you can't let my horse die!"

"I said it's not a job for the police."

"Why not?" The second officer finally spoke. He was big, about six feet two inches tall and close to three hundred pounds.

"Oh, c'mon, Bob," the first officer began.

"Look, Tim, we got nothing else happening, and our phones are on." He turned to Gregory. "We get a call, we gotta respond, and then you're on your own."

"Okay."

The EMS crew rushed through the door. "Over here, fellas," Bob called. He turned to Tim. "I want you to take a quick look around. If you don't find anything, I want you to drive to Doc Jenkins's office in Honey Brook. Bring him here. Use your siren if you need to."

"Are you sure we aren't going to get into trouble?" Tim asked.

"No," Bob answered. "But I'm sure this is what we need to do."

The first officer sighed and left to look around. The two EMS "fellas" were women. A tall one in a crisp, dark-blue work shirt, young, around twenty-five. And a shorter woman, whose skin was beginning to wrinkle but whose firm biceps revealed that she still kept herself in excellent shape, knelt beside Bo and made a quick assessment. "He needs CPR," she said.

The young woman asked, "Will it work for animals?"

"Don't see why not," the older one responded. She started to work on Bo's chest but quickly realized she wasn't strong enough. "Hey, Bob, could use a little help here." Bob moved beside Bo and used his massive body to compress Bo's chest methodically. Gregory watched in silence, helpless. The scene seemed surreal — a policeman and an EMS woman doing CPR on his horse.

Nothing happened for about ninety seconds. Gregory began to perspire, even though it was a cool morning, the sun barely up. He heard the cop car speed off, heading for Doc Jenkins. *Hurry!*

"If nothing happens soon, you'll have to try mouth-to-mouth," the second EMS woman said.

"No problem," Bob replied. Since neither of them laughed, Gregory couldn't tell if they were joking or not. He only knew he would have given Bo mouth-to-mouth if it had been called for. He would have done anything.

"There!" the shorter EMS woman said, pointing at Bo's chest. It was moving more forcefully, regularly.

"How about his heart, Marie?" the young EMS woman asked.

"Go get the stethoscope, Sally, and we'll see," Marie instructed.

Sally started for the door, but her exit was blocked by the sudden appearance of Ivan. "What's going on here?" he demanded. "Why's that ambulance outside?"

"The horses, Ivan!" Gregory said, urgently. "Something happened. We're trying to save Bo's life. Dandelion and Beauty are dead."

"Dead?" shouted Ivan. "How can they be dead?" He ran to Dandelion's stall and peered in at the still body of Wanda's horse. Gregory stayed with Bo, but Bob followed Ivan.

"Are you Ivan Heminger?" he inquired.

"Yes. Why are you here?"

"Mr. Pinckney called the police."

"Why the police?" A flicker of concern crossed Ivan's face. *Could something have gone wrong already?*

"He didn't know any veterinarians to call, so he called 911," Bob said.

Ivan moved beside Dandelion's body and placed his hand on his neck, checking for a pulse. "He's cold."

"Been dead a while. You got any ideas on what happened here, Mr. Heminger?"

"No, officer. Gregory went to New York yesterday, so I fed the horses, put them to bed, went to bed myself. Just a usual night."

"So you were the last one to see the horses alive?" asked Bob.

"Yes. So what?" Ivan asked, a bit defensively.

"Just asking."

"Excuse me," Ivan said, pushing past Bob and returning to Bo's stall. "Gregory, what happened?"

"I don't know, Ivan. I came in to feed the horses, found Dandy and Beauty dead and Bo almost dead."

"Why didn't you come get me?" Ivan asked, a touch of temper in his voice.

"I was going to, but I had to stay with Bo until somebody arrived." They heard a car stopping outside, followed by another. Soon a short, wiry man with a graying mustache, about the same age as Ivan, walked briskly through the door followed by the police officer. He was carrying a doctor's bag. "Are you the vet?" Gregory asked anxiously.

"Doc Jenkins," the man replied.

"What are you doing here?" asked Ivan, angrily. He turned to Bob. "Is this the vet you called?"

"Closest one I could think of. Is there a problem?" Bob waited a moment, but Ivan didn't answer.

"Ivan might just be suffering a case of déjà vu," Doc Jenkins offered. Ivan stared at him, but didn't reply. "Now, where's the horse that's still alive?"

"Here." Gregory showed him where Bojangles lay. The EMS women greeted him. "Hello, Doc."

"Hello, Sally. Marie." The women moved out of his way, and Doc Jenkins knelt beside Bo.

"We got him breathing pretty good," Sally said. "We were about to check his heart, maybe use the defibrillator."

Doc Jenkins felt for Bo's pulse. He examined each hoof, pried open Bo's mouth, and peered inside, using a small flashlight he retrieved from his bag. He checked his ears, rolled up his eyelids, and flashed the light onto Bo's pupils. Bo didn't stir, but he continued to breathe, if barely. "What is it, Doc?" asked Gregory.

"Don't know yet," he replied. "Don't think the defibrillator's a good idea though. He's a strong horse. I'm gonna give him some nutrients and draw some blood. The blood'll tell us what we need to know. Might give him a little something for pain, in case he has any." Doc Jenkins opened his bag, took out several vials, and began filling a syringe with the contents of one of them.

"Might as well get blood from the dead horses while you're at it, Doc," Bob said.

"That's all right," Ivan said, quickly. "I'll get my own vet to do that."

"I'll just draw a little while I'm here, Ivan. I can compare them with this one's blood, see if maybe they both suffered from the same thing."

"What kind of thing?" asked Gregory.

"Probably some kind of virus, wouldn't you think?" Ivan asked quickly.

"Could be," Doc Jenkins replied. "Or something might have gotten into their food supply. Or maybe got into their blood some other way."

"Your horses insured, Mr. Heminger?" inquired Bob.

"Of course. They're racehorses. Dandelion and my daughter — Wanda! I'd forgotten all about her. How am I going to tell her horse has been killed?"

No one said anything for a moment, then Bob asked calmly, "What makes you think he was killed, Mr. Heminger?"

"Killed?" asked Ivan.

"That's what you just said," replied Bob.

"No, I don't think he was killed. I think it was some kind of virus, like I said. If I said 'killed,' it was just because that's the way it's going to feel to my daughter. Why would anyone want to kill Dandelion?"

"Collect the insurance?" Bob said innocently.

"All right, that's enough!" Ivan exploded. "We don't need you anymore, officers! You either," he said to the EMS women. "I've had a terrible thing happen here, and I don't need your insinuations about me being involved." He turned to Doc Jenkins. "Draw your blood and then leave us alone!" He turned back to the policemen. "There's the door!" he barked, pointing angrily.

The policemen and the EMS women moved toward the exit. "Fine," Mr. Heminger," Bob said. "We'll come back later and get your statement. Yours, too," he said to Gregory. He turned to Doc Jenkins. "Make sure you get the dead animals' blood samples, Doc."

"Get out!" Ivan shouted. The policemen and the EMS women left the barn. Doc Jenkins, having finished with Bojangles, moved down to Dandelion, took out another syringe, and drew blood. He went about his work silently, under the watchful glare of Ivan. Gregory stood by, helpless, not knowing what to do.

As Doc Jenkins finished, he said to Ivan, "Want me to let you know what I find?"

"My vet'll tell me."

Doc Jenkins eyed Ivan evenly for a moment, gave a small shrug, then turned to Gregory. "Sorry about your horse, son. I'll send a tech over with some fluids and look in on him later this afternoon.

"What's the prognosis?" Gregory asked, as calmly as he could.

"Too early to tell. But we'll do the best we can. Take my number." Gregory pulled out his cell phone. "610-273-9983."

Gregory punched it in and pocketed the phone. "Thank you so much, Doctor Jenkins," he said.

"Tell Wanda I'm sure sorry about her horse, Ivan," Doc Jenkins said. Ivan nodded, and Doc Jenkins left the barn. In a minute, they heard his car drive off.

Gregory returned to Bo. Ivan stood in the middle of the barn for a moment. He couldn't look at Dandelion. "Guess I'd better try to find Wanda," he said at last, almost to himself. When Gregory didn't respond, Ivan walked slowly out of the barn.

Alone, Gregory tried to stay calm, but he couldn't sit still. He rose and began pacing the aisle between the stalls, keeping an eye on Bojangles as he did. He tried to make sense of all that had happened. *They were fine when I left for New York. How could a horse — two horses — just die overnight? If there was something in their food that poisoned them, what was it? And who put it there? And a virus? One that kills so instantly? It just doesn't add up.* Gregory stopped and looked down at Bo in his stall. *If Ivan had anything to do with this, if he killed them for the insurance or something, then why would he also try to kill Bo? And could he really kill his daughter's racehorse? That's crazy!*

Thoughts like these occupied Gregory for twenty minutes or so, and then he heard a car pull up outside. *Probably Wanda,* he thought. *I wish Ivan were here. I don't want to have to show her Dandelion by myself.* Gregory braced himself for the worst. But instead of Wanda, Rebecca came running through the barn door.

"Rebecca!" Gregory exclaimed.

"Oh, Gregory. I'm so sorry! Where's Bo?" She ran to where Gregory stood and spotted Bo in his stall. "Bojangles!" she cried, and bent near his head. "Dear sweet Bo," she murmured. "Don't worry, I'm here now." She stroked Bojangles gently with her soft hands.

"Rebecca, how did you know?" Gregory asked, kneeling beside her.

"I was in the post office when Sally Thornton came in, telling everyone what had happened. I asked her for a ride, and she brought me right out here."

"I'll tell Sally to leave. I can take you home."

When he returned from thanking Sally and sending her on her way, Gregory found that Rebecca had placed Bo's head in her lap and was gently rubbing him behind his ears, cooing words of comfort. "Good ol' Bo. You're so strong. I'm sorry something hurt you, but you'll get better, won't you? For me? And for Gregory? You're such a good horse. Good ol' Bo."

A wave of gratitude swept over Gregory. He squatted beside Rebecca and, for a moment, they both rubbed Bo silently. Gregory felt himself begin to relax for the first time in…He wondered how long it had been since he'd first discovered the horses. He had no idea. And he didn't care. Rebecca was here. With Bo. The two most important people in his life. *People?* Gregory almost smiled. Yes, Bo felt like a person to him. And somehow Gregory knew that Rebecca wouldn't let him die.

Rebecca also felt herself relax. She had been terrified when Sally had first told her about Bojangles, but now that she was there, the terror had lessened, replaced by what might almost be confidence. She was confident in Gregory. She was confident in Bo. She was confident in herself. They almost felt like a family, the three of them, huddled together in the stall. *We belong together*, Rebecca thought.

Preoccupied with thoughts like these, neither Gregory nor Rebecca heard the car stop outside. The barn door opened, and Wanda walked in. "Hi, Gregory. I saw your car. You still feeding the horses? You wouldn't believe the party I went to last — " Wanda stopped, looking into Dandelion's stall. "What's wrong with Dandelion?" She quickly knelt beside her horse. "Gregory, what's wrong with Dandy?" She touched his side. It was cold. Her scream split the air. "Aiiiiiiiii! Dandelion! Dandy!"

Gregory raced to her side. "I'm so sorry, Wanda."

"He's dead, Gregory! He's dead!" She flung herself into his arms, sobbing.

"I know, I know." Gregory held her.

"He can't be! No! What happened?"

Gregory explained as best he could, holding Wanda as she sobbed into his chest. Looking up, he saw Rebecca standing outside the stall. A kind of hurt skirted the corners of her eyes. *Could she be jealous?* "I'm so sorry, Wanda," Rebecca whispered, then returned to Bo's stall.

Ivan appeared and silently led his daughter to the house, placing his arm gently around her shoulders. Gregory felt exhausted. "I'll take you home now," he said to Rebecca.

"No, you should stay with Bo. I'll walk." She noticed the fear in Gregory's eyes. "I'll get some covers so you can spend the night. Dat can bring me in the buggy. I won't be gone long."

"Thank you," Gregory said.

Rebecca took his hands in her own. "Bo will be all right, Gregory. I know it." She smiled and left the barn.

Questions flooded Gregory's brain, his mind hopping from one topic to another. *Why did Rebecca get distant when Wanda arrived? Is Ivan involved? How? Why would he be? What did Doc Jenkins mean by that comment to Ivan about déjà vu? How could this have happened? Two dead horses! Is Bo going to be all right?*

Gregory settled against the wall in Bo's stall. He was so grateful, knowing Rebecca would be back soon. *I don't think I can get through this without her.* He furrowed his brow for a perplexed moment. *Is that true? Do*

I need Rebecca that much? He didn't want to think about the answer. It was too…what? Scary? Exciting? Confusing? Disturbing?

He looked at his horse, lying on his side, barely breathing. *I don't know about me, but Bo needs her. And that's enough for now.*

CHAPTER 15

Omar King preached in German as he stood between the living and sewing rooms in the Kings' home. Benches had been set up in both rooms, but the genders were segregated: women in the sewing room, men in the living room, and Omar standing so he could pivot to speak to both sides. In the Amish tradition, he mainly preached to the men, letting the women receive his message secondhand.

We're never the main focus, thought Rebecca from her place on the bench next to Madie. *Why would I have such a thought; it never used to bother me?* She decided that "bother" was too strong a word, she was just "noticing," that's all. She tried to focus on what Omar was saying. Something about the sin of lust. But since her return from New York, she was having a hard time focusing on anything.

Had it only been eight days? So much had happened. Gregory had discovered the horses a week ago Saturday, and Rebecca had been working nonstop ever since. In addition to her chores and her work at the quilt shop, she had spent the time nursing Bo, going to Cedar Ridge Farm every time she had an hour or more to spare. She'd helped Gregory set up a pallet and some old feather pillows for sleeping in Bo's stall. Gregory was reluctant to leave Bo's side, but sometimes she had been able to persuade him to go outside and get some rest while she tended to Bo.

Often, when she'd come to tell him she had to leave, she'd found Gregory asleep. She liked to watch him sleeping, his long brown hair falling over his tanned face, the curve of his cheek, his thin lips relaxed, the steady rise and fall of his breathing. He looked so peaceful, she hated to wake him to the anxieties that awaited him.

And then there was New York. What was she to make of that incredible experience? New York had overwhelmed her. So many people, so many cars, so many buildings, lights, sounds, smells — she felt almost numb from the experience. Numb, but curiously alive as well. So many feelings! She'd never been stimulated like that before. How placid her life was compared to that of a New Yorker. Did she like her life so calm? Did she crave more stimulation? Would she like to be able to visit art galleries and museums? Or would she rather be sitting on a bench in a farmhouse with other Amish, all dressed in their Sunday best: the adult women in black capes, black aprons, and plain-colored dresses, the little girls in white capes with white aprons covering their dresses, and the men in black clothing and black hats. *But is my world too black and white?* she wondered.

Bo was getting better, and Rebecca didn't need to do much nursing. The tech had shown her how to change the IV fluid. She placed wet towels on Bo's body from time to time. That was it. Doc Jenkins had decided that the best course of action was supportive care: let Bo's body work to cure itself. He'd even let Gregory bring Bo back to the Zook farm. But Gregory had insisted that Rebecca's mere presence was helping Bo to mend. "He feels your love" was the way he had put it. So she had continued to care for Bo whenever possible.

Or was she coming to be with Gregory? And why had she been so disappointed when she found him with Wanda? Upset, almost. She didn't want these feelings — she wanted to feel nothing but sympathy for Wanda — but she was powerless to stop them. It was all so confusing.

Rebecca decided to distract herself by paying attention to what the preacher was saying. The words came softly to her in the inner room. Something about the temptation of the flesh. "Even if you lust in your heart, you have sinned," Omar preached. "I know we've all had that feeling, that desire. I've had it m-m-myself." Rebecca smiled, thinking how hard it was to imagine Omar, tall, thin, bewhiskered Omar King, who walked with a cane and had a tendency to stutter, lusting after anything. But she knew he was right. Every adult male in that room had no doubt had that feeling. And so had every adult female.

She thought again of New York. "Becca, turn your eyes, don't look!" Hanna had cautioned her when they'd seen a small statuette of a nude male in a store window on Fifth Avenue. Rebecca had seen Gregory suppress a laugh. Did he think all Amish were prudes? Probably. *Why do I care?*

But she did care. She didn't want Gregory to think she was a prude. She was a woman. She had feelings. Those kinds of feelings. Stirrings. Was she to be ashamed of them? Was she to turn her eyes? Well, she hadn't. She'd looked at the statuette. And now she was seeing it again, sitting there in church, imagining it clear as day. The muscled arms, the taut belly, the expansive chest — *What am I thinking? And in church!*

Rebecca composed herself. At the end of the bench, Mabel and Hanna were sitting with their hands in their laps, listening intently. Seated next to her, her good friend Madie suppressed a yawn. The services were long. Three hours. But the Amish were used to it. From an early age, Rebecca had been taken to church and made to sit still hour after hour, just like all children. After getting accustomed to it, she hadn't minded. She enjoyed being still. Except today. Today she was restless, her mind wandering.

An agent! Was Mr. Goldfarb really going to be her agent? She hadn't known what that was, but Gregory had explained it to her on the drive home. Mr. Goldfarb would "represent" her. He would negotiate the price for her artwork. Her artwork? Rebecca had only six wall hangings. She'd have to get busy, make lots more. But when? Harvest time, the busiest time of the year, was fast approaching — and with it, the decision about marrying Jacob. What if she didn't have time? Worse, what if she didn't have any new ideas? She wasn't sure she wanted an agent. But apparently she had one.

And that nice Mr. Snow. He had bought her wall hanging for $1,000, including the gold frame. Mr. Goldfarb had sent her an additional $250, with a note that he split proceeds fifty-fifty with his artists. *That made five hundred dollars!* And Mr. Snow had asked her to autograph her work, as if she were some kind of celebrity. *Stop it! Omar should be preaching on the sin of pride, not lust.* But despite her best efforts, Rebecca did feel proud of what she'd accomplished. She even felt proud now, sitting in church.

Oh, it's so hard! Why am I proud, despite myself? Why am I happy about my quilt hanging? Rebecca pondered this question a moment. *It's because my efforts have been recognized and rewarded.* Yes, that was it. In the Amish way of life, her talents weren't rewarded, they were simply expected to be put to good use. Amish were very sparing in their praise of anyone's talents. Rebecca didn't really want praise, exactly. She was quite happy simply making her quilts. But to know someone else liked them. Well, what was wrong with that?

"Is that your boarder in church today?" Madie whispered. Rebecca nodded. Gregory had indeed joined them in church. Her mother, Mabel, had been forced to invite him out of politeness. She'd been asking Rebecca all summer why Gregory didn't go to church on Sundays. "I'm going to talk to that boy about why he's not going to church," she had threatened. Rebecca had advised her against it. It was Gregory's relationship with God, after all. But her mother had brought the subject up on their ride to New York.

"Are you going to church this Sunday, Gregory?" she'd asked him right out. "There are lots of churches around: Baptist, Methodist, Mennonite, Catholic — you're not Catholic, are you?" she suddenly had asked, concerned.

"No, ma'am," Gregory had answered.

"Good," Mabel had replied. "I mean, I know some nice Catholics, but you can't pay the church to take your sins away. And they drink!" She'd let other opinions remain unspoken, not wanting to venture further into that territory.

Then Gregory had surprised her. "Why don't I come to your church, Mabel? That is, if you allow English to come."

Mabel had been taken aback. "Well, I…" Hanna had finished: "We allow 'em! Come to church with us, Gregory!" Mabel had opened her mouth to speak, but, realizing she was trapped, she'd closed it again.

Gregory hadn't come that first Sunday, because of Bo. But since he'd moved Bo back to the Zook farm, he felt comfortable leaving him for a while.

And now there he was in the next room.

His presence didn't helped Rebecca's attempt to focus on God. "He's handsome," Madie whispered again. Rebecca thought, *I know he is, Madie. I'm not blind!* But she contented herself with another nod, and a small smile.

"You saw who else came to church today, didn't you?" Madie seemed determined to have a conversation right there on the bench in the middle of the sermon. Again Rebecca nodded. Yes, she had seen.

Johnny Schmucker. Of all people. His baseball team must have had a game nearby, and he'd come home to see his folks. And to see Rebecca? She didn't know. He had smiled at her on their way into the house for church, that same alluring smile that had always stirred her. Those blue eyes, white teeth, square jaw. He was a handsome man, too.

And Jacob. Maybe not handsome, but all-right looking. And solid, dependable, nice. Jacob was in the other room, too. Three men, all interested in Rebecca. *What am I thinking?! Gregory's not interested in me, at least not that way. And Johnny? Who knows? He's been gone so long, he's surely found a new girlfriend by now. Not that I care.* But Rebecca did care. Not about what Johnny felt. Or Jacob. But Gregory.

Omar announced, "We shall c-c-close with 'Gott Ist Liebe.'" Finally! No one needed a hymnal for that one, it was known by everyone and Mabel's favorite. Rebecca sang happily with her pretty, high soprano voice. She could hear Hanna's loud alto from the end of the bench, slightly off-key. And her mother's weak treble, but sung with gusto. After this, there'd be food and socializing. Rebecca would be busy serving, so she wouldn't get a chance to visit much. That suited her just fine. What if she were visiting with Jacob and Johnny came up? Then Gregory? She'd have to introduce Gregory to Johnny. What would they all talk about? Baseball? No, best to keep busy serving food.

After the hymn and the final benediction, the men rearranged the benches for eating as the women prepared to serve the food. It was hot and humid, a typical mid-August day. The older people ate first, men and women still segregated. The children and the other men went outside.

While Rebecca was putting out the schnitz pie, she noticed through the window that her brother Henry was talking to Gregory, Johnny, and Jacob. *He's done that on purpose, I bet. Just like Henry! Probably drawing the conversation toward me in some way, too!* Rebecca returned to the kitchen for more food. *There's that pride again. What makes me think they'd be talking about me?*

When all the men had been summoned, served, and had finished the simple meal, the women sat down to eat. Giving up his seat on the bench to Rebecca, Henry told her, "Really enjoyed your pie, Becca."

"Thank you, Henry."

"I told your boyfriends you'd made it and to be sure to try some." He smiled a mischievous smile.

"What boyfriends?" Rebecca asked, as innocently as she could.

"The three musketeers over there." Henry gestured toward the table where Gregory, Johnny, and Jacob sat, talking.

"Very funny, Henry," Rebecca said, and started off.

"I told 'em I'd be glad to referee a wrestling match for you, winner take all!"

"You did not!" she said. Henry burst into laughter. Her hunger suddenly gone, Rebecca grabbed her dinner plate, took it back to the kitchen, and made her way outside.

She noticed her father standing under a pine tree, talking to Samuel Glick, another Amish farmer. Mr. Glick was leaning in, apparently speaking softly. Elam suddenly straightened, grasped Mr. Glick's arm at the elbow, and said something urgently. Mr. Glick nodded solemnly, and Elam released his arm. Elam's shoulders sagged noticeably, and he hung his head for a moment. Mr. Glick touched Elam's shoulder sympathetically, whispered a few words, and then wandered off. Elam just stood there, head down. She went to him. "Dat, are you all right?" she asked anxiously.

Her father seemed to suddenly come back to the world. "Oh, Rebecca," he said, his voice dry.

"I said, are you all right?"

Elam made an effort to regain control of himself. "Yes…yes," he said. "Why wouldn't I be?"

"I don't know. I was watching you talking to Mr. Glick, and it looked like he said something that upset you." Rebecca looked at her father with concern.

He returned her gaze with fierce eyes. "Let's go home." Elam moved off to find their horse and hitch him to the buggy. Rebecca watched him go. He seemed in a great hurry — all the more unusual on a Sunday, the Amish day of rest. She watched him yank Brownie's bridle, leading him harshly to the buggy. *Something is wrong with Dat.*

Rebecca went to find Henry and say her thanks to Omar and Lydie King. She found them talking to Gregory. "Hello, Rebecca," Omar said. "We were just t-t-talking to Gregory about coming back to church again. Wouldn't that be n-nice?"

"Yes," Rebecca replied.

"And Lydie's most interested in his past," Omar continued.

"Omar!" Lydie said. Rebecca noticed that Lydie blushed. Lydie never blushed. She was the calmest person Rebecca knew, always in control of her feelings.

Omar chuckled. "It's quite an interesting p-p-past. Did you grow up in South Carolina?" he asked, turning to Gregory.

"Yes, sir," Gregory responded. "Lived there all my life. I really like it."

"Then what brought you up here?" Lydie asked.

"To tell you the truth, I'm looking for my mother," Gregory said. Lydie's eyes widened. Omar, too, was a bit surprised by Gregory's response. "How do you m-mean?"

"I'm adopted," Gregory told them. "But I got a clue from a social worker that my mother was from Lancaster County."

"You did?" Lydie blurted out, then asked, more calmly, "How would she know that?"

"She remembered her name. Mae. Mae Yoder."

"Lots of Yoders up here," Omar observed.

"That's what I'm finding out," Gregory said.

"Did she tell you anything else about her?" Lydie asked intently.

"That's all."

"And your adoptive mother, did she take good care of you?" Lydie continued.

"Yes, ma'am."

"So you're not looking for your mother because you had an unhappy childhood?" Lydie asked.

"Not at all," Gregory responded.

"Excuse us, Lydie and Omar, but I think Dat is in a hurry to get home," Rebecca interrupted.

"I'll go find Henry," Gregory said. "Nice to meet you," he said to the Kings, and walked away.

"Don't be a stranger," Omar called after him.

"How are you today, Lydie?" Rebecca asked. "I haven't had much chance to speak to you."

"I'm fine," Lydie said softly.

"I've got to tell you about our trip to New York sometime. Maybe at the next quilting bee."

"Yes," said Lydie, distractedly. "Excuse me, I need to put away the food."

"Let me help you."

"No, you go home with your Dat," Lydie replied, and scurried away.

What's wrong with everyone today? Rebecca thought.

Omar seemed to have read her mind. "Lydie hasn't been herself lately," he told Rebecca.

"Is she sick?"

"No, just…I don't know, distracted is more like it."

"Please let me know if there's anything I can do."

Johnny wandered over to where Omar and Rebecca were standing. "Hello, Omar," he said, his smile as big as ever.

"Hello, Johnny. G-g-glad to see you in church," Omar answered.

"I had a game nearby, and the next game's not until tonight, so I thought I'd come home. Hello, Becky," he said, turning his dazzling smile on her.

"Hi, Johnny." She couldn't think of anything else to say except, maybe, what are you doing here? But Johnny had already answered that.

"Excuse m-m-me," Omar sputtered, stepping away. "I have to say good-b-b-bye to the Fishers. Have a nice day," he said, and walked off to say his farewells.

Johnny wasted no time in pleasantries. "Becky, would you mind if I gave you a ride home?"

Rebecca was staggered for a moment. She hadn't seen Johnny since he'd left for spring training over a year ago, why would he want to take her home? "I don't know, Johnny, Dat's already hitched up the buggy."

"We'll probably beat him home, if that's what you're worrying about."

"I'm not worried about anything," Rebecca responded, unconvincingly. Gregory and Henry came up. "Oh, Gregory, hi. This is my friend, Johnny Schmucker."

"We've met," Gregory said.

"Are you ready to go, Henry?" Rebecca asked her brother. "Dat seems in a hurry to get home."

"I don't mind waiting if you three have things to talk about," he said, a twinkle in his eye. "You got anything to talk about?" he asked Gregory.

"No," was his simple reply, though he looked a bit confused.

"How 'bout you, Johnny?"

"As a matter of fact, Henry, I do. I just finished asking Rebecca if I could drive her home so I could talk to her."

Rebecca saw Gregory suddenly look up at this news.

"What'd she say?" Henry asked genially, as if Rebecca weren't even there to answer for herself. He looked at his sister, clearly enjoying this awkward moment she found herself in.

"I was just waiting for an answer," Johnny said, and turned to face Rebecca. As did Gregory. There was a long pause while they all awaited Rebecca's answer.

Suddenly Rebecca realized that the last thing she wanted was to go home with her family. Or Gregory. Best to get away from all this emotional turmoil for a while. If Johnny was going to offer to drive her home, she was going to let him. But she didn't want to hurt Gregory's feelings in any way, so she answered as nonchalantly as she could, "Johnny, if you want to drive me home, that'd be fine." She quickly looked at Gregory after she'd said it and saw a touch of something in his eyes. *Jealousy?*

"Then let's go!" Johnny said, never one to waste a minute. He gestured toward his car, and Rebecca and he walked away side by side.

"Who's he?" Gregory asked Henry.

"An old friend of Rebecca's. Plays ball."

"Any good?" Gregory wanted to know.

"Best from around here for a while." He looked over at Elam standing impatiently next to the buggy. "We'd better go." They walked over to Elam and got inside the buggy. Elam snapped the reins hard, and they headed for home.

Johnny led the way to a bright-red Mustang with black racing stripes. "How do you like it?" he asked Rebecca, s he pushed a button to put down the convertible top.

"It's so fancy!" gasped Rebecca, amazed at Johnny's newfound wealth.

"They pay me real good in the league. Hop in." He held the door open for her.

Rebecca seated herself. Johnny closed the door, went around to the other side, then hopped over the closed door rather than open it. He started the engine, which roared to life then settled into a smooth purr as Johnny eased the Mustang into the road.

"So, how have you been, Becky?" Johnny was the one person Rebecca allowed to call her "Becky." She didn't like the nickname, but somehow when he said it, she didn't mind.

"Good. Busy. Harvest time is coming soon, plus I'm busy in the shop, and I have…other work to do." Rebecca hesitated. She hadn't seen Johnny since he'd gone to spring training last over a year ago. There was a lot to fill him in on.

"What work?"

"Well, I'm making some quilt wall hangings. I sold one of mine, and there's a customer who wants me to make some more." Rebecca didn't see much point in telling Johnny the whole story of the trip to New York, especially since she still hadn't really absorbed it all herself.

"How much did you get for it?"

Rebecca remembered that Johnny was often focused on money in a way that bothered her. "Actually, I got quite a lot for it. $500!"

"Not bad."

"Hey, aren't you turning here?" she suddenly asked Johnny, as they passed the road to her house.

"Let's go the long way, okay? Do you have to get home right away?"

"It's Sunday, so I guess I have a little more time."

"Good." Johnny turned down a less-traveled road and gunned it. The car sped along, cornfields flashing past in a blur. Rebecca decided to let go and enjoy the ride. She put her head back and allowed the wind to blow on her face and hair. The afternoon sun warmed her, and she closed her eyes.

But instead of relaxing, she found her head crowded with thoughts. *What am I doing, racing along with Johnny? How'd he get back in my life? Is he back in my life? Do I want him back in my life?* She peeked a look at Johnny behind the wheel. A very handsome profile, she had to admit. Square jaw, tousled blond hair blowing in the wind, head bobbing to some interior song. Johnny was fun. And, of course, he was more than fun. *Remember those kisses?* Rebecca curled her toes. Yes, Johnny had his pluses.

She felt the car slow and opened her eyes, as Johnny edged the Mustang off the road under the shade of a large oak. He parked the car, turned off the engine, and looked at Rebecca.

"Becky," he said, "I missed you. Did you miss me?" Rebecca was somewhat taken aback. She hadn't anticipated such a question. Johnny noticed her pause. "Oh, I didn't expect you to be thinking about me every day," he went on. "That's not what I meant. But were there times when you thought about me?"

"Of course," Rebecca answered honestly.

"We had some fun, didn't we?" Rebecca nodded. "I think we could have a lot of fun together, Becky. And I've been thinking. You get a lot of time to think when you're on the road with a baseball team, staying in motels, watching too much TV. And I've been thinking maybe a life in baseball isn't a life I'd enjoy."

"You love playing baseball, Johnny!"

"I do. But I know I'm not good enough to make the majors."

Rebecca was shocked. "What else would you do?"

"Farm. That's what I was going to do before I decided to give this a try. The question's not what I'd do, but who I'd be doing it with. I'd like to do it with you, Becky."

Rebecca sat up straight. "Me!" For a minute, she didn't know what to say. "Johnny, I'm seeing Jacob."

"I know. But I heard that maybe you weren't that serious about getting married to him. I haven't heard much news that you'll be part of the November weddings this year. Will you be?"

Johnny was certainly being direct. That was another one of his good qualities. He didn't go round about. If he wanted to know something, he just flat-out asked. "I don't know," Rebecca answered. "I told Jacob I'd let him know at the end of harvest."

"I know this is kind of sudden, Becky," Johnny said. "And I don't expect you to say yes right away. Besides, I've got to finish the season, save as much money as I can, if I really am going to settle down."

Settle down? Johnny? Rebecca could hardly picture it. But when she looked at him, she could see that he was sincere. "You really want to farm?"

Rebecca wasn't sure if she was happy about that or disappointed. She realized she thought of Johnny's breaking away from the Amish lifestyle as perhaps pointing the way for her. Yet he had not asked her to join him in the world of the English; he'd asked her to join him in the Amish world. And that meant it was a question she had to take seriously.

"I always liked farming," Johnny answered. "My dat's got a good farm, and one day it could be mine. I'd join the church, of course. Just think about it, will you, Becky? I'll be home in a couple of weeks, unless we make the playoffs. We can talk about it more then, okay?"

"Okay, Johnny."

He smiled, reached over, and squeezed her hand, then started the car and headed off to the Zook farm. All the way home Rebecca's head was swimming. *Three men!* How would she choose? When would she have to? And were there really three?

When they pulled up in front of her house, Rebecca saw her father standing by himself outside the barn. He wasn't doing anything, just standing there. She said her good-byes to Johnny, and he drove off. Rebecca waved gaily at her father. "Hello, Dat!"

For an answer, Elam simply moved off, not even acknowledging her greeting.

Yes, thought Rebecca. *Three men. But it's my dat I'm worried about.*

CHAPTER 16

Ivan was hot. The heat and humidity seemed particularly bad this year. Or maybe it was just his foul mood. It had been ten days since the killings — Ivan tried to think of them as "accidental deaths" so he wouldn't make another Freudian slip, but he never really succeeded. Especially when he had been drinking. And Ivan had been drinking plenty of late, as he sweated out the time until he had the answer on the toxicology tests done on Beauty and Dandelion.

Sitting on his veranda, he poured himself another vodka on ice, hoping the fading light would bring a cooler night. He could have gone inside, of course, where it was air-conditioned, but Liz was watching TV, and he preferred to be alone. Wanda had said something about a house party and had sped off in the early afternoon. So there he sat. Alone. And hot.

The insurance company, not surprisingly, did a reasonable job protecting itself against fraudulent claims. When Beauty and Dandelion had first been insured, the company had sent a veterinarian's assistant to look at the horses and take a blood sample from each, so they could match the DNA of both horses and see that they were, indeed, Dandelion and Beauty. Ivan wasn't worried about that part. But the blood samples the insurance company had taken and sent to Penn State for analysis were another matter. The vet had said it would be about ten days before the results were available. That might mean, at most, two weeks. And Ivan's worries — and drinking — had increased with each day.

Even if the tests had come back positive for drugs, there was absolutely nothing that could tie Ivan to whatever chemicals were in Rex's concoction. An investigator could go through Ivan's Internet searches, purchases, and any other records that they might seek, and they would find nothing. And Ivan would try to blame Tommy, the farm hand he'd fired, or even Gregory, but that would delay the payment from the insurance company and take time.

And time was one thing Ivan didn't have. He knew the date Vinny expected payment: October 1st. If the tests results came back by the end of the week or even early next week, Ivan would have just about six weeks for the claim to process and for him to receive his money. It would be tight, but it could work.

The insurance investigator, although puzzled about what had happened, was almost through his checklist and hadn't seemed concerned about anything specific. He had done a quick review of Ivan's financial situation and, although Ivan had a fair amount of debt, there were no outstanding judgments — maybe not surprising since guys like Vinnie don't file liens. True, Dandelion's recent race hadn't gone very well, but the investigator had reviewed the tape of that race and had not noticed any specific problems. Dandelion wasn't injured. She had just had a bad day.

No, the main issue was time. Time, and the Lancaster *Intelligencer Journal.* Ivan pulled it out from under the vodka bottle on the table before him.

Strange Deaths at Cedar Ridge Farm

> *Last week, two seemingly healthy and heavily insured racehorses at Heminger Stables were found dead. A third horse nearly died but was resuscitated by an EMS crew. The cause of death of the two horses is unknown. Interestingly, a similar event occurred nearly twenty years ago when a healthy, heavily insured horse died suddenly at the same location. One month later, the horses' forty-three-year-old trainer, Rex Smith, died of an apparent heart attack.*
>
> *Gregory Pinckney, a stable hand, found the horses when he arrived on the morning of August 4 to feed them. Mr. Pinckney indicated that he had seen the horses on a daily basis for the past month, and they appeared fine the entire time. Mr. Pinckney is also the owner of Bojangles, the horse that nearly died. "As soon as Bo gets better," he added, "I'm going to help the authorities as much as I can to find out what almost killed him."*
>
> *Cedar Ridge Farm is owned by prominent Lancaster attorney Ivan*

*Heminger. A call to Mr. Heminger
was not returned.*

Ivan slammed the paper back down on the table and refilled his glass. *How did that investigative reporter find out about all this? Did Gregory tell him? I've got to keep my eye on him; he could be trouble. But Gregory wouldn't be making the Rex Smith connection; he doesn't even know how Rex died? Or when? Who's talking to this reporter?* Ivan took a swallow. He had to try to stay calm and focused. When his head was clearer, he'd turn his attention to solving this newspaper business.

An hour later, Ivan had almost finished the bottle and was thinking about going to bed, when a car drove up and parked. It was dark now, so Ivan couldn't see who got out of the driver's seat and went around to open the passenger door. But he didn't need to see to recognize Wanda's voice.

"Aren't you the gentleman!" she'd giggled. She made her way unsteadily around the back of the car, the man holding her by the elbow. Ivan could tell she was drunk. *Like father like daughter*, he thought grumpily. But his sour mood changed to something much worse when the couple entered the light from the veranda and Ivan saw who was escorting his daughter home.

Vinny! What's he doing here?

"Hi, Daddy!" Wanda called out. "We had a wonderful time at the party."

"Hello, Ivan," Vinny said. "You've got one heck of a daughter. She's a lot of fun." Wanda smiled at him warmly as they both ascended the stairs to stand next to Ivan on the veranda.

Ivan tried to stay calm, but the foremost question on his mind came out anyway. "Have you two been seeing each other?" He couldn't mask the note of surprised anguish in his voice.

"I met Vinny at that party I went to the night Dandelion died," Wanda said. "He just showed up."

I bet, thought Ivan.

"Yeah, I'm real sorry to hear about two of your horses dying, Ivan," Vinny said with just enough irony and sarcasm that Ivan noticed, but Wanda didn't. "Well, at least they were insured." Vinny looked directly at Ivan.

Ivan was trapped in a conversation he definitely did not want to be having. *He's taunting me! Mocking me!*

"I still can't believe Dandelion is dead," Wanda said sadly.

"I told you, I'll help you look for another horse," Vinny offered. "I've got a few friends in the horse business."

Yeah, right! thought Ivan.

Vinny pulled Wanda to him and put his arm around her. "Just leave it to Vinny." Ivan could swear he almost winked at him. There was his daughter and this gangster he owed half a million dollars snuggling right in front of him!

"Want a drink?" he offered Vinny. Without waiting for a reply, he returned to his bottle. He certainly wanted one.

"No thanks, Ivan," Vinny said. "Tomorrow's another business day. By the way, how's it going with the insurance thing. You heard anything yet about the blood samples?"

Ivan took this opportunity to reassure him. "Not yet. Should hear the end of the week. But the insurance company has completed everything else, so when the results come in negative, I can file right away."

"How long do they estimate it'll take?" asked Vinny.

"About six weeks."

"Let's see," said Vinny, "That'll make it just about October 1st. Hope it doesn't take longer than that," he said, looking directly at Ivan with obvious purpose.

Ivan took a drink of vodka. *Did he come by here just to twist the screws?* He could feel the sweat starting to form under his shirt. *Probably just to make sure things are on track and to remind me to stay focused.*

"I'll call you, babe," Vinny said to Wanda.

"You'd better!" She gave him a quick kiss.

"See you soon, I hope, Ivan," Vinny said with a smile.

He's almost laughing at me! Ivan said to himself.

Vinny retraced his steps to his Mercedes, gave Wanda a final wave, got in, and drove off. Wanda and Ivan both watched him go.

"He's such a nice man, Daddy," she said. "I'm really glad you introduced me to him."

Ai yi yi, the irony! Ivan could hardly believe what he was hearing.

"Well, good night," Wanda said, and started for the door.

"Wait a minute, Wanda," Ivan said. If Vinny wanted him to stay focused, then he knew he needed some answers. "I want to talk to you about Gregory."

"Gregory?" Wanda asked, surprised. "What's wrong?"

Ivan picked up the newspaper article and held it out toward his daughter. "What's wrong is this."

Wanda glanced at the paper, but she knew what he was talking about. "Yeah, Vinny showed me that."

So that's why he came by. Wanted to see how I was reacting to the article.

"They had no right to write that!" Wanda said, outraged.

"I work my whole life to build my reputation and then someone writes an article suggesting that there's something wrong with my stables," Ivan said fiercely. He paused for a second, before exploding angrily, "What the hell is Gregory doing, talking like that to a reporter?"

"I don't think he meant any harm," Wanda said.

"I'm suing 'em. Maybe I can't stop Gregory from talking to them, but they can't just wreck my reputation."

Wanda was puzzled. "What did they say that wrecked your reputation?"

"They said I didn't return a phone call. That suggests that I didn't call them back because I had something to hide. I don't have anything to hide. The problem is that they never called me in the first place."

Wanda stammered for a moment. "Uh-oh."

"Uh-oh what?"

"Daddy, someone from the paper did call a couple of days ago. I forgot to give you the message. I'm sorry."

Ivan started to explode, but then thought better of it. After all, he wasn't really going to sue, and it wasn't his reputation he was so worried about but the idea that Gregory might start snooping around to find out what had happened to his horse. "That's all right, darling," he said. "People make mistakes. When did you last see Gregory?"

"I've only seen him once since…that day."

"Did he ask any questions about my business or about insurance?"

"No. He was worried about Bojangles."

"Are you dating Gregory?"

"Daddy! We're just friends." Then she added, almost as an afterthought. "He's not even interested in going out with me."

"What's he doing here, anyway? He's from someplace in South Carolina. Why did he and his horse move to Pennsylvania? It seems strange."

"He moved here to find his mother."

"His mother?"

"You don't understand, Daddy. He was adopted. He thinks his mother is from this area, and he came here hoping to find her."

"Interesting. Why didn't you tell me that before?"

"It didn't seem like a big deal. There are lots of adoptees who try to find out about their background. One of my profs explained that to us in a sociology class. It's easier than it used to be, but it's not easy. My professor spent twenty years on this, and he still hasn't found his mother."

"Has Gregory had any luck?"

"Not really. But we haven't talked too much about it. All he knows — or as he puts it, all that he thinks he knows — is that his mother's name is Mae Yoder."

"That's not much of a clue. There are lots of Yoders around here."

"Exactly."

Ivan didn't care about Gregory's past or his useless search for his mother. He cared about what Gregory might do in the present. "Talk to Gregory. Try to find out how this whole newspaper business came about. Let me know what his thinking is about Bojangles, will you?"

"Why?" asked Wanda.

"Because I said so!" Ivan snapped. Then he changed his tone. "Because I feel bad about what happened to Bojangles. It happened in our stables. I want to make sure the horse gets better, and I want to know if Gregory needs any help. With anything. Okay?"

"Sure, Daddy. Can I go to bed now?"

"Of course, darling. Have a good night."

"You, too, Daddy. See you in the morning."

"Good night."

Ivan watched his daughter enter the house, overheard her "Goodnight, Mom" call to his wife, and listened to the night settling back into silence. He slumped back into his chair. He was tired. *I really gotta cut back on the booze. Just as soon as this mess is over. Maybe take some time off, maybe even go on a little trip with Liz.* Ivan almost smiled. He hadn't thought of spending time with his wife in a while. Maybe it was time to relax a little. It was certainly time to stop gambling. *At least for a while.* Ivan never could convince himself to give up gambling completely, any more than he could completely stop drinking. *Moderation in all things,* he thought, *including moderation.*

Ivan got up, stepped down the veranda steps, and walked to the end of the stone-slab walkway. He looked across at his barn. Bojangles was gone. *Good riddance!* For a split second, Ivan wished he'd given Bojangles another injection. *I could still do it. The drugs are right up there in my office. All I'd have to do is —* Ivan suddenly opened his eyes wide. *The drugs! I never moved them from my freezer! I knew the insurance people can't go snooping around without a search warrant, but Gregory...*

He moved quickly across the courtyard, entered the stable, and took the stairs to his office. He hurried to the refrigerator, ignored the bottle of vodka chilling on a shelf, and opened the freezer compartment. He withdrew the small box containing the vials of the remaining concoctions and placed it on his desk, closing the refrigerator door. He opened the box. Yes, there were the drugs. *Now where can I put them? Gotta keep them cold. Who knows, might need them again. Where's the safest place I can hide them?* The obvious answer made Ivan shiver. It was not his favorite place to be.

He exited the barn and headed for Rex's shack. Ivan had had plenty of other employees stay there over the years, but he still thought of it as Rex's shack. It was a converted tobacco shed that Ivan had fixed up when he'd hired Rex, putting in plumbing and a new kitchen. At Rex's suggestion, he'd had the contractor hide a small freezer behind a false wall underneath the kitchen sink. That's where Rex kept his "pharmaceutical supplies," as he liked to call them. And that's where Ivan was headed with the vials. He had buried the syringes, but he hadn't been able to part with the drugs. He was confident no one would ever find them in the hidden freezer.

The shack was dark when he entered. He quickly flicked on a light. It smelled dank, there was dust everywhere, and a few spiders had built their homes in some corners. The front door opened onto a small living room with a chair, a table, lamp, a TV on a stand, and a dining table whose chairs were pushed back helter-skelter. An old couch nestled against one wall. Ivan tried not to think about that table, but he couldn't help himself. It was where he'd found Rex's body the morning of his death. Standing there years later, Ivan could remember it all perfectly.

"Mr. Heeminger, we need to talk," Rex had said to him one Saturday morning, while Ivan was reading his newspaper on the veranda. "We're partners now." He had a smile on his lips that revealed his yellowing teeth.

"Partners?" Ivan had asked. Rex had never called them that before.

"Well, sure, Mr. Heeminger. Because of what I did for you. With the horses. And the insurance." Rex's smile had brightened a little.

"Let's step off the porch, Rex," Ivan had said. *What's he talking about this now for? he wondered. That was six months ago. And on the veranda, where anybody might hear him?!* Ivan had moved under a walnut tree that stood in a corner of the yard. "What's this about?"

"It's about a woman. She's got, you know, a leetle one on the way, and she thinks I'm the father."

"Are you?"

"I don't know, Mr. Heeminger, and that's the truth. I sometimes take too many drugs and I sometimes do things I do not remember. You know how it is. Anyway, I need some cash right quick."

"We had a deal, Rex. A deal that involved quite a bit of money for you, as I remember."

"Yes, Mr. Heeminger, and I'm real grateful. But that was then, and this is now." The smile had stayed fixed on Rex's face. It had begun to anger Ivan. "But since we were partners in crime, I don't see why we can't still stay partners, if you know what I mean."

What Ivan had known was that he was looking at a potential lifetime of Rex's blackmail to keep from spilling the beans about how he'd helped Ivan kill his horse to collect the insurance. "Rex, this is too important a conversation to be having here and now. How about if we put it off until tonight."

"Sure, Mr. Heeminger. Want me to come to your barn office?"

"No, Rex, I'll just come down to where you're staying, bring a few beers, and we can talk about it. Say about nine o'clock?"

"All right. I'll be done with the horses by then. Thank you, Mr. Heeminger."

"My pleasure, Rex."

Ivan had worked on his plan the rest of that Saturday, but it really hadn't been much of a plan. If the concoctions could kill a horse, they certainly could kill a man. But Rex wasn't going to hold out his arm and say, "Inject me." That's where the other kind of Rex's concoctions had come in handy, the kind that had allowed Ivan to have his way with the one woman who had resisted his charms.

At nine o'clock that evening, Ivan had showed up at Rex's shed with a six-pack of Coors beer. He had previously fortified himself with some vodka, but he wasn't going to bring that to Rex's. That night wasn't about drinking, at least not about the fun kind. It was about business. That's why Ivan had brought beer mugs, too. "Pour you a beer, Rex?" he had asked.

"Sure, Mr. Heeminger, thanks." Ivan had stepped over to the kitchen sink, popped open a beer for Rex, then carefully reached in his pocket and poured a yellow liquid into the beer, keeping up a conversation to distract Rex. "All the horses okay, Rex? I thought I saw Rake's Progress with a little limp."

"No, it is nothing. I have a concoction for him, fix him right up."

"You have a concoction for everything, don't you, Rex? Here you go." Ivan had handed Rex his beer and kept the one he had also poured for himself. *I bet you don't have a concoction to fix this,* he thought.

To encourage him, Ivan had taken a big swallow of his beer. Rex had done the same. "Now, what is it you wanted to discuss about our partnership, Rex?"

"This woman, she is demanding $10,000 for child support."

"Do you need to pay it?"

"She says she will go to the police if I don't. I just don't want the police asking questions about me, not about that, but, you know, about other things." Ivan had been sure Rex was into "other things" he didn't care to know about.

"Well, I might be able to advance you a loan."

Rex had swallowed some beer. "Not a loan, Mr. Heeminger. Let's just call it a further payoff for a job well done. Maybe it's a bonus." Rex smiled. "Yeah, a bonus, I like that. This is good beer," he offered, sitting down. "Strong for a Coors."

"A bonus, eh?" Ivan had said. "About how many bonuses do you think you might need down through the years?"

"You pay me good here, Mr. Heeminger. And I usually know how to stay out of trouble. I don't think there will be too many times for more bonuses."

"But there might be more?"

"Well, Mr. Heeminger, a man's gotta live."

Not long, Rex. Ivan had smiled.

"And besides, you might need some of Rex's little concoctions again." Rex had swallowed some more beer. "I don't feel so good." He had looked at Ivan. Ivan had looked back with a steady gaze. "Hey, Mr. Heeminger, did you — " Rex had tried to stand up, but he immediately slumped back into his chair.

"Yes, Rex, I did. But don't worry, it won't kill you." Ivan pulled a syringe out of his coat pocket. "This is what will kill you."

"No!" Rex had shouted. He had tried to rise again, but could barely move. Ivan had just smiled. With a last desperate look into Ivan's cold eyes, Rex had fallen forward, his head on the table. Ivan had stepped forward and held Rex's wrist. There had been a pulse. *But not for long.*

Ivan had looked at Rex's arm. There were needle marks all over it. Rex had a drug problem. *Now you'll have a real drug problem, Rex.* Ivan had smiled. He had jabbed the needle into Rex's vein and squeezed the plunger. Rex had not moved. He never would again.

Yes, Ivan remembered that day; how could he forget? But what surprised him was how easily he'd managed to live the past twenty years knowing he had killed someone. At certain moments, he actually regretted what he had become. But this wasn't one of those moments.

He walked quickly with the box of drugs to the sink. He opened the cabinet doors underneath and pushed a small indentation hidden behind the sink's bowl. He heard the click of a release from inside the wall, then pushed the wall aside, revealing a small freezer. An electrical outlet had been installed in the floor next to it. The AC cord was unplugged, so Ivan plugged it in. He heard the freezer start up, a small humming noise.

Ivan opened the door, and a light came on. The freezer was empty. Ivan shoved the box of drugs inside and closed the door, then slid the wall back into place, hearing the latch click. He pushed on the panel to make sure it wouldn't open by itself, then stood up and listened. Only the faintest sound of a motor running came through the wall, a sound no one would notice unless specifically listening for it. He closed the kitchen cabinet doors, then washed his face in cold water in the sink. The drugs were hidden. *Now to get out of this creepy shack.*

When he opened the door, the person standing there caused Ivan to literally leap backward. He'd seen her around town the last twenty-five-odd years, but he'd never spoken a word to her since their final meeting so many years ago. She was dressed in a plain, dark-green dress and simple blouse, and she had a covering on her head. She spoke barely above a whisper. "Hello, Ivan."

"What do you want, Lydia Mae?" Ivan asked when he'd regained his composure.

"I want to speak to you for a minute. I saw the light, took a chance it was you. May I come inside?"

"Just say what you want from right there."

Lydie regarded him a minute, then shrugged. "It's about that newspaper article. I was sorry to see it."

"Me, too. But it shouldn't concern you, so I don't know what there is to say about it."

"But it does concern me," she answered calmly. "Do you know why Gregory is up here, Ivan?"

"Wanda told me he came to look for his mother." Ivan stood stock-still. He was beginning to understand.

Lydie made sure he did. "Any idea who that might be?"

He stared at her with wide-eyed amazement. *She is Gregory's mother?* His mouth went dry. He needed a drink. "What makes you so sure?"

"After you had your way with me, South Carolina is where I went to put my baby up for adoption. My father knew some people down there who would look after me."

"A lot of people are from South Carolina." Ivan was trying to stay calm, but this conversation was the last thing he needed on a day that had already been stressful enough.

"True, Ivan," Lydie responded, with the same calm that had driven him crazy all those years ago.

He looked at her in the light that spilled from the ceiling fixture inside the shack. She was still a fine-looking woman. For a moment he thought about how beautiful she had been as the teenage Amish girl who cleaned his parents' house. Her next words brought him sharply back to the present. "But not a lot of people from South Carolina carry with them the baby quilt their mother made for them while she awaited delivery. Nine squares with butterflies inside them. Maybe you've seen it."

Ivan remembered the quilt he had seen draped over Bojangles' stall. He'd thought it was a "bunch of boxes." But they easily could have been squares. He swallowed hard. "You say Gregory is your son, so what?"

"Have you had any thoughts about Gregory since you read the article?" Lydie asked. She hadn't moved an inch since Ivan had refused to invite her inside. But Ivan now took a step backward and wiped his brow with his hand. "I thought so," said Lydie.

"Thought what?" Ivan shot back, pulling out his handkerchief and wiping his brow some more. *It's so stuffy in here! But I'm not going outside with her.*

"Thought you'd be having some evil thoughts."

Evil. Ivan remembered how she had called him an evil man all those years ago, when he had first tried to grab her late one afternoon when she was sweeping the living room and his parents were gone. She'd pushed him away with her broom. "Get away from me, you evil man!" she had said to him, not really raising her voice but letting her hard, cold stare convey her meaning. "What are you going to do, kill me with your broom, Lydia Mae?" Ivan had scoffed. "I just might," she'd replied. And Ivan had believed her.

So he'd decided to use another method. Slipping her some of Rex's concoction in a glass of milk he'd offered her some weeks later, he found it had worked just as Rex had promised. A few minutes later, Lydia Mae had fallen to the floor, the broom at her feet. Ivan had carried her to his bedroom, done what he was lusting to do, then placed her in a rocking chair on the veranda.

When his parents had returned home, he'd said, "I think Lydia Mae's drunk," pointing to her slumbering figure in the chair. His parents had wakened her and sent her on her way, But about three months later she had confronted him outside the general store when no one else was around. "I'm pregnant," she'd said with that same steady calm. "The baby is yours. I need money to go away and have it."

"Get on your broom and ride away, Lydia Mae!" Ivan had laughed at her.

"You are an evil man," Lydia Mae had spat at him with a vengeance in her voice that had caused Ivan to actually squirm.

And now here she was, some twenty five years later, giving him that same chilling stare and calling him evil again. Remembering all that, Ivan squirmed again. "Don't be ridiculous," he said to her. He wanted to brush past her, maybe push her out of the way, but he knew she wouldn't budge. Nor did he want to get too close to her.

"I know what a man like you is capable of, Ivan," Lydie continued. "I promise you Gregory is your son. And I hope even someone as evil as you wouldn't think of harming his own son. But if you do, it will be the last person you'll harm." From any other woman, such a threat would seem absurd. From Lydia Mae, Ivan believed it. With a final look of complete hatred, she turned away and walked slowly into the darkness.

Ivan stood in the doorway, breathing hard, as if he'd been exercising. The first thing to do was to get out of Rex's shack, get away from all the bad memories. He turned off the light and quickly closed the door. Standing in the darkness, Ivan tried to think. The day had been so confusing. Rereading the newspaper article, then Vinny with Wanda, and now this. *My world is crashing in on me! Gregory is my son? That's crazy!*

But even as he thought it, Ivan realized it was true. He had seen the blanket himself. And what other possible reason would Lydie have had for coming to his house in the dark to confront him? Still, just because Gregory was his son didn't mean anybody had to know. Lydie certainly wasn't going to tell anyone. So, what difference would it make if Gregory were Ivan's son?

Like a blow to the gut, Ivan suddenly knew. He tore off through the night, heading for his office. He opened the barn door and sprinted to the second floor, flinging open the door to his office and running to his desk. He frantically searched through drawers. *I know I saw it here. Just a piece of paper I'd written it down on, just because...Where is it?* He opened a drawer. Nothing but a half-empty vodka bottle. The next drawer contained some magazines, a couple of issues of *American Lawyer*, some horse newspapers. He pulled them out and quickly shuffled through them. Nothing again.

Ivan yanked open the middle draw and spilled its contents on top of his desk. Pencils, sticky-note pads, business cards, some stray stamps, a few sheets of paper — some with writing, some not — paper clips, a stapler. Ivan scattered the objects this way and that, searching frantically. He was about to stop and head for his filing cabinet when a small, green sticky note caught his eye. It was folded in half. Ivan quickly grabbed it and read in his own hand: "If you can prove you have the will, / A dandy death will cure your ill."

Ivan turned it over. There it was. "But nothing can be done at all / When your son shall cause your fall."

The prophecy! Could it possibly be true?

CHAPTER 17

The dogs began to bark as soon as Gregory had parked his truck and was approaching the front door of the kennel. He passed the small sign stuck in the yard: "Dr. David Jenkins, Veterinary Medicine, Professional Skill, Personal Care." When Gregory rang the doorbell, the dogs barked even louder. Gregory liked dogs. *But you have to really like them to run a kennel,* he thought.

Having lived with the Amish for three months, he was even more appreciative of quiet. So when Doc Jenkins opened the door and the cacophony of barks and yelps and woofs and snarls pounded Gregory's ears, he actually flinched. Doc Jenkins noticed and smiled. "It's a nice day," he said. "Why don't we sit on that bench over there and talk?" He led the way to a wooden bench shaded by two large cedar trees, offered Gregory a seat, then sat next to him.

It was a typically hot and humid late August day in Lancaster County. Doc Jenkins wiped his brow with a handkerchief and asked, "Now, what can I do for you?"

"I suppose you saw the article in the newspaper about the dead horses," Gregory began.

"I did. Your name was prominent."

"Yes, I didn't know the investigative reporter would use it so often. Probably get me in trouble with Ivan."

"I've had my troubles with Ivan for years, and I don't think we'll ever work it out."

"Why not?"

"Don't think either of us wants to."

"Why is that?"

"Happened around twenty years ago, when Ivan lost another horse in a mysterious manner. He wanted me to sign the insurance report saying the cause of death was heart failure, but I wouldn't."

"Why not?"

"I wasn't sure it was. So Ivan got another vet to sign off on it. He then took all his business elsewhere, which is all right with me. In case you haven't guessed, Ivan Heminger is not my favorite person. That's why I was happy to talk to that reporter."

"You talked to him?" Gregory exclaimed. "Why didn't he put your name in the paper?"

"Because I told him I wouldn't talk to him unless he promised he wouldn't," Doc Jenkins said slyly. "Is that why you came to see me, to find out what happened to Ivan's horse back then?"

"That, and to find out if you know anything about this Rex Smith character. It seemed odd that the reporter put in that line about Smith dying of a heart attack. Why would he think the two were related?" Gregory looked at Doc Jenkins. "But now that I know you talked to the reporter, I'm thinking maybe you put that notion in his head." For an answer, Doc Jenkins only smiled. "So, what do you know about Rex Smith?"

"Not much, really," he replied. "He was Ivan's trainer for years. Came from Ocala, Florida, he once told me. I guess that might have explained the Mexican accent, but it doesn't really explain how someone who looked and spoke like that would be named Rex Smith."

"That does seem odd," Gregory said. "He and Ivan got along?"

"Far as I could tell."

"Anything else?" Learning that Rex Smith was from Florida didn't really provide many clues.

"Well, there was one thing that always struck me as rather curious."

"What's that, Doc?"

"Ivan once had a horse that was really sick. This was before he and I had our little tiff. Well, I couldn't figure out what was wrong with him for the life of me. The blood tests didn't reveal anything unusual. But he had a kind of a shiver, the horse did, and I was afraid he might actually die. I told Ivan that one day, right there in the stables. Ivan was mad, he called me some name or other and stormed off. Tell you the truth, Gregory, I was feeling pretty small. I mean, I'm supposed to help animals, and I couldn't help this poor horse at all. But after Ivan had left, Rex said to me, 'Wait here, Doc.' And he went away. He was gone, oh, about fifteen minutes, and when he came back, he had a syringe in his hand."

"A syringe!"

"I thought it was strange myself, him having one. He was a trainer, but trainers don't usually inject horses with something. They call the vet." Doc Jenkins paused, remembering. "I believe I objected, but Rex just asked me if I had any better ideas, and I had to admit I didn't. And danged if he didn't inject that horse then and there. And danged if two days later the chills were gone and a week later that horse was running like he'd never been sick."

Gregory pondered what he'd just heard. It seemed almost magical. "Did he ever tell you what was in the syringe?"

"I asked him, of course. But he just said, 'Oh, a little concoction I cooked up.'"

"A little concoction, huh?" Gregory mused out loud. "A Mexican from Florida with an English name who knows how to mix…concoctions.

So, you think there may have been a connection with Ivan's horse that died and Rex Smith's heart attack a week later?"

"Rex was young, healthy as a horse — if you don't mind the expression." Gregory smiled. He liked Doc Jenkins; he had a sense of humor. "For him to die suddenly like that. I mean, he was able to make a concoction that could save a horse. Maybe he could also make one that could kill one. And kill a human, too."

Gregory looked at Doc Jenkins, who pulled out his handkerchief and wiped the back of his neck. "But Rex Smith isn't around to have caused these latest deaths," Gregory said.

"No," Doc Jenkins replied. "But maybe his concoction still is."

Driving back from Doc Jenkins' kennel, Gregory thought over the situation. *Two dead horses, and Bo almost dead. No evidence of foul play. He hadn't heard what the results of the blood tests were yet, but assuming Rex had been responsible for the earlier death of one of Ivan's horses and that Ivan had collected on the insurance, it made sense that Ivan might try the same scheme again. So it wouldn't be surprising if the blood tests came back negative this time, too. That is, if Ivan had had the horses poisoned. But by whom? Why not by Ivan himself? Maybe Rex helped him the first time, and maybe that's what got him killed. And maybe Ivan decided not to have any partners this time around. It was just a syringe into a horse's neck; he'd be capable of doing that easily.*

If he still had some poison left. And, if he did, where would he keep it? Somewhere on the farm? A freezer somewhere; he'd have to keep it there to preserve it. But where? Ivan's office, maybe? He certainly got the ice for his vodkas somewhere.

I wonder how Wanda fits in with all this? I like Wanda. A little vain, maybe. But she's got a lot to be vain about. Gregory called up a mental picture of Wanda in her riding clothes: jodhpur boots, and hip-hugging breeches hugging some very nice hips. *Then why aren't I more attracted to her?* The answer came immediately: a mental picture of Rebecca, barefoot in a cape and apron, light purple dress coming halfway down her calf, revealing just a few inches of smooth, white skin.

Somehow those few inches were more beguiling to Gregory than all of Wanda's blond beauty, even when wearing a tee shirt and shorts, as she often did around the farm. *And Rebecca's eyes! Blue-green, never seen anything like 'em. With that wonderful freckle in her left eye. When she's looking at me, do I feel special!* Gregory thought about that for a moment. Was he feeling more special to Rebecca lately? Was she looking at him in a different way? He snapped to in time to see his truck wandering off the lane a little. He yanked it back onto the road, shaking his head to clear it. *Wow, she's really gotten to me!*

As he parked near the stables, Gregory refocused on the task at hand. He looked around. The place seemed deserted. No cars, not Wanda's or Ivan's or Liz's. Gregory entered the barn and headed for the stairs to Ivan's office on the second floor, opened the door, and entered.

The midafternoon sun poured through the two windows that opened onto the courtyard below. Desk, chair, filing cabinet, bookshelf. Gregory scanned the shelf. Books on horses and on horse farms in Kentucky, Florida, California; treatises on racehorses; manuals on feed; various account ledgers. Gregory opened one and flipped through several pages of line items and numbers, none of which meant anything to him. Besides, who knew when someone might come back home; he didn't have time to go through any ledgers. *Ivan wouldn't be so stupid as to leave evidence right here in his accounts anyway.* He opened the filing cabinet and quickly scanned a few labels. Contracts. Purchase orders. A file stuffed with pictures of Wanda at various ages on her horses. *He's not going to leave incriminating evidence in his files either.*

Gregory next checked the small refrigerator standing against a wall. He opened it. Empty. He opened the freezer compartment. It hadn't been defrosted in some time. At the bottom, a thin layer of ice had formed. Looking more closely, Gregory noticed an indentation in the ice, about the size of a small box. *Something's been removed.*

He crossed to the desk. *Why so messy?* It was obvious someone had dumped the contents of a drawer onto the desktop. Gregory shoved pencils and paperclips to the side. *Nothing here.* He opened the first of the two drawers and saw the bottle of vodka, nothing else. He closed it and opened the second drawer. *Magazines and newspapers.* Gregory picked them up. A *Forbes*, a *Fortune*, a *Time*, a *Newsweek*, each at least three months old. Same for the horse newspapers. *No big deal. Ivan's just behind keeping up with his periodicals.*

He was about to replace the pile when he noticed a sheet of paper sticking out of the middle of the *Newsweek*. He pulled it out. It was a letter from Ephrata National Bank denying Ivan an additional loan on his property. *Ivan applied for a second mortgage?* The letter was from a senior vice president, explaining that Ivan's current mortgage was over 90 percent of the property's appraised value. "In the current regulatory environment it is impossible for us to increase your loan." *Wow, Ivan's mortgaged to the hilt, he needs more money, and he's not getting it from the bank.*

The letter was dated two months earlier. Behind it was a handwritten paper that contained dates and figures. Gregory looked at it, trying to puzzle out its meaning: $250,000 with a date of March 1. $40,000 dated March 20, with a total on the right-hand side of the paper of $290,000. On April 1, an additional $27,500 brought the total to $327,500, but on April 15 there seemed to be a payment reducing the total to $302,500. Gregory quickly looked at the bottom figure, which was underlined: $500,000. *Are these debts?* He looked at the final scribblings on the page: two dates, the first one, October 15, was crossed out; the second date was October 1.

He wasn't sure, but it looked like Ivan owed half a million dollars to somebody and the due date was October 1. *Here's the motivation for killing Dandelion and Beauty: to get the insurance money!* Gregory excitedly took the paper over to the copying machine in the corner, turned it on, and waited impatiently for it to warm up. *Come on, come on, somebody might come back!* When the machine whirred to life, he placed the sheet of paper on the glass, closed the lid, and made a copy. He stuffed the copy in his jeans, turned off the machine, put the original back between the *Newsweek*'s pages, and carefully replaced the magazines in the drawer, doing his best to make it appear as if nothing had been disturbed. Then he quickly exited Ivan's office.

Outside the office, Gregory found that he was breathing rapidly. His adrenaline was up. *Not really used to sneaking around. But now that I've started...* He walked down the hallway a few feet and opened the next door. It looked to be some sort of storage room filled with stools, barrels, broken chairs, an old tractor tire, some discarded clothing — all of it dusty. Gregory thought he might poke around, but the room obviously hadn't been entered in a while. *Maybe later.*

The next room stretched along the entire back wall of the second floor. It seemed to be some sort of combination conference and trophy room with a long table, chairs, lots of pictures of horses on the walls, and a couple of bookcases filled with trophies of various sizes. Gregory walked quickly through the room. Stairs at the far end led back down to the stables. He stood with his hands on his hips, thinking. *Rex Smith...I know he lived at Cedar Ridge Farm. But where?*

Gregory descended the stairs and stepped outside. He blinked in the sunlight, waiting for his eyes to adjust. When they had, he looked around. No cars had appeared in the driveway. *Still might have some time. Where is Rex's room?* He looked down the back pasture and saw the shack. *Tommy! The farmhand — he'd lived there. I bet Rex lived there, too.*

Gregory ran the fifty yards to the shack and opened the door. A living quarters. A small room with a kitchenette off to the side, and a door at the far end that probably led to a bedroom. He approached the small table next to the couch and opened the drawers. Empty. He pulled the pillows off the couch, lifted up a rumpled quilt, felt down between the cracks. Nothing. He knelt on the floor, looking under the couch. Collected dust. He rose and surveyed the room. A TV on a stand, another table without a drawer. Very sparse. And why not? Rex was a trainer. He lived and breathed horses. Probably used this place only for sleep.

Might as well check out the bedroom. Gregory opened the door and stepped inside. A single bed, stripped. He opened the closet door. Empty, just a few hangers. He felt along the top shelf, found nothing. *I wish I knew what I was looking for.* Gregory gave the room a hard look. *Look under the bed?* Gregory was beginning to feel a little foolish. *Who do I think I am, some detective from a TV series?* He decided not to bother looking under the bed. *Just a lot of dust, I bet.*

Exiting the bedroom, Gregory crossed the small living room and walked toward the kitchenette. He paused to look out the window, but still no cars had returned, and no one was about. He stepped into the kitchenette, where he opened all the cabinet doors. A few glasses, a bowl or two, salt and pepper shakers. In a drawer were some utensils and a couple of kitchen knives. A frying pan hung from a nail over the stove; an empty pot rested on top of one of the burners. A small refrigerator. Gregory opened it, but it was empty, not even plugged in.

He decided to look underneath the sink, opened the cabinet doors, and found some bottles of cleanser and a few rags. *Nothing.* He had closed one of the two cabinet doors when he stopped. Looking more closely, he saw an outline in the dust between the rags. *A handprint!* Gregory quickly knelt, opened the other cabinet door, and carefully placed his own left hand over the print in the dust. To do so, he had to lean forward into the space under the sink. Looking straight ahead, Gregory could see dust disturbed on the back wall of the cabinet. *Somebody was looking for something.*

With his right hand, he began to move his fingers slowly over the back wall, feeling for anything unusual. When he moved his hand to the top, or the underside of the wall containing the sink bowl, he found it behind a pipe: a slight depression. Gregory pushed down and heard a click. Then he slid the back portion of the wall to the side.

A freezer! With the wall moved aside, he could hear the slight hum of its motor. *It's on.* Gregory seized the small handle and pulled back. There was only one thing inside. A small box. He withdrew it, closed the freezer door, stood up, placed the box on the kitchen counter, and opened it. Inside were three vials containing liquids of various colors. Gregory took the cork stopper out of one of them and sniffed. It was an acrid smell.

He started for the front door of Rex's shack, then stopped. *What if someone comes looking for this box and doesn't find it? I can't just take it with me.* He considered for a moment. *This might be evidence. I can't tamper with it. But the police can. If I can convince them it's here. Doc Jenkins knows those police officers who were here. Gotta talk to Doc Jenkins.*

Satisfied that he had accomplished more than he could have imagined, Gregory replaced the box, closed the cabinet doors, and hurried outside with one overwhelming urge: get off Ivan's property fast. A quick glance showed that no cars had returned. He half-jogged to his truck, got in, turned it around in the driveway, and headed out. Only then did he relax and breathe easily. *Made it!*

Up in his bedroom, Ivan stood at a window and watched Gregory's truck disappear. *But nothing can be done at all / When your son shall cause your fall.* The prophecy echoed uneasily in his brain. *Nothing at all? We'll see about that.*

The phone rang. Ivan picked it up and listened to the voice on the other end. "Mr. Heminger, hi, it's Bud Smith from Autoworks. Your car's ready. Want us to drive it out to you?"

"That would be great, Bud."

"Sorry it took so long. Hope you weren't too bored, hanging out at home for a while."

"No, Bud, not bored at all. The day has been very interesting." Ivan replaced the receiver with a cold, satisfied smile. *Very interesting indeed.*

CHAPTER 18

As Elam sat down to the family meal, everyone bowed their heads in prayer. It was Friday night. *Two weeks since New York,* thought Rebecca. *Tomorrow is two weeks since the horses' deaths. I wish my life would slow down a little.*

After a quick, silent prayer, Rebecca's thoughts turned to her father. He didn't seem to have much energy and went about his work in silence, mostly. Elam had been silent before, of course. Silence was a way of life with the Amish, an honored way of life. But there had been power in the silence, noise in the silence, *something* in the silence. Lately, however, there had been nothing. Her father had ceased his walks after supper and usually went straight to bed. Rebecca had even noticed a certain dullness about his eyes, which used to sparkle with joy. And all of this had happened since that moment in the Kings' yard after church, when her father had heard some kind of news from Mr. Glick and had hurried the family home right away.

"Corn's looking good, Pop," Henry said, when the prayer was finished. Elam only nodded.

"You need more potatoes than that, Elam," Mabel said, attempting to spoon some onto his plate.

Elam held up his hand and suddenly burst out, "No, I don't!"

For a minute, everyone was silent. Mabel passed the potatoes along the other side of the table. Finally, Rebecca could stand it no longer. "Are you all right, Dat?" she asked. Elam nodded and poked at his food. "You seem a little upset — "

"I said I was all right!"

Hating the tension, Hanna began to chirp away. "These are good beans, Mabel. We had a good garden this year, 'specially for beans. Potatoes, too. Radishes didn't grow so well. I think it was that dry spell we had in August. What do you think, Becca?"

"That was probably it, Hanna," Rebecca answered quietly. For a minute, everyone ate in silence, the clanking of fork, spoon, or knife the only noise emanating from the usually boisterous family table. After a while, Rebecca stopped eating. She'd been ravenous before, but now she had no interest in food.

When the meal was finished, Elam pushed his plate back and looked at his family. "I have something to tell you," he announced. All eyes turned to him.

"I've had some news," he began. Rebecca sucked in her breath. She knew something hadn't been right. "You know, Mabel, but the others probably don't. A while back, I invested some money with Noah Glick. Quite a bit of money. Around $200,000."

"I told you, you should've done it sooner," Mabel said. "All kinds of people were making money from Noah."

"Yes, that's what it looked like," Elam said. "That's why I did it. But it wasn't true."

"What do you mean, Pop?" asked Henry, leaning forward.

"I mean, the money's gone," Elam said simply.

"Gone?" Henry cried.

Mabel gasped. "What do you mean, *gone*, Elam?"

Elam looked at them all steadily. "I mean, there's no more money left. No more of mine, anyway, and probably no more of anybody's. Noah's brother, Samuel, gave me the news last week at church. He'd invested, too. Betraying his own brother…" Elam's voice trailed off in disbelief.

"But where'd it go?" asked Henry. "It can't just disappear."

"Apparently it can," said Elam. "It's something called a Ponzi scheme. Noah's been engaging in it for years. He'd take money from some people and invest it, then he'd raise money from other people to pay the first people wonderful dividends. Others would hear how much money Noah was making for his clients, then they'd invest. But some investments were bound to go bad, and when they did, Noah needed to raise more money to keep paying those good dividends. Those in the beginning of the scheme might do all right, if they took out a lot of money before the whole thing collapsed. But those at the end…" He looked at Mabel. "Those like me."

If there had been silence before, it now settled over the room like a thick fog. Rebecca felt as if she could hardly breathe. She looked at her family. Mabel was staring dumbly ahead. Hanna was carefully eating every last scrap of food on her plate.

Henry was looking at his father, eyes glaring. He finally asked evenly. "Just what does this mean, Pop?"

"It means I've been thinking that it might make more sense to sell the farm sooner rather than later."

"No!" Henry implored.

"What do you mean, no?" Elam shot back.

"I mean you can't sell the farm just because you made some stupid investment!" Henry shouted.

"You will not speak to me in that tone of voice, Henry Zook!" Elam shouted back, rising from his chair.

"Tone of voice? Tone of voice!" Henry screamed. "What kind of tone am I supposed to use when you've thrown away a hundred and fifty years of Zook history on this farm? When you've thrown away my life? Is this the right tone?' He spoke in a mockingly sweet voice. "Oh, poor Pop, I'm so sorry you made a little mistake, but that's okay."

Elam threw back his chair and started for his son. "How dare you!" he screamed.

Henry stood up, too, ready to fight, but Rebecca rose and blocked his path. "No, Henry!"

He grabbed his sister, about to throw her aside, but when he saw the look of terror in her eyes, he hesitated, then turned and ran from the room.

Elam yelled after him. "Come back here! Come back here this instant! I will straighten you out!"

Rebecca held her father back. Her brother escaped. Her mother gripped the table with all her might, trembling. And her aunt began to quietly weep.

After the altercation at supper, Rebecca went looking for Henry but couldn't find him anywhere. She then looked in at home, but saw no one in the living room. *They must be in their bedrooms. Not to sleep, it's too early yet.... But I don't want to lie there, tossing and turning...and sad. What has happened to my family? Arguing over money...No, it's not the money with Henry; it's his dream of being a farmer for the rest of his life. Is it the money with Dat? He's got a dream, too, of opening a leather and harness shop. A dream of doing something creative. That's not much different from my dream.*

Her head filled with such thoughts, Rebecca decided to go for a walk around her farm, the farm she had known her whole life. She ambled over to the hen house. There were a few chickens rooting around in the yard. The rest, she knew, were already settled in their nests. How many times she'd been in that house, gathering eggs. Having to shoo the hen off her nest, picking up the small eggs, still warm in her hand, then carrying them to the kitchen for cooking. It made her feel part of the natural cycle of life. She fed the hens, the hens laid eggs, she and her family ate the eggs, she fed the hens, and it started all over again. Simple. Nourishing. Complete.

She heard a snort from inside the barn. Bo was in there. *I wonder if Gregory's there, too.* But she didn't want to see Bo or Gregory just then. Instead, she walked over to the tobacco shed and slid back the large wooden door. There were the rows and rows of tobacco stalks, curing in the night air. Rebecca drew a breath. The sharp, acrid smell of tobacco filled her nose. She'd always loved that smell.

She smiled, remembering when she and Henry were younger, how he'd rolled a tobacco leaf into a kind of cigarette, and talked her into taking a puff. How she'd coughed! And how Henry had laughed! That had cured her of ever wanting to smoke. She could almost hear Henry's laugh again. But then she remembered his angry shouts at his father. *Where is he? Surely he wouldn't just run away?* Rebecca shook her head, freeing herself from such thoughts. If she was on a journey of remembrance, she was determined to remember only the good things.

She stepped outside the tobacco shed and looked around. There was the old icehouse. They didn't use that anymore, hadn't really been using it even when Rebecca was little. But she had used it, oh yes. It had been one of the best places to hide during hide-and-seek. Henry hardly ever looked there. He was afraid of spiders. *Funny how big, strong men can be afraid of the littlest things.*

Rebecca wasn't afraid of them. Come to think of it, there wasn't much that Rebecca feared. Nothing in the natural world, anyway. Horses, cows, pigs, sheep, goats, bugs, snakes, spiders, mice — none of them bothered Rebecca. She felt part of their lives, as they were a part of hers.

No, nothing in the natural world caused her fear. But the other world, the world of people — that world sometimes caused her to be afraid. Afraid when the natural order of things was upset. Like when a son defied his father, and the father threatened to beat the son.

She hastened toward the crick, drawn to it. *My favorite place on the whole farm.* She remembered wading, looking for tadpoles. Or frogs. Or salamanders. Anything that lived in the world of the crick. Often she'd taken off her shoes and socks and just sunk her feet in the cool water. Or even scooped up a handful of water and sucked it down. *So fresh!* She hadn't told her mother about drinking crick water, of course. Mabel would have been worried about disease. But Rebecca, though hardly a daredevil, thought that surely God wouldn't put disease into something so pure, so refreshing, so natural. After all, it was God's crick, too. Sure enough, in all the years and all the scoops of water she'd swallowed, Rebecca had never gotten sick from it. *The crick is my friend.*

She sat down on the bridge over the crick, as she had so many times in her life, and watched the water meander underneath. It hadn't rained in a while, so there wasn't much water in the crick. Rebecca saw the stone she thought about so often, rising even higher from the crick bottom now that the water was so low. *My life. Stuck in the crick.* The water was moving lazily past the stone, under the bridge, and on to wherever it was bound. Going somewhere, true, but not necessarily rushing to get there. *Maybe I'm going somewhere, too. But I don't have to rush to get there. Maybe it's all right to just be a stone for a while, until I figure out where I want to go — or if I want to stay.*

Rebecca looked up. Evening had settled in while she'd been taking her little walk about her farm. The first star was beginning to peek through. The crickets had finished their symphony. A stillness was beginning to cover the earth. In the distance, an owl hooted mournfully, then hooted again. Rebecca closed her eyes and took a deep breath. Peace. *Dat and Henry will be all right. Somehow it will all work out. I won't lose my family, my way of life. God will take care of things. Like always.*

She got up and began walking toward the house. But as she neared it, her footsteps turned toward the barn instead, as if drawn by an irresistible force. She told herself she just wanted to say goodnight to Bo. But in her heart she felt a twinge of hope that someone else would be there with him. Someone else to say goodnight to. Someone else to simply be with.

She opened the barn door, letting in the remaining light from the darkening skies. Bo's stall was at the very end. The opened door cast just enough light to reveal a shadowy figure standing outside Bo's stall, rubbing Bo's face. *It's him.* Rebecca smiled a small smile. Closing the door behind her, she called out softly, "Gregory?"

"Rebecca, hi," came the voice from the shadows. "Come see Bo. Just a minute."

Rebecca started down the aisle between the stalls. It was a warm night, and all the cows had settled down to sleep outside in the pasture. She'd walked this path so many times she could do it with her eyes closed. Or like now, with hardly any light peeking through the cracks in the wooden walls. Suddenly a match flared. Gregory lit a lantern and hung it on a hook. Rebecca drew near. "How's he doing?" she asked.

"Much better. 'Specially since his favorite person's been taking care of him."

"I believe that honor belongs to you," Rebecca said, patting Bo's neck.

"Used to. Not anymore. I've been replaced, haven't I, Bo?" Gregory held Bo under the chin and nodded his head for him. Rebecca laughed. "And who replaced me?" Gregory swung Bo's head to point at Rebecca.

"Maybe you should take this act on the stage," Rebecca said, laughing.

"We just might. 'Now presenting, Gregory Pinckney and his Nodding Horse!'" Rebecca applauded, and Gregory made Bo's head bob up and down in a kind of bow. "Thank you, thank you, thank you!"

"Bo, where did you ever get such a silly master?"

"Picked me up in the sands of Carolina. Felt sorry for me."

"Gregory, do you ever miss the sands of Carolina?" Rebecca was still full of the feeling of home from her walk about the farm and wondered what Gregory felt about leaving his.

"Tell you the truth, I miss my parents a little. But so much has happened lately, I haven't had time to reflect on my life. Except to know, somehow, that it feels right to be here." He looked at Rebecca. His eyes smiled.

She covered her own smile by stroking Bo's neck. "You are doing better, aren't you, boy?"

"I don't know why I ever took him away from here," Gregory said.

"He needed more space, remember? He had other horses to run with. And you had someone to ride with."

"Wanda?"

"I've seen her ride. She's really good. And she looks really good on a horse." *Why did I add that?*

"What's that got to do with it?"

"Nothing. It's just that…it must be fun to ride with such a really good rider," Rebecca stammered.

"It is. But the looking-good part, what's that all about?"

"Well, nothing. Wanda's beautiful; everybody knows that. That must make it kind of fun, too, that's all." *How did I get into this conversation about Wanda? How do I get out of it?*

"I suppose Wanda's beautiful, but so what? So are you."

Oh my goodness, now we're talking about my looks! "That's not what I meant. I wasn't fishing for a compliment, Gregory."

"And I wasn't just tossing one out. You're just as beautiful as Wanda."

"Oh, well, thank you." Rebecca hoped she wasn't blushing. "That's nice of you to say, but I'm sure most men wouldn't agree with you."

"Then most men don't see you the way I see you," Gregory said firmly. "At least, I hope they don't."

What does he mean by that? He doesn't want most men to think I'm beautiful? Why not? Does that mean he'd be jealous?

"Of course, I haven't seen you in your full beauty, Rebecca. I haven't seen you with your hair down."

Goodness me, I have got to change the subject! "Anyway, Bo's much better; that's what's important," she said. To move away from Gregory, she entered the stall and patted Bo's side and then whacked him affectionately on the rear once or twice. But Gregory followed her inside the stall.

"Yes, that's what's important. And I really thank you, Rebecca, for nursing Bo so faithfully. He wouldn't be as recovered as he is without your love." Gregory stroked Bo's side.

"It was easy. I do love Bo." Rebecca looked up. Gregory was standing right next to her. It was almost as if she were trapped. There wasn't room to pass him by. She could probably squeeze behind Bo and go down his other side and out the stall. But that would be awkward. *Besides, do I really want to leave?*

Her hand was resting on Bo's back. Gregory was rubbing Bo's side. He moved his hand up, still rubbing. It was next to Rebecca's now. She stopped moving her hand. Slowly, delicately, Gregory placed his hand on top of hers. She raised her head. He was looking at her. His eyes shown. They pierced her own, but she didn't look away. Instead, she looked deeply into Gregory's eyes and held her breath. Slowly he began to move his face nearer and nearer. She could see his lips coming closer. She closed her eyes in anticipation.

The barn door suddenly swung open. "Rebecca, you in here?" Henry peered toward the lantern.

Gregory quickly withdrew his hand from Rebecca's, straightened, and moved out of the stall. Rebecca, staggered for a moment by the sudden intrusion, gathered herself and answered. "Down here, Henry." She unconsciously smoothed her hair. Nothing had happened to ruffle it, but she felt as if it had.

"Hey, Henry, just checking on Bo," Gregory said, as Henry approached.

"How is he?" Henry asked.

"Lots better, thanks."

"You all right?" Rebecca asked her brother.

"Been better."

Gregory sensed something was wrong. He had no idea what, but since Henry had come looking for Rebecca, he thought it best to leave. "Guess I'll be turning in," he said, giving Bo a farewell pat.

"Don't go!" Rebecca said impulsively. Gregory stopped. Henry looked at Rebecca. She swallowed. "Henry, would you mind if we told Gregory about our problem? He might be able to help."

"An Englisher?" Henry said doubtfully. He liked Gregory, but he couldn't quite see how an outsider could help in this family matter.

"That's just why he might be able to help," Rebecca explained. "He's seen more of the world; he might have run across such a situation. He went to law school, remember?"

"I don't see how knowing the law can help," Henry replied. "But I guess it can't hurt. If you want to air our dirty laundry, Rebecca, go ahead."

"I don't think it's dirty laundry. Problems happen to everyone. It's just life."

Rebecca told Gregory about Elam losing his money in a Ponzi scheme, about how he had decided to sell the farm right away, and about how Henry had always looked forward to running the farm on his own someday, when Elam passed it down to him.

When she had finished, Gregory thought for a moment. "We need to find some reason why Elam doesn't have to sell the farm, some reason that allows it to stay in the family so Henry can inherit it." He pondered some more. "How much money did Elam lose?"

"About $200,000," Henry said.

"Does he need it all back right away?"

"I don't think so," said Rebecca. "He mainly wants to have enough to start a leatherworks business, making saddles and harnesses and whatnot. I actually think Dat's just tired of farming. Don't you, Henry?"

"Could be. I don't blame him for wanting to try something else. I just wish it didn't mean selling the farm."

"Maybe it doesn't have to," Gregory said. "Do you know about the Lancaster Farmland Trust? I read about it in the paper. They've helped preserve a lot of farms around here."

"Aren't those the folks that go around buying up property to keep it from being developed?" Henry ventured.

"They don't buy it," Gregory answered. "They get land to protect by having someone give them the development rights. It's called a conservation easement."

"Why would anyone want to give away his land?" Rebecca asked.

"To keep it out of the hands of developers. If your dad opted to preserve his farm, he'd still own it, but he could also sell it to Henry. In any case, it would always be a farm." As the idea grew on Gregory, his voice became more animated.

But Henry wasn't convinced. "I still don't understand what's in it for Pop."

"At a minimum, a tax deduction, when you contribute the development rights," Gregory replied. "A deduction that might be enough for your dad to start his own leather business. With the easement he could also sell you the farm at a price you could afford without having to worry about tax consequences."

For a moment, no one spoke. Gregory could tell Henry was thinking it over. "I'm not sure I understand it all, but it sounds like you do," Henry finally said. "Thanks, Gregory. I think it's worth trying."

"I'll look into it right away," Gregory said. He saw Henry smile. Rebecca smiled, too. A sense of relief settled over them all.

"I'm going to bed," Henry said. "Coming, Rebecca?"

"Yes. Goodnight, Gregory." She looked at him warmly. The magic moment had been interrupted, but she could still sense some passion in the look he returned to her.

"Good night, Rebecca. Henry. See you in the morning."

When Rebecca lay in bed later that night, she thought how the two men she loved most in life might end up getting what each wanted, and the third man she loved would be the one who had made it happen. *Love? Is that really what I feel for Gregory?* She didn't really know what love felt like. Love for a father, a brother, a friend, a mother, an aunt, sure. But that other kind of love?

She remembered Gregory's lips coming closer to hers. She closed her eyes and could imagine their soft pinkness, their fullness, the way they slightly opened. She remembered how her heart had fluttered. And the smell. Of Bo, of the barn, of Gregory. So earthy. Vital. Sensuous. It was a moment Rebecca had never experienced before. As she drifted off to sleep, she hoped it was a moment she would experience again.

CHAPTER 19

As she walked to Mrs. Ansbacher's shop the next morning, Rebecca had no reason to feel that this day would be different. She would work at the shop all day, as usual. True, often her thoughts strayed to Gregory and all that had transpired since that day when he had driven up to their house with his horse trailer and Hanna had rented the abandoned cottage to him. Gregory at the family table, Gregory in church, Gregory in the barn, Gregory in the shop, Gregory helping harvest the tobacco. It almost seemed as if Gregory had become part of the family.

He fit in easily, despite being an Englisher. Rebecca hardly even thought of him as an Englisher anymore. And now he was helping them figure out how to keep the farm in the family and still let her father follow his dream of opening a leather shop. Yes, Gregory had become a part of their lives. Did Rebecca want him to become a permanent part?

Despite her best efforts, that question was intruding more and more into her thoughts and dreams. *Not that I can do anything about it. It's up to Gregory. And God.* Yet the question remained, threading through her mental pictures of Gregory: his easy smile, his kind, blue eyes, the way the muscles in his back responded when he lifted a bale of hay, the graceful way he would mount Bojangles, how he would suddenly burst out laughing as if he'd just heard a private joke. *So many images crowding my brain!* So many, in fact, that she sold a bolt of fabric to Lydie King and said, "Thank you very much, Mrs. Gregory." *Mrs. Gregory!*

Lydie looked at her sharply. "Why did you call me that?"

"I'm sorry, it just slipped out."

"Nothing's wrong with Gregory, is there?" Lydie asked, concerned.

"No, of course not, why would there be?" Rebecca answered. She remembered Lydie's intense interest in Gregory after the last church service. *What's going on?*

"Keep an eye on Gregory, Rebecca," Lydie pleaded. "Stay with him as much as you can."

"Why?"

"Just do it," Lydie blurted out, startling Rebecca. "I'm sorry, Rebecca," she softened. "Just indulge an ol' friend, won't you? Where does Gregory sleep?"

"In an old cottage behind the barn."

"I don't suppose Henry might sleep there for a few days?" Lydie pondered, then answered her own question. "No, of course not."

"Lydie, why are you acting this way? Is Gregory in danger?" Rebecca pressed.

Lydie returned to her usual self, masking her feelings. "I'm sure everything's all right. I'll go pay Elizabeth for the fabric."

Lydie's strange behavior worried Rebecca all the rest of the day. She desperately wanted to go home to see Gregory. Finally it was time to leave. But Mrs. Ansbacher stopped her on the way out the door. "May I speak with you a minute, Rebecca?" She was standing near the fabric bolts, checking the tags and writing the yardage information into a small black book. When Rebecca approached, she put the book in her pocket. "Do you have anything you have to do right away at the farm?"

"No. Mam and Hanna are canning chowchow, and Dat and Henry are doing field work."

"You make sure your mother saves me some of that chowchow, you hear? She makes the best I've ever had; I couldn't make it through a winter without it."

"I will."

"And what's Gregory doing?" Mrs. Ansbacher asked, a smile playing at the corner of her mouth.

"Gregory?" Rebecca answered, surprised. "Why should I know?" *Why is everybody so interested in Gregory all of a sudden?*

"Just thought you might," Mrs. Ansbacher replied, feigning innocence.

"Taking care of Bo, I guess. That's what he does most evenings. That, and reading."

"So you do know what he does!" Mrs. Ansbacher said.

Feeling herself about to blush, Rebecca turned aside to search for a pencil and paper on the countertop. "Do you want me to help you mark what we've received?"

"No, I want to talk to you about an idea I have. Let's sit at the table in the front." Mrs. Ansbacher led the way to the bay window in front, bringing her book with her. She sat, and Rebecca joined her. "Ah, it's good to get off my feet," she said, leaning down to rub one foot.

"You work too hard," Rebecca replied sympathetically.

"Coming from an Amish woman, I consider that the highest compliment." Mrs. Ansbacher smiled warmly at Rebecca. "As a matter of fact, that's kind of what I wanted to talk to you about. I believe I'm ready to work less. A lot less." She paused, gathering her thoughts. Rebecca waited patiently for her to continue. "Rebecca, how would you like to buy my shop?"

Rebecca's eyes widened. She didn't know what to say. *Buy her shop! How?*

Mrs. Ansbacher, sensing how the question had stunned her, spoke to Rebecca reassuringly. "We've talked about it before, remember? I know, we always said 'One day' and 'Wouldn't it be nice?' Well, maybe 'one day' is here, and maybe it would be nice. Wouldn't it?"

Rebecca found her voice at last. "I've always dreamed of owning a quilt shop, but now?"

"Do you have too much to do on the farm?"

"Not really. Mam and Hanna do fine with the gardening and washing. Henry does more and more, and Dat…" She knew that if her father gave up the farm, she would need a place to work, need a dream of her own to fulfill. If he didn't, and Henry took over, she knew her brother would be only too glad to have her work in the quilt shop. Henry could always get some hired help to replace Elam. In fact, more and more Rebecca had been fantasizing that that someone might be Gregory.

"Then what is it?"

"I don't have enough money to buy your shop, Mrs. Ansbacher."

"I've thought about that, Rebecca. I thought you might consider using that money you made from selling your quilt in New York as a down payment. Five hundred dollars, wasn't it?"

"Yes, but that wouldn't make much of a down payment."

"I don't need much." Mrs. Ansbacher opened her little book. "Then I would rent it to you for $1,000 a month until you got enough money to get a mortgage. As you know from doing the books, we've got a good business here. This summer…" She leafed through a page or two. "This summer we've made about $5,000 a month profit, so if you bank $4,000 a month, you could probably get a mortgage in a year or two. And if you sell any more of your quilts, it could be sooner than that." Mrs. Ansbacher paused, waiting for Rebecca's response. "Meantime, I don't mind waiting. I know you'll be good for the money."

"But what will you do?" asked Rebecca.

"Retire," replied Mrs. Ansbacher with a smile. "Maybe move to Pinecraft."

"Florida?" cried Rebecca. Pinecraft was a community of Amish people established near Sarasota many years ago. If she were to own a quilt shop, Rebecca would feel more comfortable if Mrs. Ansbacher were around to ask for advice.

"Don't worry, Rebecca. I wouldn't move anytime soon," Mrs. Ansbacher said. "And I might just go only during the winter. The point is, you don't have to worry about me; I'll be fine. At the very least, I'll have time to make my own quilts for a change. Then I can give them to you to sell!"

My own quilt shop! I could set up quilting bees right here in the shop, maybe even start a class for Englishers to teach them how to quilt. "I don't know what to say, Mrs. Ansbacher. Thank you."

"You don't have to say anything right now, Rebecca. Think about it, that's all." Mrs. Ansbacher closed her book. "I have no idea what your plans are. I know you want to get married someday and raise a family. Owning a shop is actually easier when you're raising children than when working a farm, I've always thought. And you'd have your brother and others here to help you through any rough patches. You Amish are wonderful at supporting each other. You'd have to work more hours and have more responsibilities, but I don't think your life would change all that much. Do you?"

Maybe it wouldn't. Getting married would be the biggest change. And that might not be happening anytime soon. I don't want to marry Jacob. I've decided. Marrying Johnny would be fun, but he's just not stable enough. So there's really no one, except maybe…What am I thinking?

"I said, 'Do you?' Rebecca?" Mrs. Ansbacher leaned forward to get her attention.

"Oh, sorry," Rebecca said. "No, I guess maybe my life wouldn't change all that much. I would love to own the shop, Mrs. Ansbacher, you know that. And I thank you for helping me see how I might afford it. I definitely will think about it. Thank you so much for the offer."

"Rebecca, I would like nothing better than to see you take over this shop. I've put a lot of years in here. It's a good shop, a good business, and I don't want to just sell it to some stranger. But I'm ready for a little less work and a little more rest. Speaking of which," Mrs. Ansbacher continued, "would you mind helping me put away this order before you go home?"

Desperate as she was to see Gregory, Rebecca knew she had to stay and help, especially in light of Mrs. Ansbacher's generous offer to sell her the shop. So about forty-five minutes later Rebecca found herself walking home more briskly than usual, a big smile on her face. She was happy with the thought of owning a quilt shop. She could work on her own quilts in the room out back, especially during the winter, when business was slow. She would be with people. Rebecca had always enjoyed the company of others. And she would be earning a living, not just being a farmer's wife. She knew that her mother and many of her friends were a lot more than "just" wives. They worked hard; many of them even ran the business side of the farm. They raised happy and respectable children. And they had a great deal to be proud of — if they had been prone to pride. But there was nothing wrong with running a shop for a living. Plenty of Amish did it. Why not her?

Since Rebecca often worked late on Saturdays, she knew the family meal would be finished and a covered dish of food left for her on the table. But she had other things on her mind besides food. As she passed the house, she could see Hanna and her mother moving about the kitchen, canning. She hurried to the barn, entered, and looked quickly down to the end. She could see that nobody was there, only Bo. Rebecca walked to the horse and petted him. "Hello, Bo. Where's your master?" Bo nuzzled her playfully. He was feeling frisky. Gregory had said that soon he would be ready to ride.

Rebecca reached into her pocket and pulled out a small sugar cube, which she gave to Bo. "Not here, huh?" She gave Bo a final pat and walked out the barn.

In the far field she could see her father and brother, working until the last rays of the sun would force them to quit. They had mended their relationship enough to be able to work together. Rebecca had no doubt that time and a little patience would do the rest. And there was always the hope of Gregory's land trust idea to mend all fences. She turned toward the cottage in back of the barn. "Gregory!" she called out. After a moment, he stepped outside.

"Hi," he said. Rebecca noticed the taut, bronze skin of his chest as Gregory finished buttoning up his shirt. "Sorry, I was reading, but it's so hot in there…" He turned his back on her and tucked in his shirt, then turned back. "What's up?"

"Gregory, are you all right?" Rebecca asked, the concern obvious in her voice.

"Sure, why wouldn't I be?"

"It's just, Lydie King said some strange things in the shop today, almost like you were in danger or something. Are you?"

Gregory paused before answering. He had told Doc Jenkins about the box full of vials. Doc had advised him to wait until the results were back from the blood-sample testing, which would probably be on Monday. It might not even be necessary to go to the police, he'd explained, if the samples were positive. Or, if they were positive, the police would have more reason to believe Gregory when he told them about the hidden freezer. But all day Gregory had been debating if he should tell Rebecca. He didn't want to frighten her, but he also felt a tremendous urge to let her know what was going on.

"I've found out some things I want to tell you about," he began. "I think I know what happened to Dandelion and Beauty, and what almost happened to Bo. I think they were killed."

"Killed! By who?"

"By Ivan Heminger."

"Why would Mr. Heminger want to kill his own horses?"

"To collect the insurance. I think he did it once, about twenty years ago, and got away with it."

"I do remember hearing about one of his horses dying suddenly."

"Did you also hear that Rex Smith also died suddenly about six months later?"

"Who's he?"

"Ivan's trainer. And probably his partner in crime. His name wasn't Rex Smith. It was Juan Garcia. Juan had studied at a pharmacy school in Florida."

"How do you know all this, Gregory?"

"I called a lawyer friend of mine in South Carolina. He does a lot of cases that require investigation. It wasn't too hard for him to get one of his investigators to snoop around and come up with something. I figure that in pharmacy school, Rex — I mean, Juan — learned how to mix chemicals. And he may have learned how to mix some that would kill a horse and not leave any evidence. And if my theory holds true, they wouldn't leave any evidence if they were used on a human either."

"You think Rex Smith was killed by his own poison?"

"As administered by our friend Ivan," Gregory said confidently.

"Why would he do that?"

"Maybe Juan was in on the horse killing. And maybe he decided he wanted a little more money for his silence. Blackmail is an old and honorable tactic among thieves."

"I never much liked Mr. Heminger," Rebecca said. "But I never thought he was a murderer."

"I can't prove it. But there's some potentially damning evidence sitting in a freezer in Rex's old kitchen. Some vials with liquids in them. I told Doc Jenkins about them, but he thinks we should wait for the insurance company's blood-sample results."

"How did you find them?"

"I went snooping."

"Gregory! Did anybody see you?"

"Nobody was home, as far as I could tell."

"Does Lydie King know about this?"

"I don't see how she could."

"But she was so concerned today in the shop. Oh, Gregory, don't do anything careless, all right? Don't do any more snooping!" In her desperation, Rebecca grabbed Gregory's arm.

He put his hand over hers, gently. "I won't, Rebecca. From now on, I'll let the police do the snooping." Rebecca tried to be reassured, but she wasn't. It all seemed too frightening: killing horses for insurance and killing Rex Smith.

Gregory decided that this was enough talk about Ivan and horses. "How was your day at work?" he asked.

In her concern, Rebecca had almost forgotten her good news. "Mrs. Ansbacher wants to sell me her quilt shop!" she said excitedly.

"Rebecca, that's great! Really?"

"Yes, really! She has it all figured out, financially and everything."

"I'm so happy for you," Gregory said, his own voice rising. "What did you tell her?"

"That I'd think about it. Will you help me think about it, Gregory? It's such a big decision."

"Of course, Rebecca, I'd love to help in any way I can."

"You can do the legal things, help me figure out a mortgage, maybe, go over the numbers with me — " Rebecca stopped herself. She was practically babbling. She took a deep breath and said more calmly, "Anyway, that's my big news."

"I've got big news, too. I'm going to take Bo for his first real ride."

"When?"

"Tonight!"

"That's great, Gregory. I'm so happy for you."

"Come with me to the cottage a minute, will you?" Rebecca nodded and followed him out of the barn and down to his cottage. "Wait here," he said, and ducked inside.

Rebecca sat on the bench outside his door. She was tired, she realized, from the excitement about the shop and tired from worry about Gregory.

When he returned, he was carrying a pair of his jeans. "Think these might fit you?"

"Are they yours?"

"Yep."

"Why would I want to wear your jeans?"

"Well, I didn't think you'd want to ride in your dress." Gregory smiled at Rebecca, a mischievous smile.

"Ride? What do you mean, ride?"

"I mean on a horse. On a horse named Bo, to be exact." The mischievous smile changed into a huge grin. "If he's ready to ride again, I think the person most responsible for his being able to do so should ride him." He held out the jeans to Rebecca.

"Me? I can't ride."

"It's not *verboten*, is it?"

"Not exactly. It's just Dat and Mam never allowed us to. Didn't see much use for it. And they were afraid we might get hurt. Like Hanna."

"You know Bo is gentle, don't you?" She nodded. "But as for being useful, I admit, it won't be a useful ride. But it sure will be fun. Why not have a little fun to celebrate the day you got offered the quilt shop?"

"I'm not even sure I know how to ride," Rebecca mused.

"That's where the magic solution comes in," Gregory said. "I'll ride, too. I'll ride in front; all you'll have to do is hold on."

"Both of us ride Bo? Won't that be too much for him?"

"Not with what you weigh." Gregory laughed. "I bet he won't even feel you. Except he will know that he'll be carrying his two favorite people. And for a symbol that Bo has returned to his old self, I don't think you can beat that. You go up to the apple orchard; I'll saddle up Bo and pick you up there. Henry and Elam are in the far field. Your mother and Hanna are in the kitchen. We'll ride away from the farm. No one will even know."

"You have it all figured out, don't you?"

Gregory smiled at her again. But this time it wasn't his mischievous smile. This time it was his kind, gentle smile. Rebecca might almost say it was his loving smile. "I confess I've thought about it a lot since last night in the barn." He held out the jeans again. "You can change in the cottage." Rebecca took the jeans. "See you in the orchard."

He turned and walked quickly toward the barn. Rebecca considered the jeans in her hand. *I'll look stupid.* Then she had another thought. *I don't care!* She went into the cottage, put on the jeans, and almost ran to the orchard.

When he led Bo to the orchard, Gregory found Rebecca leaning against a tree, eating an apple. She did look a little strange, his jeans peeking out below the hem of her dress, and he almost laughed. "Don't you dare!" she warned him, but with a smile. "If I look silly, it's all your fault."

"You look wonderful. Here you go, Bo." He reached up, plucked an apple, and offered it to his horse. Bo grabbed it with his mouth, chomped down on it twice, and it disappeared down his throat. He shook his mane in appreciation.

"Ready?" Gregory asked.

"I guess so."

He led the horse a few feet away while Rebecca followed. Then he swung himself up into the saddle and stretched a hand down to her. She grasped it, and he hauled her up behind him. She circled his body with her arms. "You all right?" he asked.

"Yes," she answered simply. In fact, she felt more than all right. She felt fine, sitting astride Bo, high off the ground, his strong body between her legs. Rebecca shuddered a little. Not from any chill in the gathering dusk. From a tingling of joy.

"Okay, here we go," Gregory said, and he clucked Bo into motion.

At first they simply walked the horse, letting him get used to them. Rebecca's body swayed a little, left to right. Holding onto Gregory, she felt his swaying, too. It was as if they were doing a little dance, sitting on top of Bo. Their two bodies moved as one to the easy rhythm of the horse beneath them. Rebecca closed her eyes. The evening air smelled sweet, the only sound the noise of Bo's hooves as they struck the soft earth. She sighed. *I'm so content.*

They reached the end of the apple orchard. An empty field stretched before them. "A little faster now," Gregory said, and he kicked Bo's sides lightly. Bo started into a canter. At first the new rhythm jostled Rebecca, and she had to hold on more tightly to Gregory. He was bouncing to his own, different rhythm. For a short distance they jostled back and forth as Bo sped over the earth, trying to find a harmony of motion. It was a bit awkward, banging into Gregory's back with her body, but it wasn't an unpleasant feeling. Rebecca found it strangely exciting.

At last their three bodies settled into the same rhythm, and they cantered across the field. The wind felt good on Rebecca's face. She could feel her covering beginning to slip, but she didn't want to let go of Gregory to try to fix it. She didn't want to let go of Gregory at all.

"This is fun!" he yelled back at one point.

"It is!" she shouted back. And then an impulse came over her, an impulse she couldn't resist, one which, thinking back on it later, astounded her with its intensity. Rebecca suddenly dug the heels of her sturdy black shoes into Bo's flanks — one, two, three times — and Bo broke into a gallop.

Rebecca pulled her body hard against Gregory's back, holding him with all her might. Up and down together they went as Bojangles flew across the ground. Rebecca buried her face into Gregory's neck, smelling his strong, masculine sweat. She inhaled deeply. The smell of him filled her nostrils. She clasped her body to his ever more tightly. On and on they pounded over the earth.

Gregory screamed. "Yeeeehiiiiiiii!" His voice boomed over the land, a cry of pure ecstasy. Rebecca heard the noise from Gregory's lungs through the ear pressed into his back. It sounded primeval.

She lost track of time. She had no idea how long they had galloped together when Gregory pulled up on the reins and slowed Bo into a walk. The transition forced her to open her eyes and lift her head. She was panting a little from the excitement. She didn't recognize where she was, but she didn't care. She was with Gregory.

He pulled Bo to a stop, swung his leg over Bo's neck, and jumped down to the ground, stretching his arms out to Rebecca. She leaned forward, and he grabbed her under the arms, lifted her off Bo, and set her down in front of him. He didn't remove his hands, but instead circled his arms around her back. Rebecca looked up into Gregory's face. The look he gave her took her breath away. And then he kissed her, gently, almost delicately. She put her arms around him, pulling him toward her, running her fingers through his hair. She wanted to gobble him up. She wanted the kiss to never end.

Finally it did. Gregory pulled her into himself, clasped her head to his shoulder, and embraced her so tightly that Rebecca could feel his heart beating inside his chest. "Rebecca!" he murmured. "Rebecca..."

Rebecca didn't say anything. Her heart was too full to speak. She just held Gregory as hard as she could, feeling the aliveness of her body, feeling the blood rushing through her veins, wanting to mold her body into his, to make them one.

He kissed her neck and pulled back to look at her. For a moment they stared at each other, too dazzled to speak or even to move, as if any extraneous word or movement would break the spell. He slowly tugged at her hair. What was he doing? Then she realized. Her covering! It had come loose during the ride. Gregory pulled it all the way out of her hair and let it fall to the ground. He gently undid her bun, pulling her hair down around her shoulders. *No one has ever seen me this way,* she thought. *It's like I'm naked.*

With both hands Gregory laid her hair out about her neck and shoulders. "You are so beautiful," he whispered. "So beautiful." And he leaned in and kissed her again.

Later that night, Rebecca and Gregory lay in separate beds, but they were thinking the same thing. *It was wonderful! I can't wait to go riding again! And the kiss!...* With the sweetest of thoughts of each other and of their special day, they drifted off to dream of love.

Over at Cedar Ridge Farm, Ivan Heminger had other dreams.

CHAPTER 20

Ivan had spent a restless Saturday night planning, plotting, and dreaming of his ultimate release from the demons that had been haunting him ever since he had witnessed Gregory snooping around his property. He had managed to make it through a long afternoon, and now he waited impatiently on his veranda for Gregory to arrive.

He wasn't drinking — at least, not heavily. He wanted all his senses about him on this night. He would need them if his plan was to succeed. There hadn't been a hitch so far. He had called Gregory on his cell phone — the number provided him by Wanda — and told him that he had some news about how the horses had died, news that might make Ivan rethink his theory that a virus had been the cause. Gregory had been surprisingly amenable to coming over that evening so Ivan could "show him something." *Probably thinks he's got me*, thought Ivan. *Well, I'm not so easily got.*

As for arranging to be alone with Gregory, Wanda had told him she was going out with Vinny. To her surprise, Ivan had acted pleased. *Who knows, having Vinny in the family might be a good thing. But only if I settle up first.* He had taken care of Liz by handing her $300 and reminding her about the special pre–Labor Day sale at the outlet malls. He'd even asked her to buy him some shirts, something she was always begging to do and which he always denied her. So Liz had been pleased to jump in her BMW and speed away. The way she loved to shop, Ivan knew she wouldn't be home for hours.

He had unfurled a tarp in back of Rex's shack. In case Gregory proved too big to carry back to his car, he could drag him. He had the beers on ice in a cooler in the kitchen, two mugs chilling in the freezer, some cashews in a bowl on the small table on the veranda, and, most important of all, a vial of one of Rex's concoctions ready to go. He pulled the vial out of his pocket, held it up to the fading light, and smiled. *This will knock him out. And then…*Ivan looked at his watch: 6:45. He'd told Gregory to come around seven. He popped a couple of cashews into his mouth and sat down to wait. He chewed the cashews. *Extra salty. That'll make him want a beer.*

Gregory had been shocked that Ivan had called. His first impulse had been to say he was busy — after all, if his theory were true, Ivan had killed before and wouldn't hesitate to do so again. *But he's got no reason to suspect me of anything. He doesn't know I know about the vials in the hidden freezer. Or about Rex Smith's past. So what could it be?* He knew Rebecca would be worried, however, so he didn't tell her where he was going, just "out for a little while." He'd promised not to snoop, but this wasn't snooping.

What a wonderful Sunday it had been. Gregory had slept like a child the night before. When Henry had come to invite him to come to church with them again, Gregory had been elated. Ever since he'd awakened, he had ached to see Rebecca.

On the ride to church, Henry had prattled on about the corn, praising some crops as they passed by, criticizing others. Gregory had tried to uphold his end of the conversation, but he hadn't succeeded very well. He had been too busy watching Rebecca's every move in the buggy in front of them. Through the small window in the rear, he could see the back of her head. When she'd turned to speak to Hanna at her side, he had been able to see her profile. Once, she had turned all the way and smiled back at him. It had caused Gregory to break into a big smile himself. *Just the way she looks at me makes my heart jump.*

After the long church service, Gregory had been glad that the men and women ate separately. He hadn't wanted to chitchat with Rebecca in front of others. He had wanted to speak with her alone. He had finally gotten the chance when they'd returned home, and everyone had gone about their business.

She had met him outside his cottage, and they had walked to the woods at the back of the farm. They had moved in silence, each feeling the awkwardness two people sometimes feel when something of significance has occurred, but they don't know how to begin to relate to each other again. They can't simply start kissing. Yet it seems somehow silly to talk about anything less significant than the momentous question of how they feel about one another.

When they were out of sight, Gregory had taken Rebecca's hand. This simple gesture had freed her feelings so much that a flood of words had flown from her mouth. She'd told stories of how they'd had picnics in these woods when she was little, how her great uncle Elmer, who'd married an Englisher, had always brought soda pop and her grandmother had always made a big pot of chicken noodle soup, of how she'd once spied a hawk's nest and had climbed the tree and actually seen the baby hawks in the nest. Gregory had let her talk, relishing the sweet melody of her voice, until he finally had not been able to resist and had taken her in his arms and kissed her, right in midsentence.

The words had then ceased and the intimacies had followed. Lingering kisses. Rapt gazes. Gently stroked cheeks. Soft "I love you's" whispered into ears or murmured into warm necks. Rebecca had taken off her covering and loosened her hair, and Gregory had run his fingers through it, over and over, exulting in its luxuriance. Every touch of her had filled him with a happiness he had never known, nor ever dreamed of knowing. He had passed the afternoon in a daze, yet he had simultaneously never been more alive.

As he parked in Ivan's driveway Sunday evening, Gregory sighed at the sweet memories of his joyous afternoon. But he forced the pleasant thoughts from his mind. The matter at hand would need his full attention.

"Up here!" shouted Ivan, and Gregory mounted the veranda stairs. "Hello. Thanks for coming."

"You have news about the horses; of course I came."

"We can get to that in a minute. There's something I want to show you. But first let's sit and talk for a minute." He showed Gregory to a chair, sat down, and offered him some cashews. Gregory took a handful, and Ivan stuffed a few into his own mouth. "You know, Gregory, I never did get to offer my apologies for what happened to your horse on my property. I feel kinda bad about it."

"It wasn't your fault, Ivan." Gregory had decided that remaining friendly was the best strategy, even if it involved hiding his real feelings.

"I'm glad you think that, Gregory. I thought maybe you sought out that reporter because you were angry."

"I didn't seek him out, Ivan. He came to me."

"Really? Why?"

"To satisfy his curiosity, I guess."

"Any idea what made him so curious? Or who?"

Gregory pondered his answer. He wasn't about to bring Doc Jenkins into the conversation. "Sorry, Ivan, you'll have to do your own snooping."

"Snooping, yes..." Ivan looked at Gregory, a small smile on his lips. Gregory had an instant's concern. *Does he know I was here?* But Ivan changed the subject. "Wanda tells me you're from South Carolina, up here looking for your biological mother."

"That's right."

"Any luck?"

Why all this interest in my past? "To tell you the truth, Ivan, I haven't had much time to focus on that. And with what happened to Bo, even less."

"Got any clues?" Ivan took some more cashews. Gregory took a handful and began eating them one by one.

"Just that her name was Mae Yoder. And that she left a baby quilt she apparently had made for me."

"A quilt, huh? What's the pattern?"

He's interested in the pattern on the quilt? What's going on here? And what does any of this have to do with the horses' deaths? "Nine squares with butterflies appliqued inside them. Are you interested in quilt patterns, Ivan?"

"No, no, just curious," Ivan answered. So far, what Lydie had told him was panning out. Gregory might indeed be his son. But Ivan had spent the night convincing himself that even if he were, he still needed to do what he had to do. "Let me know if there's anything I can do to help you find her, Gregory."

"Thanks, Ivan, I will."

"These cashews are making me thirsty. I'm having a beer. You want one, Gregory?"

"Yeah, they're real salty. Sure."

"Got some on ice. Might take the sting out of the day. It's always too hot in August up here."

Ivan went into the house. Gregory got up and looked out across the courtyard at the barn and the pastures beyond. A lot had happened since Wanda had ridden into his life that day months ago. He felt sorry for her, having Ivan for a father. *He poisoned his own daughter's horse. That man is capable of anything. Stay alert!*

Ivan returned with two beers poured into frosty mugs. He handed one to Gregory. "Cheers!" he said and raised his glass. They both drank. "Oh, that tastes good. Yours all right?" he asked Gregory.

"Fine."

Ivan took another swallow, ate some cashews, then drank more beer. He held up the bowl to Gregory. Gregory took a handful, ate them, then took a swig of beer. When Ivan didn't speak, he decided to get things moving. "Now, what did you find out about Bo?"

"It's something in Rex's shack." Ivan took a swallow of beer. "Bring your beer, and I'll show you."

He led the way down the stairs and back toward the shack. "That newspaper article made it sound like there was something suspicious about Rex's death. That's ridiculous, of course," Ivan began. *Of course,* thought Gregory. "It was a heart attack, says so right there on the death certificate." *Of course.* "If it wasn't a heart attack, what are they implying, that Rex was killed? By me? The best trainer I'd ever had? That's even more ridiculous." *Of course.*

They had reached the shack. Ivan opened the door, gestured for Gregory to enter, followed him, and closed the door. With the curtains down, and the sun sinking fast, there wasn't much light inside, but Ivan didn't turn on any lights. "Follow me," he said, and led the way to the kitchenette.

Gregory had to pretend he'd never been inside this place, although he remembered it in vivid detail. "Anybody stay here after Rex?"

"All my trainers, sometimes a farmhand. But mainly Rex." Ivan stopped when they'd reached the kitchenette. "Notice anything peculiar?"

Gregory answered honestly, "No, looks like any other kitchenette."

"How about now?" Ivan asked, opening the cabinet doors underneath the sink.

Gregory was beginning to feel uncomfortable. He took another swallow of beer before answering. "I don't see anything peculiar, Ivan."

"That's because you're not looking close enough, Gregory. Look there; see how the dust's all disturbed underneath the sink?"

"Yes. So what?"

"So somebody's been in here snooping around."

Gregory was beginning to perspire. *It's so stuffy.* He tried to answer calmly. "Why would anyone want to snoop around underneath the kitchen sink?"

"Because of this." Ivan knelt, found the indentation, released the lock on the back wall, and moved it slowly aside. He looked back up at Gregory. "Bend down and see." Gregory placed his beer on the countertop and knelt beside Ivan. "It's a hidden freezer," Ivan said. "Open it."

Gregory was beginning to feel weak, and more than a little dizzy. He shook his head vigorously, attempting to clear it, then opened the freezer. He knew what was inside, but pretended he didn't. "What do you see?" Ivan asked.

"Some sort of box."

"Take it out," Ivan commanded, standing up.

Gregory took out the box and stood up. He had to steady himself by holding onto the countertop. Ivan took the small box from his hands and opened it. He held it for Gregory to see inside. "Vials. Any idea what's in them?" Gregory asked.

"Drugs," Ivan answered.

"What kind of drugs?" Gregory unbuttoned the top button of his shirt. He was beginning to perspire.

"You tell me, Gregory," Ivan said, with the hint of a smile.

Gregory noticed that one of the vials was missing. "How should I know?" he asked.

"You're right, you don't know. At least not yet. You haven't had time to test them. So I'll tell you." He looked straight at Gregory. "The kind of drugs somebody might use to poison a horse."

"What?" Gregory managed. He could hardly talk. Now he was really feeling woozy. *I gotta get some air!*

"Isn't that what you thought when you found this box last week?" Gregory wanted to protest, but he couldn't find the words. "That I used these drugs to kill Dandelion and Beauty, and almost Bo? And Rex before that? And you know what, Gregory? You're absolutely right!" Ivan smiled maniacally at Gregory. "But you know what else? There's another kind of drug in these little concoctions of Rex's. They used to call it a mickey in the old days. I don't know what they call it now. But its effect is the same. Feeling a little strange?"

Gregory tried to answer. "I…You…" He couldn't complete the sentence. He gulped for some air. *I've got to get out of here.* He started for the front door, took two steps, then his knees buckled and he fell to the floor, semiconscious.

"Now you're not feeling much of anything, are you, Gregory?" Ivan stood over his inert body. "And you won't be feeling anything for a long, long while. Like forever." Ivan placed the box on the counter, took the vial out of one pocket, a syringe out of another, removed the plastic cap, and filled it with the orange liquid. He put the empty vial on the counter and moved toward Gregory with steady purpose. He knelt beside him and took his pulse. Satisfied he was still alive, he pinched Gregory's skin and prepared to insert the needle. "Sorry to do this, son. If you really are my son."

As Ivan moved the needle slowly toward Gregory's arm, a calm voice from the shadows stopped him. "Is that how you did it to me?"

Lydie King stepped forward. Ivan dropped Gregory's arm and stood up. "Lydia Mae!" he shouted.

"Drugged me, then dragged me to your bedroom and raped me?"

"What are you doing here?" he cried in complete bewilderment.

"I've been keeping an eye on you. When I overheard Gregory tell Rebecca at church he had something to do this afternoon, I decided to see if that something included you. So I walked over here. Saw all your careful preparations. When I watched you add salt to those nuts, I had an idea what you were up to. When I saw you withdraw that vial on the porch, I knew my idea was right."

"Get out of here!"

"Would you really kill your own son?" Lydie asked calmly.

"This is none of your business!"

"A son is always a mother's business, Ivan."

"How are you going to stop me?" he asked, lowering his voice to a menacing growl.

"I would have said, 'Reason with you,' but I can see by the look in your eye that that won't work."

"Then get out of here and leave me alone," he snarled. "Go back to your home and sweep. That's all you've ever been good for, Lydie Mae, cleaning house. I used to watch you every day when you worked for my parents. So meticulous. So perfect. Never leaving a speck of dirt. In your simple covering and plain, brown dress. But that dress couldn't hide your beautiful body. It only made me want you more." He approached her. "You wouldn't let me kiss you then," he leered. "How about now?"

For an answer, she slapped him hard across the face.

"Why you little — !" Ivan lunged at her, but Lydie dodged him. Spying a broom leaning in a corner of the kitchenette, she grabbed it and stepped back into the living room, where she'd have more room to swing it. Ivan laughed at her. "You're going to stop me with a broom, Lydia Mae?"

He took a threatening step toward her. She raised the broom and jabbed him in the stomach, stopping him. Surprised, Ivan narrowed his eyes and raised his arm to hit her, but Lydie swung the broom, catching him full on the side of his face. His head snapped to the right. Lydie tightened her grip on the broom. "You don't do that to me," he growled.

Ivan feinted to his left, Lydie swung the broom to respond, but he moved quickly to his right and backhanded her across the face, knocking her down. "How'd that feel, Lydia Mae!" he screamed.

He tried to kick her, but Lydie rolled out of the way. When he turned and moved toward her, she quickly stuck the broom handle between his legs, tripping him. Trying to break his fall, Ivan hit the floor with the hand holding the syringe, forcing him to drop it. It skittered across the floor in her direction.

For a frozen minute, both Ivan and Lydie looked at the syringe. Then they both scrambled to reach it. Ivan was closer, but Lydie swept the syringe toward her with the broom. She grabbed it as Ivan lunged. Lydie scrambled to avoid him, but the needle accidentally plunged into Ivan's side as he fell toward her, the force of his fall pushing the plunger down as he hit the floor.

Ivan screamed. He rolled over and yanked the syringe from his side, flinging it away. Lydie scrambled to her feet. "I'll kill you!" he shouted, wild with rage.

He started toward her. "Stop, Ivan, stop!" Lydie shouted. "You don't have time!" She held the broom in front of her to ward him off if he continued. Ivan stopped, puzzled. "You could probably kill me. Gregory, too. But that would take time. Time you don't have, Ivan.

"What do you mean?" he spat out, advancing again.

"The poison! The poison, Ivan! It's working its way through you. Your only chance is to get to a hospital fast!"

Ivan stood still, unclear what to do. She ran to him. "It was an accident. I didn't mean to do it. I just wanted to stop you from harming our son." She turned him toward the door. In his confusion, he let her push him forward. "Please, Ivan, go! Drive as fast as you can. Go!" She shoved him. He turned, murder in his eyes. "Save yourself, Ivan!" Lydie pleaded.

For a frozen moment, neither of them moved. Then Ivan's eyes widened with understanding, and he bolted out the door. Lydie followed him outside the shack and watched as Ivan sprinted toward his car. "Dear Lord, don't let him die," she whispered.

Ivan yanked open the car door, jumped in, and sped away, tires squealing.

Lydie ran to Gregory and knelt beside him. She took his pulse. Stable. She wasn't too worried. She remembered that when Ivan had drugged her all those years ago, she had eventually simply awakened. She'd felt a little confused, but there'd been no side effects. At least, not from the drug.

Lydie's first impulse was to drag Gregory to his car, using the tarp, as Ivan had intended. But when she'd struggled for many minutes and had managed to pull him only as far as the front door, she abandoned that idea. Gregory would wake up. He'd remember following Ivan to Rex's shack, and that would probably be all he'd remember.

She made him comfortable by placing a pillow under his head. She found an old quilt and covered him. It was August, and not that cold, but she couldn't help herself. She felt an overwhelming urge to mother her son to make up for all the lost years. So, she tucked in her child.

With Gregory comfortable, Lydie turned her thoughts to the scene at hand. She figured out that the box of vials must go back in the freezer, since its door was still open under the cabinet sink. She used the broom to sweep away any indication of a recent disturbance, then placed it back in the corner. The syringe, however, presented a problem. She could leave it as evidence of what Ivan had tried to do, if he died and the police investigated. Or she could dispose of it elsewhere, assuming Ivan would live, and Gregory would simply go home. And then what would happen? *Too much to try to predict,* she decided. So she tucked the syringe into her pocket.

Satisfied that she had done all she could, Lydie knelt beside Gregory and looked lovingly at him. He was breathing regularly. His features were relaxed. She bent forward and whispered, "I love you, son," kissed him gently on the cheek, rose, and walked quietly out the door, feeling strangely content. As Amish women had done for centuries, she had taken care of her men. Both of them.

CHAPTER 21

"The water supply is really an asset," said Mr. Lowery, the man from the Lancaster Farmland Trust. Gregory and the whole Zook family were standing on the banks of the crick, watching the water rush by. A huge thunderstorm had rattled the skies the night before and with it had come a downpour, followed by a steady rain. "*Hoch wasser!*" Hanna cried delightedly. "High water!" The crick was so full it looked more like a river. But the sun was blazing now, midafternoon, as Mr. Lowery finished his walk about the property that Elam might preserve through the land trust.

Gregory had really enjoyed the walk. There were parts of the farm he hadn't paid much attention to, and it was nice to see them through the eyes of Mr. Lowery, someone with a passion for land and its beauty. He had particularly admired the apple orchard. He'd dug up soil in various places around the property. "So rich! No wonder you want to keep farming it," he'd said to Henry. Henry had beamed, and Gregory could see that even Elam was proud.

Near the woods at the back of the property, Mr. Lowery had stopped several times to point out flowers that were worth preserving: buttercups, violets, corn flowers. "*Sheny blumen,*" Mabel had murmured. Pretty flowers, indeed. "Adds to the preservation value of the land," Mr. Lowery had confided.

"I thought they were just weeds," Hanna had exclaimed.

"They're not weeds, Hanna," Mabel had responded. "Now, don't interrupt Mr. Lowery. It's not polite."

"I'm not interrupting; I'm just talking."

In another part of the woods, Hanna had smiled and said, "Hey, Mabel, 'member when we used to sneak in here and wade in the crick? We weren't supposed to go in the crick, 'cause our parents would warn, 'Snakes!'" she'd explained to the others.

"No, I don't remember!"

"Sure you do, Mabel. That's how you met Elam, 'cause our farms were next to each other. And the time we went home barefoot, but didn't see the cow patties — oh, Pop was mad about that, bringing manure into the house."

"Hanna!"

Henry had added a few memories, too. Of how he'd snuck into the woods to try to smoke some of the tobacco leaves he'd rolled up to resemble a cigarette. "'Bout coughed myself to death! Dumbest thing I ever did."

"Not hardly," Elam had replied, to everyone's amusement.

"How 'bout you, Pop? You grew up here, too."

"Well, seems like your mother and me might've had a few dates in these woods."

"Elam Zook!" Mabel had cried out, blushing. And all had laughed some more. Except Gregory and Rebecca. They'd exchanged a quick look. These woods now held happy memories for them, too.

The walkabout had reignited many such memories for the whole family. They'd been so busy farming, working the land, going on with their lives, they'd forgotten about all the beauty of where they lived. And of all the living that beauty had witnessed. *If nothing else comes of this land trust idea, at least it's reminded us of the wonder of God's green earth,* Gregory had thought.

But it seemed that something might come of the idea. Gregory had done some research, Rebecca and Henry had persuaded Elam to at least talk to the Trust, and, surprisingly, Mabel had been quite strong in pushing the idea herself. And so Elam had made the call, the Trust had been interested, and there they were, having completed the walkabout.

"Seventy acres, right Mr. Zook?" Mr. Lowery asked, looking past the crick at the surrounding fields.

"That's right," said Elam.

For a minute, everyone turned and looked. Corn as far as the eye could see, the next field flush with hay, burnished by the sun, cows chewing contentedly in the pasture, workhorses and mules grazing nearby, the glistening white house, the barn, the tobacco shed, the corn crib. A beautiful place. A place worth preserving.

"I think the Farmland Trust will be very interested in continuing the conversation," Mr. Lowery said. Then he addressed the group. "I'll be frank with you. These transfers often get bogged down because of family disputes." He looked at each Zook carefully. "Are you sure you want to give away the development rights to this land, in perpetuity?"

"As long as Henry can still farm it," Elam said. The others nodded.

"He can, and his descendants can, if we make it a charitable remainder trust," Mr. Lowery said. "But we can talk about all that later." He took off his hat and wiped his brow. "All right, then, we'll get started on the paperwork and the rest. If all goes smoothly, we can have the deal in place in three to four months."

"Thank you, Mr. Lowery," Elam said, shaking his hand. He seemed relieved.

Taking action always helps, Gregory thought. He was so glad he had helped bring the family back into harmony.

They said their good-byes, and Mr. Lowery drove away. Elam turned to Gregory. "Thank you, Gregory. Where'd you learn about conservation anyway?"

"I trained as a lawyer."

"We don't like lawyers," Hanna proclaimed.

"Speak for yourself, Hanna," Mabel said. Then she smiled at Gregory and began walking toward the house, Hanna following.

Is she warming up to me? wondered Gregory. *Even though I'm English?*

"Well, it might be Labor Day, but that don't count for farmers," Elam said. "Come on, Henry, let's see to that corn."

"Sure thing, Dat!" Henry answered happily.

Father and son headed toward the barn, walking side by side, in earnest conversation about farming.

Gregory and Rebecca found themselves alone at the edge of the woods. "Why were you so quiet during the tour?" he asked her.

"Just enjoying my family, the farm, being with you." She looked at Gregory, her eyes sparkling.

It felt good to relax for a change. The last few weeks had been hectic. After his visit with Ivan, Gregory had awakened in Rex's shack, terribly confused. The last thing he could remember clearly was standing in the kitchenette. Yet he had regained consciousness near the front door, with a pillow under his head and a quilt covering him. It just didn't make sense.

All he knew was that Ivan had died at the hospital that night. He'd checked himself in, screaming about some kind of poison, but the doctors could not identify it in time to find an antidote. How had the poison gotten inside him? The police had investigated and had turned up the same evidence of Ivan's debt Gregory had found. When they'd talked to Gregory, he'd told them about his visit with Ivan and about his blacking out.

They had tested the drugs they'd found in the vials in the kitchenette. Matched with a sample of Gregory's blood, they'd learned that one of the vials contained a drug that would indeed knock someone unconscious for a while. And drug testing had become much more sophisticated since Rex had invented his "leetle concoctions," so when the results from the dead horses' blood samples came back with a positive match with another of the vials' drugs, the police had determined that Ivan had killed the horses to collect on the insurance.

Ivan was dead and there was no evidence linking Gregory or anyone else to his death. They were still investigating, but the last time Gregory had talked to them, the police were leaning toward thinking Ivan had killed himself.

Wanda was devastated, of course. She'd loved her father. And Ivan had loved her very much, in his way. Spoiled her with his love, in fact. She and her mother would have to sort through Ivan's affairs. So far, no one had come forward to claim the debt indicated by the papers the police had found in his files. Vinny was out a lot of money. But no one knew that, not even Wanda. She only knew that Vinny had been particularly solicitous, bringing food for Liz and her, taking Wanda out to the movies to distract her, even helping her move back to Penn State to start her senior year. Gregory was glad that Wanda had school to get back to, with all its activities and friends. *She'll have the rest of her life to sort out her feelings*, he thought.

As I will mine. There were many questions in his mind about the events of that evening, but the one that really plagued him had nothing to do with Ivan's death. As he and Rebecca strolled back to the house, Gregory asked again the question that had been plaguing him. "I keep remembering Ivan calling me his son, Rebecca. His *son!* How could that be?"

"Are you sure that's what you heard?"

"No, not sure. I don't even know if I was conscious." He paused, trying to remember the event. "I just heard a distant voice, almost like hearing it through a curtain or something. And I remember a female voice, too."

"How could that be? Wanda wasn't there, was she?"

"No, she wasn't. Neither was Liz. But somebody was. How else would that pillow and quilt have gotten there? I could swear this voice called me 'son,' too. Could it have been my mother? What would she have been doing there?"

Rebecca didn't answer. There really were no answers.

"Ivan's son?" Gregory continued, considering the consequences. "What if it's true? What do I do?"

"Nothing for now, Gregory. It will all be revealed as God wills."

He looked at her. There was a time when this answer would not have satisfied him. He would have taken action: talked to the police more about what they thought happened that night, pumped Wanda and Liz for any information about her Ivan, resumed the search for his mother. But seeing Rebecca standing next to him, noticing the serenity of her smile, inhaling the sweet purity of the air around them, Gregory knew that all those questions would have to be answered later, if at all. For now, yes, he was content to leave it in God's hands. *Another change I've undergone in Amish land,* he thought with a smile.

He took Rebecca's hand, and they walked silently toward the crick. How good her hand felt in his. How warm the sun felt on his back. How grateful he felt that he'd had the courage to leave South Carolina and go looking for his mother. *Looking for myself, too.* He hadn't found his mother, but maybe he'd found something just as good: a place that felt like home. With a woman at his side who made him feel like he belonged there.

There'd be time to resume the search for his mother another day. For now, Gregory was content that his search had helped him find a part of himself he'd lost without knowing it. His love for the simple life. And maybe he'd even discovered a simple love.

As they crossed the bridge over the crick, Rebecca suddenly stopped and yelled, "Gregory, look! It's gone!"

"What is?"

"The stone! The stone in the crick!" She pointed at the water.

"What are you talking about, Rebecca?"

"There was a stone there, right there in the middle of the crick. I always used to see it whenever I crossed the bridge. It looked so solid, like it would be there forever. And now it's gone!"

Gregory had no idea why the disappearance of a stone would mean so much to Rebecca. "Do you want me to look for it?"

"Yes! I mean, no! No, don't look for it. I don't want to know where it's gone, just that it's moved to a different place. All that water from last night's rain must have done it." She crossed to the other side of the bridge and looked down. "No, not on this side either." She crossed back to stand next to Gregory, then suddenly grew silent, and spoke softly to herself. "It's no longer there. It's gone somewhere. It's *going* somewhere." She looked up at Gregory, her face radiant. "Just like me."

Gregory put his arm around Rebecca and drew her close. Together they stared at the water rushing by in the crick below. Rebecca was overwhelmed with joy. And wonder. *If the movement of a single stone can mean so much...*

Simple, so simple. And so profound.

THE END
of
STONE IN THE CRICK
REBECCA ZOOK'S AMISH ROMANCE, BOOK ONE

AUTHOR'S NOTE

Growing up in Greenville, SC in the 1950's, I confess I had never heard of the Amish. After an education in the northeast, I had heard about them, but knew nothing about them or their faith or culture. Imagine my surprise, then, to end up married to a woman raised in her grandparents gross-daddy house on their Amish farm near Lancaster, PA, a woman who would be the first in her family to be educated past the eighth grade. My delighted surprise, I hasten to add. For I soon came to admire the Amish for their simple ways, their profound faith, their love of the land, and their deep sense of community.

Some time ago my wife's cousin, Howard, came up with the idea of my writing an Amish novel. The novel began as an attempt to tell a funny story about the challenges my wife, Reba, experienced marrying outside her faith, especially from members of her own family. She, her cousin, and I had many story conferences, and the more we talked, the more the novel changed from being a series of humorous family anecdotes into a real Amish romance, one overlaid with mystery and attempted murder. As I know from a lifetime of writing for the theatre, the final work is often a far cry from the initial idea, but never have I been more surprised to find out that I am the author of not only one, but two Amish romances, with a third on the way, to complete my *Rebecca's Amish Romance* trilogy. I decided to write a novel and I ended up writing three!

I couldn't have done it alone, of course, so thanks are due. To Howard, for the inspiration and detailed notes, especially concerning the Mafia storyline. To Reba's family, Mabel, Anna, and Lydia, for answering my endless queries about Amish life in general and their own Amish experiences in particular. To my sister-in-law and author, Diana Martin, who provided invaluable advice about plotline and character. To members of my immediate family — Mary Wyche, Frank, and Ben — and my friend Elizabeth Neely for reading the early drafts and giving valuable feedback. And last, but far from least, to my wonderful wife, Reba, for helping me not only with storyline but with all the intricacies of Amish life, from what to call their bonnets to how to harvest tobacco, and myriad details in between.

And to Rebecca, Gregory, and all my other characters for coming to life and surprising me in such delightful and intriguing ways!

If you enjoyed my story, remember that Chickadee Prince Books, the publisher who brought this to you, is a small independent artists' collective press devoted only to quality work, and it needs your word of mouth to survive. Please tell a friend and write a review on Amazon and Goodreads of this book or other CPB books.

Granville Wyche Burgess
November 2017

OTHER BOOKS FROM CHICKADEE PRINCE THAT YOU WILL ENJOY

Fork in the Crick by Granville Burgess
Rebecca Zook's Amish Romance, Book Two - 978-0991327492

Rebecca Zook loves her Amish life. But with each step beyond its boundaries, she faces painful choices. Run a quilt shop or pursue her passion of being an artist? Obey her religion or follow her heart, which yearns for the love of Gregory Pinckney, a man outside her faith who came into her life so unexpectedly, and who seeks to uncover the secrets of his own family history? This gripping tale of thwarted romance and attempted murder in a peaceful Lancaster community is filled with surprises and threaded through with the abiding love that knits the Amish world together like stitching on a well-worn quilt.

*

There's More Than One Way Home by Donna Levin
ISBN: 9780991327461

"A witty, modern voice delivers a captivating tale about a mysterious death."
— *Kirkus Reviews*

Anna Kagen seems to have it all: She's young, beautiful, and married wealthy, prominent man. But within the walls of her San Francisco mansion spends her time dodging her husband's barbs and hunting down potential fri for her son, Jack, a 10-year-old on the autistic spectrum.

That old life suddenly seems idyllic when, on a school field trip, she make small error in judgment that sets in motion a chain of events that leads to an boy's death. Suddenly Jack is a suspect, her husband's career is in jeopardy Anna has to choose between loyalty to her son … and what may be her chance at happiness.